MASON JARS
IN THE FLOOD

And Other Stories

By
Gary Carden

Appalachian Writers Association's
Appalachian Book of the Year 2001

2000

Parkway Publishers, Inc.
Boone, North Carolina

Second Printing 2002

Appalachian Writers Association's
Appalachian Book of the Year 2001

Library of Congress Cataloging-in-Publication Data

Carden, Gary.
    Mason jars in the flood and other stories / by Gary Carden.
       p. cm.
    ISBN 1-887905-22-7
       1. North Carolina--Social life and customs--Fiction.
    2. Mountain life--North Carolina--Fiction. I. Title.

PS3553.A658 M37 1999
813'.54--dc21
                               99-058227

Cover Design by Bill May, Jr.
Editing, Layout and Book Design by Julie Shissler

I'll go my own way,
And drink my own whiskey,
And sing until morning,
The old-fashioned songs.

- Ian Tyson, "The Renegade."

This book is about dreams and memories;
Memories that never happened but should have;
Some that did happen, or might happen yet.
Dreams so tenuous that any attempt
to recall them, alters them.
Many are like sun-bleached photographs
placed in an old blue Schrafft's candy box
and kept in the attic until now.
Who are these people?
What day was this?
What happened to this child?
Where are they now?

This book is for

Richard and Louise Jackson in Banner Elk
(They know why)

and

Marcianne Herr in Akron, Ohio
Marilyn McMinn McCredie in Asheville
Jean Kirkland, M.A., in Sylva
Patricia Myler in Atlanta
John Quinnett in Bryson City
Dot Jackson in Six Mile
(who did the final edit on this book)
Michael Kesselring in Bryson City
David Thompson, SMMH, Sylva, NC
Dwain Edwards in Oceano, California
Richard Craven in Charlotte
Sara Louise who is up on the hill
the wicked woman in Tennessee
my dog, Teddie,

and for Lee Smith, who made me believe that I could write.

ACKNOWLEDGMENTS

Lafcadio Hearn
Vance Randolph
Thomas Wolfe
Jorge Luis Borges
Gabriel Garcia Marquez
Bernice Kelly Harris
Joseph Campbell
Bailey White
Jonathan Carroll
The Brothers Grimm
Edvard Munch
Egon Schiele
Gustav Klimt
Nina Simone
Dinah Washington

Arthur and Agnes Carden
John Lyndon Carden
Irene Mimms
Uncle Albert
Uncle Frank
Hunter Library, Western Carolina University
The Ritz Theatre
E. C. Comics
The Inner Sanctum

I owe a special debt to the Internet since the majority of this book
first appeared on AOL's Storytelling folder in "The Writers' Club"
during 1998 where it was read and critiqued by participants.
Many of the subsequent revisions are based on the comments
of hundreds of e-mail posters.

INTRODUCTION

I told my first stories to 150 white leghorns in a dark chicken-house when I was six years old. My audience wasn't attentive and tended to get hysterical in the dramatic parts. It wasn't an auspicious beginning, but I guess it helped me develop a sense of structure. A few nights before my debut, I had heard a Pentecostal preacher describe the most terrifying aspects of hell: molten brimstone, roasted flesh and endless pains on the Devil's rotisserie. As I sat, mouth agape, and watched this inspired performance, I found myself memorizing details. When he described the screams, weeping and lamentations of the tormented, I heard a Mormon Tabernacle choir of grief and saw the lurid red lights. As he stalked the platform miming the antics of the damned - writhing, whispering and shouting, I sneaked a look at the people behind me. They were riveted, hanging on every word, swaying like trees in this aural wind. "Wow!" I thought, as the hairs stood up on my neck, "I want to do that!" And so, I came to that dark chicken-house with an inspired and graphic message about chicken-hell.

Eventually, I got a human audience. In the third grade my class-mates encouraged me to repeat the stories that our teacher had read aloud. If I said, "You've already heard it," they responded, "Not your version!" I enjoyed telling "augmented" renderings of Saturday westerns, Tarzan movies and continued serials. I loved the attention I received, and I enjoyed the suspense in discovering what I would say next. Well-meaning teachers sometimes brought me home and made diplomatic comments to my anxious grandmother about problems attending "an overly active imagination." They noted that I spent too much time in the world of "make-believe," and that could cause problems when it came to adjusting to the "real world." My grandmother usually said, "Well, he can't help it. His grandfather on his mother's side told lies, too." The teachers were right, of course. An uncontrollable desire to "improve on the truth" has caused me endless problems.

My first attempts at writing this book gave me a shock: It was much harder than telling stories. My transcribed tales were filled with repetition, ambiguity and clichés. Of course, there are good reasons for that. Repetition, ambiguity and clichés are the singular attributes of a good storyteller. However, trapped on the printed page, these same marvelous, protean qualities become dull and uninspired.

Consider this: I don't memorize the stories that I tell. This is a debatable point, but I believe that the best storytellers advocate the same practice. "Don't memorize," they say. "If you do, you will sap the story of its vitality." (There is an interesting paradox here, for much of great literature seems to be diminished when read aloud.) Both storytellers and writers have noted that written words are "fixed and frozen" whereas spoken words are "fluid and changeable." As a result, memorized stories often have an awkward, stilted quality, whereas the tale of a storyteller who trusts to inspiration may become vitally alive.

When telling stories before an audience, I'm never quite sure what I am going to say next. With a good audience, a twenty-minute story may stretch to 45 minutes or more. Storytellers learn to "read" a responsive audience, and will elaborate on details that the audience endorses. Frequently, this "elaboration" is the inspiration of a moment, composed of the chemistry of the speaker, the audience and the story. It may be elusive, transitory and gone at the conclusion of that story told to that audience.

Writing and storytelling share a common goal: to interest, and if possible, enthrall the listener/reader. Out of twenty years of experimentation, I am left with this modest conclusion. I find that I can metamorphose a spoken story into a written one if I figuratively maintain the image of the reader's face as I write. I am, after all, still trying to communicate to the same rapt faces that I saw in the Pentecostal church (and did not see in the chicken-house). Within me is a voice that says, "I may have his/her interest now. How can I keep it?" Each image, each sentence should be structured to maintain and hopefully, increase that interest.

This is a recent discovery. The sentences, the images that I chose to write down are different from the ones that I use in storytelling. In writing for that singular, attentive face, I can be more thoughtful and the images can be more descriptive. The eyes reading my words are, after all, representative of all the readers that my written work will ever have. So, I have an opportunity that I do not have in an extemporaneous story. I can think, revise, expand and polish. I can put the written story in a drawer, and when I take it out a week or a year later, it has not evaporated like an inspired passage in a "spoken" tale. There it is, just as I left it, and I can revise, remove a trite image, omit repetition, and sometimes something gleams through like a precious metal under the prosaic words.

So, I begin with a story, one of the many versions of the one I have told. The written story is just beginning, for when it is fixed (can't move, can't wiggle away), it is time to start the "labor of the file" under the attentive eye of my reader. When it is finished, and when my figurative reader finally approves, I can put it aside. Later, when I read it again, it will be the same, but the paradox continues. This fixity, which is the bane of a good storyteller, has become a wondrous attribute in the written (and published) story. It will not change. Each time the book is opened, there are the words as they were finally crafted - a fact that is both gratifying and humbling.

Gary Carden, Winter, 2000

SECTION I
The Harley Stories

SECTION II
The Granny Stories
(Granny in Four Seasons)

SECTION III

SECTION IV

SECTION V
Quirky Pieces

MASON JARS
IN THE FLOOD

MASON JARS IN THE FLOOD

My grandfather loved two things beyond all else: the sound of rain that comes in the night and sleeping in a feather bed. His greatest joy was when the two came together. When I was a child in my grandfather's house, there were summer nights when I would wake to hear him shuffling blindly through the kitchen; I would rise to see him, clad in his white long-johns, climbing the narrow attic steps. Sometimes, I would follow and find him deep in the old feather bed by the window.

"Hush, now. Don't talk, just listen," he would say. I would creep through the warm darkness where befuddled wasps, alarmed by our presence, droned about and bumbled on the dusty windows. "They won't sting you if you leave them alone. Now, lay still."

"Okay, Papaw."

I would climb into the bed and curl against his body, listening to the rain sifting through the branches of the big poplars, pattering on the tin roof of the canning house, and dripping into buckets and cans. My grandfather actually placed objects around the house to catch the drip from the eaves. I remember the soft "doc, doc," from an old bucket, the "ting, ting," of rusty cans and the faint drumming of the shingled roof, all blended into a symphony of percussions.

"Jerusalem oak seed," he would whisper. "Lespedeza and jimson weed," the beginning of his evocation to sleep. He didn't call it that, of course, but he believed that repeating the names of plants and flowers would produce a growing drowsiness. "Sweet juniper, sheep's tongue and love lies a-bleeding."

Once, I asked him if he liked the feather bed so much, why didn't he sleep in it all the time? "Moderation," he said, "like the preacher says. Some things are sweeter if they are taken in sensible doses." After a moment, he added, "Besides, Agnes would take it amiss."

There was a night when my grandfather woke me.

"Wake up, Harley. Wake up and listen." Instead of a soft drip and patter, there was a harsh discord of clattering and thunder. Wind shook the windows and the liquid sound of rushing water was everywhere.

"Cloud-burst," he said, and we stumbled down the steps to the kitchen where he jiggled a dead light-switch.

"Power's out." I felt a rising excitement. This was not going to be an ordinary day! In moments, my grandmother appeared with a kerosene lamp, and peered out the kitchen window. Then my grandfather found his big three-celled flashlight and we were all on the front porch. Silver needles fell through the beam, and a loud gurgling came from the branch. We could see muddy water lapping at the foot-log. Our little branch was turning into a creek! When the slender beam was directed toward Painter Knob, it didn't go far. The rain was so thick, we couldn't see across the yard.

"Ain't seen one of these since I was a boy."

My grandmother retreated to the kitchen, and in minutes I could smell coffee and frying bacon. I stayed on the porch listening to the hearty chuckles and thumps that came from the darkness.

By daylight, the creek had become a river! We watched logs, brush and barrels come bouncing down the holler, rush through our front yard and disappear into the fog. I got pretty excited about the unique turn of events and started rushing back and forth on the porch, calling out the names of the items that whizzed by - pig pens, bushes with live possums in them, dead chickens and Willard Carnes' outhouse!

"Harley, go put some dry clothes on and stop acting like a fool," said my grandmother. "You seem to think this is fun." It was! The water was up in the yard now, a dark chocolate flood that swirled around the steps and ran through the big boxwoods around the house. By the time the rain stopped, most of the new corn in the bottom was on its way to the Tuckaseigee River. This was better than the Cherokee Fair! Suddenly, a large collection of barrels and buckets, followed by hundreds of jars, rode by, the contents of somebody's can-house, and I tried to imagine their journey. From here to Cope Creek, then into Scott's Creek and then into the Tuckaseigee. The journey got a little vague after that, but I was pretty sure that the

Mississippi and the Gulf of Mexico couldn't be far. Then what? France? Africa? Alpha Centauri?

Papaw went off to check on his oil truck, which sat fender-deep in the muddy water. Granny went to the barn to feed the cow, who, although well out of danger, had been bawling mournfully all morning. That is when I decided to do it. In minutes, I had hauled all of my grandmother's canning jars out of the can-house, and I lined them up on the porch. I wrote each note in my Blue Horse notebook. Generally, they went like this.

Hello!

My name is Harley Teester. I am nine years old and I live in Rhodes Cove, North Carolina. School is out and I don't have anybody to play with. Why don't you come and see me? I like Lash LaRue, the Squeaking Door, Captain Marvel and Pepsi Colas.

Your Friend, Harley Teester

I rolled each note like a scroll, put it in a Mason jar with a "seal-tight" rubber ring and screwed on the lid. Then, I threw them one by one into the flood, and watched as they rode away on their way to the ocean.

My grandmother "took a fit." She canned a lot of stuff and was proud of her stock of jars. She used a lot of mayonnaise jars that summer. I was pretty optimistic for a couple of weeks and spent a lot of time on the porch looking down the trail that ran through the swamped cornfield, waiting for someone with one of those jars - a kid about my age, maybe with an elderberry pop-gun, a cigar box full of marbles and a complete set of Captain Marvels.

"Why are you staring down the trail, Harley? Expecting somebody?" Granny would rock in her old white oak rocker and shell peas.

"No, just looking."

"Think somebody might bring some of my jars back?" Sometimes, she would tell me, "The only person who is likely to come up that trail looking for you is the folks down at the insane asylum at Morganton. Sometimes, they come looking for little boys with what your teachers call 'an overly active imagination' and they give them....the cure."

"What's the cure?"

"I've been told that it is mostly hard work. They make you hoe corn, chop wood, milk cows....all them things you don't like to do."

"How would they know about me?"

"Somebody would have to write them a letter, I guess. It would be a letter that went by post office, not by Mason jar. Now, why don't you make yourself useful and go get a load of stove-wood for your poor old Granny."

I figured she was "just funning," but I got the wood anyway.

POSTSCRIPT

As the years passed, I still thought about the jars. Sometimes, I had elaborate dreams about them. In my teens, I sometimes dreamed that the jar-bearers finally appeared, but now, they were usually female and looked a lot like Debra Paget in "Broken Arrow." Captain Marvel wasn't as important as he had been, and in my dreams, Debra's clothing was getting skimpy. The years passed, flowing away like the little stream in front of my grandparents' home. I went to college, married, taught school, got divorced, taught college and got divorced again. Now, I am back, sitting on that same porch in Rhodes Cove, and on summer evenings, I sit in the old white oak rocking chair and watch the light fade in the Balsam Mountains.

I still dream of the Mason jars and see a weary traveler who finally arrives at the foot of the steps. The face is indistinct now, but the traveler says, "It has taken a long time to find you, Harley. Do you still want to play?"

The attic is still up there, of course, still filled with trapped wasps and forgotten relics; but the one I dream about is the one with the feather-bed (gone now) and the soft rain and the warmth of my grandfather's body - and the sense of security that he gave me in the warm darkness. Sometimes, on rainy summer nights, I climb the stairs and unroll a sleeping bag on the floor.

"Lespedeza and jimson weed," I say. "Jerusalem oak seed."

WHEN THE MUSIC STOPPED

Granny and me was on the porch shelling peas in the moonlight. She liked to do that. I shelled too, but I wasn't good at it like Granny. Her old rocking chair moved in slow, gentle arcs like the tick-tocks in the old Waltham mantel clock. Then she would stop, her head lifting; her hands still over the pile of hulls in her lap. "Listen!" she'd say, her eyes turning to the dark trail where mica sparked and burned in the moonlight, or she would look at the abandoned springhouse in the front yard. Granny was always thinking that she heard things at night. She raised a finger at me like Mrs. Luck, the librarian. "Shhhhh," she whispered. "You hear that?"

Sometimes she was serious and sometimes she was just having a little fun with me, like if she said she heard a baby crying, she was getting ready to tell about the woman that drowned her baby in the spring-house. I'd heard it before, but Granny could still scare me, especially if she started making noises like a baby crying. Sometimes, she would claim she heard a painter scream, up on the Knob, and then she was off and running about painters that climbed down chimneys to get babies and pregnant women.

I listened. Rain-crows mourned on Painter Knob and wind stirred the big pines on the steep ridge before the house. "What, Granny, what?" She shook her head, and her deft, strong fingers began to weave again, popping pods, pushing the peas into her cupped hand with her thumb and pouring them into a tin pot. "Thought I heard somebody playing an old song," she said. Then, she started singing snatches of old hymns, her chair keeping time.

I'll meeeeeet you in the moooorning, She always sung in a high screech like a five-year-old child. *And we'll set down by the river...*

She hummed a while, and then looked at me.

"It were a night like this when your daddy brought your momma home." She turned peering down the dark trail like she expected to see somebody coming. "I was setting right here like I am now, stringing beans and shelling peas." She laughed and rocked. I knowed not to rush her; I could tell from the set of her mouth that the story was coming and this was one I had been wanting to hear for a long time.

"Arthur was out under that maple there, sharpening one of them mowing blades, just like he is doing now." I turned to where Papaw sat in his cave of darkness. He had his little emery-wheel out there, the one that set in a tub of water. He peddled it with his foot, and I could see the sparks in the dark and smell the hot blade. I could hear the water hiss as it cooled the wheel.

"That's how I knowed somebody was coming," said Granny. "Arthur stopped sharpening his mowing blade. He got up and walked up on the porch. I think he heard John Lyndon's car stop behind the barn down yonder." Granny looked at the trail that run along the branch to the house. It was bordered on both sides by rows of corn. A fog of lightning bugs rose and blinked above the tassles.

"We heard 'em before we seen 'em." She smiled and prodded her glasses up on her nose. "Laughing, they was. 'Course, your daddy was always laughing. That's where he got his nick-name, you know, 'Happy.' He was playing that song, *The Raindrop Waltz,* on his guitar. The music was all mixed up with the wind and the moonlight and them rain-crows up on the Knob. Then, we seen 'em. Irene, your momma, she was dancing. Tiny little thing in a white dress and barefoot. John Lyndon had her shoes in his coat pockets, and he was laughing and playing while she waltzed round him. They disappeared behind the spring-house and we could hear them whispering and giggling there for a while, and then they come out in the front yard."

Granny looked towards Papaw, and for a while we listened to the song of the blade on the whetstone. "Shhhhh," she said, "He don't need to hear this." Well, I hadn't said anything anyway, but I nodded. When she went on, her voice was softer like she was telling me a secret, and I guess she was.

"Oh, Arthur, he was fit to be tied!" Granny covered her mouth and laughed. "He knowed what had happened before they told it. There they stood like two kids that had done something that

6

they was half-proud and half-scared about. John Lyndon was so full of hisself, he was about to pop. 'Me and Irene, we got married in Walhalla, South Carolina tonight,' he said. Well, it weren't like we hadn't already figgered that out since it was wrote all over their faces. Irene got all low-headed and took your daddy's arm, waiting to see what would happen."

Granny got up and took her apron off. She went to the end of the porch and shook dirt and pea stems into the yard. Then, she stood there for a minute or two and looked at the moonlit Balsam Mountains that rose behind the cornfield and the barn. Wind moved through the corn stalks and made Granny's calla lilies by the old springhouse nod together like laughing children. She sighed and stooped to lift another pile of unshelled peas into her lap.

"Well, what can you do?" Granny said, shaking her head. "Of course, we'd rather they hadn't done it. The Depression was on, and work was scarce as hen's teeth. So, the next day, Arthur went with your daddy to Massie Furniture and helped him buy a bed, a bureau and a chest of drawers. They hauled that stuff home and put it in the back bedroom." I set for a while with my back against the porch banisters, shelling one pea pod to Granny's four. I listened to the water whisper on the back porch where it ran through hollow pine logs into a great trough filled with milk and butter.

"Do chickens really have teeth?"

Granny stared at me for a minute. "I swear, Harley, you are a quare boy. Where did you come up with a question like that?"

"You said jobs was as scarce as hen's teeth."

"So I did. Well, no, Harley, chickens hardly ever have teeth. That's why they are scarce. If you see any, I'll give you a quarter for 'em." After a minute, she said, "Don't go bothering the chickens, Harley. I already checked and none of them have teeth." I watched her mouth put up a fight against a laugh, and then she started singing again in that high, piping voice.

"He walks with me, and he talks with me;
He tells me I am his own;
And the sound I hear......."

The old rocker moved and her voice gave way to a hum and then silence. In a little while, she said, "Ah, Harley, I wish you could have heard your daddy play!"

"What did he play, Granny?"

"Well, that's the wonder. He played everthing. Mandolins, fiddles, guitars and banjos. George Swan said that the first time John Lyndon picked up a mandolin, he was playing it in thirty minutes."

"What *kind* of music did he play?" I said, meaning that was what I meant to ask in the first place.

"Anything!" said Granny. "I've seen him out here listening to the radio, and when music was playing, I'd notice his fingers moving, like he was playing right along with that music even though he didn't have nothing in his hands. After him and Irene got married, he'd set out here on the porch at night and play for her. Sometimes the songs was strange. Arthur would say, 'Now, what was the name of that?' Your daddy would laugh and say, "I don't know, Daddy. I just made it up." And Arthur would say 'Play it again,' and John Lyndon would laugh and say, 'I can't, Daddy. It's gone.' It were wondrous strange."

The Balsams was fading now as fog run like rivers of milk through the hollers and coves. Little by little, the mountaintops got fuzzy. Fog covered Black Rock and the moon come swimming down the holler like a lantern in the clouds. I waited, afraid that Granny wouldn't keep talking. She did though.

"Granny, what happened to my daddy?"

The tin pot slid from her lap and fell to the porch and Granny stopped rocking. She sat a minute watching the sparks from Papaw's whetstone.

"Harley, you know better than to ask that."

"Doty Womack said he was shot by a drunk man."

Granny leaned forward, speaking in a harsh whisper. "Arthur can't stand to hear about it," she said. "I made the children all swear to never mention it."

"Nobody will tell me. I don't know nothing!" I tried not to cry, but I did.

"Hush, now Harley. Just hush!" For a while we just set there. I watched the fire-flies flicker in the corn and tried to shell peas.

"Move over here, closer to my chair, Harley. Quit crying, now." I did as I was told.

"It's time, I guess. Ten years old, and you don't know what happened to your daddy." She sighed and shook her head. I was so close to her, I could smell biscuits and apples.

"Doty spoke true, Harley. Your daddy was killed by a drunk man when you was less than two years old. The man that done it was so drunk, he didn't remember doing it. The day they brought the news, Arthur was standing on the porch over there, and when they told him, he fell off the porch. Laid in the yard and cried. Tore locks of his hair out by the roots. The boys, Albert and Asbury, they carried him in the house. He didn't speak for two days." Granny stopped talking for a while. She wiped her face with her apron and shook her head. "Little Doc Nichols said it was like a fit. Epilepsy, he said. That's when we decided to never talk about it in front of your grand-daddy." Granny ate a couple of peas. "Mmmmm. Now, if I had some spring onions, some cresses and a hunk of gritted cornbread!"

"Where did it happen?" I said. Granny give me a long look. "You going to make me tell it, Harley?" She looked into the dark woods for a while.

"It were in that little service station in Moody Bottom, the one that your Uncle Albert run for a while. Back then, it had a big sign on the front that said, 'Happy's Place,'" and there was always a bunch of fiddlers or banjo-pickers hanging out there. They helped your daddy pump gas, and then, when business was slow, they would play." Granny laughed, remembering. "People would gather at night and listen. They'd bring chairs and set out there in the dark. Got to where they'd holler requests, like 'The Waltz You Saved for Me,' or 'Can I Sleep in Your Barn, Tonight, Mister?' John Lyndon would start playing, and the others, they would join in. I loved it when that happened. First, your daddy's guitar, then maybe a fiddle, then a banjo and a couple of mandolins, all of it coming together like a little stream that becomes a creek and then a river.

"They started playing dances, your daddy and them fellers that made music with him. They was always going off some place like Walhalla or Clayton or Cashiers Valley. Oh, they had fun. After John Lyndon and Irene got married, she went with the band." Granny chuckled and peered at the Balsams. "They'd come in at two o'clock in the morning laughing and cutting up, sometimes, me and Arthur would get up and listen to them tell about the dance. That's when I found out about *The Raindrop Waltz*. Oh, I'd heard it before, but Irene would tell me about how your daddy always played it last.

"She said that when the band was wore out, maybe a banjo string had broke or the fiddle bow was warped, the boys would give Happy a nod, letting him know they wanted to go home, and your daddy would start playing *The Raindrop Waltz*. It got 'til everbody at the dance knowed what that meant, and they would get up to dance one last time."

"Did my daddy write that song?" I said.

"Law, no, Harley. That song had been around a long time. Some folks said that it was wrote by a man in a prison camp in World War I. Others said that a guitar-picker who got jailed in Asheville for fighting at a dance, he wrote it. Claimed he listened to the rain dripping off the jailhouse roof, falling into a pile of jars and cans. Said he heard a song in them raindrops."

Granny made plinking sounds with her mouth and smiled.

"He heard the song in the rain?"

"That's right!"

"Aw, Granny, you're joshing me," I said. She laughed.

"No, Harley, it's true. I'll tell you what else. Nobody could play it like John Lyndon. Other folks played it, even made records of it, but nobody played it like your daddy. Sometimes, he picked it clean and sharp on a banjo; sometimes he slid the back of a pocket-knife on the strings and made the notes quaver. I've seen him set right there," she pointed to a worn patch of porch planking, "and play it on nights like this - moon and fog and wind in the leaves. Made you feel good to hear it, like life and family, everthing was the way it was supposed to be."

The whine of the emery-wheel stopped; the sparks vanished. Papaw stood in the dark and stretched.

"Tell me how it happened," I said. "The man that done it...."

"Another time, Harley," said Granny, watching Papaw walk toward the porch. "There will be other nights."

"But...."

"Hush, now, Harley," Granny said, like she meant it.

"Well, now," said Papaw, "Time to hit the hay! Gotta be on my way to the rock-crusher on Little Canada by daylight." He looked at me. "I want to hear your feet hit the floor when the tannery whistle blows in the morning."

"O.K., Papaw," I said, rising to go inside. I rode the truck with Papaw in the summer, writing the bills up in the big receipt book while he did the figuring.

I stood for a moment watching Granny light the kerosene lamp. Even though the house had electricity, Papaw liked lamplight, claiming it helped him go to sleep. Now, stripped to his long-handles, he slid under the quilts, stretched himself to his full length, closed his eyes and began to talk about the Republicans. He had a long list of things that they had done that he didn't approve of, and when he had wore that out, he started on President Roosevelt's New Deal, which he was afraid wasn't going to work. Then, he moved onto things he was worried about closer to home.

"The pasture fence is down," he'd say. "The corn ain't making anything this year and I think the pig has the scours." Papaw talked in a sing-song voice. If he run out of things that needed fixing, he would start on the Cove. That was a place in Macon County that he owned. It was on the backside of Cowee Mountain, and Papaw wanted to build a cabin there.

"So far back, I won't never hear another car horn. Don't want no roads, no phones, no lectricity." Then, he would list all of the things he would have there. "Chickens that roost in the trees. A good dog. Maybe a blue-tick. A garden. Corn, beans, onions, potatoes."

"Go on to bed, Harley," Granny said.

I used to sleep on a cot in Papaw and Granny's bedroom, but now I slept in the bed that used to belong to my momma and daddy. At first, I was afraid to be alone, but after Uncle Stoogie won me the little radio at the Cherokee Indian fair, I got used to it. The radio was pink and I had a copper wire antenna that run halfway up Painter Knob. I sometimes left it on all night, and it would light up the whole bedroom with a little, pink glow. I liked to wake in the night and see the light, maybe hear an announcer say something like,

"From high atop the Rose Room in downtown Chicago, we bring you Tommy Tucker Time!" The music would play all night, and when I looked at the wall at the foot of my bed, I could see the picture of my momma and daddy. Daddy was standing with his foot on the bumper of a car. He was playing a mandolin and laughing, looking straight at the camera. My momma was looking up at my daddy's face, her hand above her eyes, the way you do when you're looking at something real bright. She was laughing, too.

If I left the radio off, I could sometimes hear Papaw muttering in the dark. If he didn't go to sleep talking about the Cove, he would start talking about different kinds of feed, flowers and grain, which always worked.

"Alfalfa," he would whisper. "Millet, jimson weed, trillium, Jerusalem oak seed, hollyhock, jonquil. Oats and fescue. Timothy and sweet William." When he stopped talking, Granny would lean over and blow out the lamp. I know because when I slept in their bedroom, I saw her do it lots of times.

That's the way it was on the night that Granny told me about when the music stopped. Papaw quit talking, so I knowed he was asleep. Then, I heard Granny coming, her bare feet whispering on the floor, and there she was standing by my bed in her long flannel gown.

"Move over," she said. She laid down on top of the covers and started talking. "The man that done it, his name was Clyde Morgan. He was bad to drink and couldn't keep a job. Sometimes he would drink Scalf's Indian River medicine, or vanilla extract."

"Like you put in pies?"

"Yes. I've even heard that he would drink shoe polish if he got desperate enough. The day he killed your daddy, he was drinking wood alcohol. People at the trial testified that he had been drunk for a couple of days, and that he showed up at Happy's Place every morning and spent the day setting on a Coca-Cola crate outside the station. Always trying to borrow money off of people."

Granny took out her upper plate and set it on my radio. She stared out the window for a while before she went on.

"Nobody knows where he got the pistol. Found it, I guess. I seen it on the witness table at the trial. Rusty, with no handles. Didn't look like it would even fire. But it did. He shot John Lyndon while he was playing. Shot him in the top of the head." Granny touched the top of my head with a finger. "Right there." Then, she moved her finger to my left eye. "Stopped right there, behind his eye. Vernon Haskett said that John Lyndon lived about thirty minutes." Granny gave a sad little laugh.

"They tried to take him to the hospital in that car that nobody could drive but your daddy, and wrecked it at the bottom of the courthouse steps. Turned the car over on its side. Poor Vernon felt awful because he was driving, but it didn't make any difference. Little Doc Nickols told me later that there was no way he could have lived."

Granny dabbed at her eyes with her sleeve. "Clyde got clean away. Everybody just set there after Clyde shot your daddy. Vernon said that gun made an awful lot of smoke, and that Clyde dropped it and stared around at everybody and said, 'I stopped the music.' I've always wondered why he said that. They caught him a week later up near the Pinnacle in the Balsams." Granny turned the radio on and a string orchestra somewhere in Chicago began to play.

"The night before your daddy's funeral, Arthur went up to Vernon Haskett's house and asked him to get the rest of the band together. He asked them to come to the funeral and just before they closed the lid of John Lyndon's casket, he wanted them to play *The Raindrop Waltz*. They done it. Stood there behind the coffin and played. They followed the coffin out to the graveyard. It was raining, sort of a misty rain and that's when I saw all the cars and people. Over a thousand people, Harley."

She looked at me and smiled. "Now, you always remember that. You see, that little band played all over western North Carolina and people came from Murphy, Andrews, Franklin, Asheville, Clayton. People that had been at them dances. Made me proud, Harley. They stood in the rain at your daddy's grave. Vernon looked around and whispered to me, 'It's just like the dances. We played that song last because it was time to go home.' Then, he done the strangest thing. He took his mandolin and laid it on top of the flowers by the grave. I told him that the rain would ruin that mandolin, and he just smiled at me. 'That's all right,' he said and walked away."

Granny picked her upper plate up and rose in the darkness.

"You was there, Harley. Not quite two years old, and Irene not even eighteen and scared to death. It were an awful thing. I do take comfort in remembering the music, and I can still see all of them people standing in the rain."

Her hand rested briefly on my head, and then she was gone.

Now, my radio is playing "Moonlight and Roses," and I lay in the cool, pink light, listening to the water gurgle and bubble on the back porch. Sometimes, Papaw gets up in the night, and walks to the back porch where he drinks from the big gourd dipper and stares into the moonlit yard.

"Ah, boyz!" he always says when he finishes drinking. "Ah, boyz!" I asked him once what "boyz" meant, but he didn't know. He said that it was something his own father said when he was pleased. "One of them old Irish words, I guess," he said.

Granny is gone, now, and suddenly, I am dreaming of Saturday Matinee heroes who need my help to restore law and order in Tombstone: Lash LaRue, Gene Autry and the Durango Kid: We gallop into town and stop at a saloon that has a big sign that says, "Happy's Place." Then, the saloon is gone and I float on Tommy Tucker's music to the top of Painter Knob and sit with the rain-crows and the hoot owls, watching the ocean of fog drift in the moonlight, covering the house where a little boy lies asleep next to a pink radio.

THE OIL TRUCK - 1945

Papaw drives the Standard Oil truck. It is a big red and white monster with dangling hoses and little doors that open along the truck's sides. Papaw delivers kerosene and gasoline to service stations and little mountain stores. In the bedroom where him and Granny sleep, there is a picture of Papaw delivering oil and kerosene with two mules and a wagon. The mules were named Dolly and Maude. The words "Standard Oil Company" are printed on the side of the wagon. In the picture, Papaw is standing in his striped overalls with one hand on his hip and his other hand on Maude's back. He is smiling and looking right at the camera.

Papaw told me a story about when Maude died. He said he sent a telegram to the Standard Oil Company that said, "I can't make my deliveries today. Maude is dead." Later in the day, a big wreath of flowers came on the train from Asheville. The Standard Oil Company thought Maude was Papaw's wife! Granny laughs when Papaw tells the story. She says that Papaw gave the flowers to the Lovesdale Methodist Church and they put them in front of the pulpit. Granny said the flowers spelled out M-A-U-D-E, and a big gold ribbon across the middle of the wreath said "Gone Before."

Sometimes, in the summer, I ride the oil truck with Papaw. He lets me write the bills, but he always figures up the amount. I'm in the 4th grade and I can add pretty good, but I don't think Papaw believes it.

"You do the writing, Harley, and I'll do the figuring," he says.

We deliver kerosene and gasoline to the Cherokee Indian Reservation, and to the rock crushers in the head of Little Canada. Papaw also delivers oil to Boodleville, which is the name of a little valley in Cullowhee that has about one hundred trailers in it. This is where G.I.'s live who are going to college on the G.I. bill at Western Carolina Teacher's College. Papaw complains a lot about Boodleville because sometimes the G.I.'s move out in the night - just vanish without paying their fuel bills.

The first time Papaw let me go with him to the Cherokee Reservation, I was six years old. I got so excited, he thought I might have a fit.

"For God's sake, settle down! You're acting like you ain't got a lick of sense." I was bouncing up and down on the seat and rolling the window up and down. I'm ten now, and I can act pretty much like a grown person. I saw my first Cherokees walking along the side of the road. Except for being Indians, they looked like people on the street in Sylva. They had on overalls and blue shirts, which was a disappointment. The Indians in my funny books, and the ones in the Saturday westerns that Aunt Ruby had took me to see at the Ritz Theatre, wore war bonnets and carried tomahawks. I didn't see nobody riding ponies either. When I asked Papaw about it, he said, "Real life ain't never like the movies, Harley." If that is true, it's a shame.

I did see some Cherokee kids about my age swimming in the Oconaluftee River, and they were buck-naked. When Papaw parked the oil truck in front of a log store, I saw lots of old Cherokees sitting on the porch of the post office talking Cherokee. I sat in the truck and listened to them. They sounded like buzzing bees; there was something peaceful about it. Then Papaw came out of the store and called me.

"Come here, Harley," he said. "Come and see the Chief."

When I got in the store, there was a Cherokee with a big war bonnet on. He had on beaded leggings and there was a knife on his belt. He had a bow and a quiver of arrows on his back. Now this was more like it! Papaw bought a picture postcard from him, and the Chief told me that his name was Chief Walkingdeer, the "most photographed Indian in the world." He asked me if I wanted to see him shoot his bow, and we went outside where he had a big bulls-eye target set up. Every arrow he shot went in the bulls-eye. A car stopped across the road, and a man and woman got out with two little kids. The kids were jumping up and down and screaming while they pointed at Chief Walkingdeer. They acted like they might take a fit, too. When the man got his camera out of the car and tried to take

16

Walkingdeer's picture, the Chief turned his war bonnet wrong-side-out. He just reached up and pulled the feathers down so that his war bonnet looked sorta like an umbrella that the wind has turned inside-out. His head looked like the back end of a turkey! Walkingdeer held out his hand and chanted, "Tip! Tip! Tip!" The man came over and gave the Chief some money and Walkingdeer turned his war bonnet right-side-out. He picked up the two little kids so the man could take a picture. Then he sold the man some of his picture post cards.

Two Cherokee boys standing near the store asked me if I wanted to learn to speak Cherokee. When I said I did, one winked at the other and said,

"O.K., say Cee-Oh,"

"Cee-Oh," I said.

"That means, 'Hello' in Cherokee. Now, say Sty-You." I repeated it and he told me that I was now able to say 'Hello, how are you."

The other one said, "Now repeat after me, Stick-a Wa-Ta-lee. I repeated it several times, and they told me the next time I saw a Cherokee, to repeat all the words I had learned. In my mind, it became sort of a chant: "Cee-Oh, Sty-You, Stick-a Wa-Tal-ee."

On the way home, Papaw told me that President Roosevelt had come to Cherokee and made a speech up in the Smokies at New Found Gap. Papaw said that the President had created a national park, and that tourists had already started coming to the park in the summer. He said that Chief Walkingdeer had figured out a way to make a living. He would dress up like a movie Indian and the tourists would pay him to make his picture.

"You mean, he isn't the real chief?" I said.

"Not hardly."

"Does the real Chief have a war bonnet?"

"Nope, The one I met had on a Sears-Roebuck suit. He was a nice feller. Told me he was worried about the effect that all of them tourists would have on his people. He wanted to send his son to college and told me he didn't like to see Cherokees doing what Chief Walkingdeer is doing, selling pictures and saying 'Tip!' He was ashamed because saying 'Tip' was like begging. He also told me that the Cherokees never wore war bonnets anyway. Even way back, hundreds of years ago, they just wore one or two feathers."

17

All the same, I liked the war bonnet, and when I got home, I put the picture of Chief Walkingdeer in my memory box. That night when I got in bed, I said over and over to myself, "Cee-Oh, Sty You, Sticka-wa-Ta-lee." When I woke up, I could still say it.

The best trips are when Papaw goes to Cashiers Valley. Well, I enjoy them, but I don't think Papaw does. The truck roars and chugs up Glenville Mountain, always sounding like it is going a lot faster than it really is. We get down to 10 m.p.h. on the mountain, and we have a big line of cars behind us. When Papaw pulls over and lets the cars by, a lot of them are tourists that glare at him, and sometimes they yell things like "Stupid hillbilly!" That is when Papaw gets mad at the oil truck and starts talking about quitting. He says that it don't matter how hard he scrubs, he can't seem to get the smell of kerosene off his hands, not even with the pink Lava soap. He talks about "the Cove," which is over in Macon County. This is land that Great-Grandma Teester has promised Papaw, and he wants to build a house there some day, and he never wants "to see another highway or hear another car horn."

"Never wanted to make a living this way," he says. "Always wanted to farm. Ain't no way you can make ends meet, though. But one of these days," he would say, his eyes shooting sparks as he beat on the steering wheel with his fist, "I'm gonna push this damn truck off the edge of some mountain, maybe Whitesides, 'n watch it tumble into some godforsaken holler!" Then, he would laugh, kinda wild like. "Yessir, let the possums and the ground-squirrels live in it! " Then, he would look at me and demand, "And where will I be, Harley?"

"In the Cove," I would say.

"Damn right!" Papaw would say. "I'll be in the Cove, so far back that you can't hear no car horns. No sir!" When Papaw got rolling, he sounded a lot like Preacher Stiffleback, at the "jump and holler" Holiness Church. "What will I have there?" he would say. "How will I live?"

These questions were like a game that Papaw played with me, and I knew what to say to keep him going. "I guess you will raise what you need," I would say.

"That's right! I'll have chickens that roost in the trees! Wild hogs! Razorbacks! A mule, a cow and a bottomland garden. And spring water, by God! Never gonna drink water that's been standing in iron pipes. And at night, boy, at night when I set on the porch, I won't hear a thing but wind, rain crows and running water!"

I know that Papaw is just talking, 'cause he never says anything about Granny and me being with him in the Cove. He's just pretending, like I do when I'm Sergeant Preston of the Yukon or Tarzan. So, I listen while he talks about the six bee gums, and the water system that he will make out of hollowed-out pine logs (like the one we already have at home), and hunting pheasant and quail. By the time we get to Holden's Store in Norton, he is ready to pump kerosene and argue politics with the store loafers. In the summer, he sometimes lets me fish for a few minutes in creeks around High Hampton and Fairfield Inn, where the rich folks come in July. He lets me sneak down to the little creek with a cane pole and a slice of lightbread for bait. In no time at all I will catch a dozen.

"Them is stock trout, Harley," he says as he watches me unhook another one. "Ain't much sport in catching them." He is right, I guess. I bait my hook with light bread and catch a few more. "They sure taste good though, fried in cornmeal," he says. "You can eat 'em, bones and all."

In the winter, we stay in the truck, making out the bills with numb fingers. And when we are too far away to go home for dinner, we eat sardines and crackers while Papaw keeps dreaming, "Maybe I need a bluetick hound, you know, to keep the possums away from the chickens. So far back, soooo far back, I'll never hear another stripped gear!"

The return trip from Glenville is always exciting. Papaw gears the big truck down, and sometimes, when we come down Glenville Mountain, the brakes smoke. Papaw tells me scary stories about runaway trucks and the men who rode them to their deaths.

"There!" he says, pointing to a big rock on the side of the road. "See them scratches? That's where old Andrew Haskett hit. He rode the ditch all the way down, lost that load of acid wood, and that truck just kept going. He blowed the horn to let people know he was coming and lost control right here where the big water pipe goes over the mountain to Glenville Lake. Didn't find enough of him to make a decent burial. I guess there is still parts of Andy down in that holler." I look down through the treetops in the dim holler and imagine pieces of Andy buried in the woods...maybe a moss-covered leg bone.

19

Once when we were creeping down Glenville Mountain, Papaw rolled down his window and pointed. "What the hell is that?" he said. Something was knocking down corn stalks in the field below us. Papaw stopped to get a better look and the truck suddenly tilted. We had been watching the truck's left rear wheel on its way to the Tuckaseigee River. We heard the splash and saw the steam rise. Papaw looked disgusted, got out of the truck and started down the hillside to the river. The wheel had made a pretty good trail through the corn, so it was easy for him to follow. Getting it out of the river took a while, though. It was long after dark when Papaw dragged the wheel back to the truck and managed to get it back on. He skinned his knuckles and got mad at the truck. He kicked the grill and hurt his foot. All the way home, he talked about the Cove. "Some banty chickens, I think....the ones with feathers on their feet. I'd like one of them little Swiss cows, too." In the dim light from the dashboard, I could see him smiling and nodding, his blue eyes dreamy and his sunburned cheeks glowing.

The road to Little Canada makes me think of a snake; a big, looping coil that we inch up on our way to the Wolf Mountain rock crusher. It is a one-lane dirt road, and when you meet somebody, it sometimes takes ten minutes of see-sawing to get around an acid wood truck. Sometimes, we hear a horn blowing a long way off, and Papaw starts looking for a place to get off the road.

"Crazy mountain boys," says Papaw. "When you hear that horn, it means that they ain't interested in stopping, and it's up to us to get out of the way." Papaw will pull up a cattle trail and wait. When they pass, still blowing the horn, they yell and slap the sides of their logging-trucks with their hats, like cowboys riding rodeo steers. Papaw used to haul oil to Little Canada with his wagon and mules. He said that sometimes he would come around a quick turn and there would be a hat in the road. On the banks on either side would be half-a-dozen men with guns, and one of them would tell Papaw that they didn't mind him using the road, but that he "better not run over that hat." Papaw said sometimes he would back and fill for a half-hour, while his audience laughed, swigged moonshine and fired guns. "There ain't a lot to do in the way of amusement up here, and watching me trying to get around that hat was probably the most fun them guys had all week."

"If you had run over the hat, would they have shot you, Papaw?" I said.

"I wondered about that, too," he said. "At the time, it appeared to me that they wouldn't have any choice, since they had told me that they would."

After a couple of trips, Papaw got to know them by their first names, and they stopped putting the hat in the road.

"Morning, Arthur," they would say from the road-bank as they watched the wagon pass.

"Morning, boys," said Papaw. "Would you care for a ride?" Sometimes, they would climb on the wagon and ride a ways, just for something to do.

When I used to ride with Papaw to Little Canada, he usually made me stay in the truck. The one exception was Jesse's Store. It was one of the strangest places I have ever seen and I looked forward to going inside. The walls were covered with pictures of Indians, and everywhere you looked, there were barrels of arrowheads, spear-points and pottery. Little statues set between the Prince Albert tobacco cans and the Bruton's snuff: cheap carnival Indians sat side-by-side with effigy pots and honeysuckle baskets.

Jesse sat in a cane-bottomed chair in the corner and talked to his buddies. Now and then, he would rise, take a Flit spray from under the counter and pump a thin, sweet mist into the air. The counter top and floor was always littered with the dead bugs, flies and spiders. It was dark in the store because stacks of feed or strips of burlap sacks covered most of the windows. When anyone entered, Jesse and the old men blinked like lizards at the sunlight. In the back of the store, there was a doorway and sometimes "the Woman" would stand there watching us. She might have been a stack of feed sacks, she stood that still. Then, the shadow would shift and move away.

Once, when Jesse saw me looking from the walls to the statues to the baskets, he took time to spit in a Del Monte peach can at his feet, smiled and said, "I like Injuns." I knew he meant he liked "Indians."

I picked up a milky quartz arrowhead. "How much is this?"

"Oh, ain't nothin' fer sale," said Jesse. "I jest put this stuff out so's people can look at it." He smiled, and then went back to talking to the old men. I dropped the arrowhead back in the barrel. There must have been twenty people in and around the store, but nobody spoke to us but Jesse. They watched us though. I could feel

21

their eyes on me. When we left, Jesse followed us to the truck. I didn't see him until he spoke to me through the truck window.

"What's yore name?" he asked. I was writing the bill for the kerosene that Papaw had pumped into the square red tank in the back of Jesse's store.

"Harley," I said.

"He's John Lyndon's boy," said Papaw.

"The one that got killed?" asked Jesse. Papaw nodded, and looked away.

Jesse reached through the window and took the oil bill.

"Here ye go," he said. There was the quartz arrowhead in my hand.

"Mind your raising," said Papaw.

"Thank you, sir." I said.

Out in the sunlight, Jesse seemed a different person. He had a great, squashed nose covered with blue veins and the skin on his face looked like my baseball glove. His teeth were brown nubs and the creases at the corners of his mouth were stained with tobacco.

"You like Injuns?" he said.

I nodded. "I been to the Reservation and seen the Chief."

"He's seen Walkingdeer, down at Howell's Trading Post," said Papaw.

"Cee-oh," said Jesse. "Sty-you?"

"Stick-a wa-ta-lee," I said.

Jesse laughed. "I don't believe this boy knows what he just said," he told Papaw.

"That's something he picked up at Howell's Store. What did he say?"

"He just inquired about the health of my trouser worm," said Jesse.

Papaw got real mad before he remembered I didn't know what I was saying. "Let that be a lesson to you, Harley. Be sure you know what you are saying before you open your mouth."

"What's a trouser worm?" I said.

"Never mind," he said.

Jesse laughed and turned away. I noticed he was limping.

"What happened to his leg?" I asked Papaw.

"That's a long story," said Papaw, starting the truck.

Once on the way down the mountain, he said, "The woman is a Cherokee."

MASON JARS IN THE FLOOD

"What woman?" I said.

"The one in the back of the store." I remembered the motionless shadow in the doorway. "She never speaks, or comes out in the store, but she's usually back there somewheres." Papaw didn't say anything for a while. "She showed up after Jesse's wife got killed."

"What happened to his wife?" I said.

"Somebody cut her throat," Papaw said. "Beat Jesse half to death. Broke his leg 'n it never did mend right."

"Did they catch whoever done it?" I said.

"Nope. Jesse couldn't give a very good description of them."

"Why not?"

"That's a good question. I wonder about that myself." Papaw seemed to get involved in his driving. Finally, he said, "I think that Cherokee woman might know."

"I don't understand," I said.

Papaw looked at me out of the corner of his eye. "No," he said, "Not yet, you don't." It seemed that I spent lots of days learning things that I wouldn't understand until I was older.

Halfway down the mountain, a rattlesnake crawled across the road. It was six feet long.

"Wow!" I said.

Papaw ran over the snake. Then, he stopped and backed up so he could run over it again. Then, he got out of the truck and found a big stick. Papaw really hated rattlesnakes. The snake was still moving, but there was something wrong with the way it crawled. Then, Papaw saw the string around the snake's neck. Laughter came from the side of the road, and we saw two boys running into the woods. We stood and watched them vanish, the dead snake dragging behind them. Papaw threw his stick away.

"Don't that beat all!" he said. "Probably been hid out there in the bushes for hours waiting for somebody to come along, so's they could pull that dead snake across the road. Don't know what these people would do without this road for entertainment."

Papaw was quiet for a while. Then, he said, "There ain't no snakes in the Cove." That surprised me.

"Not any a-tall?"

"Well, maybe some hog snakes and a few blue racers. But there ain't no mean snakes. No rattlers or copperheads."

Papaw talked all the way home about what lived in the Cove. Pheasant and wild turkeys. Might even see deer from time to time. I asked if there would be any painters, and Papaw said no. I asked him why, and he laughed and said, "Because I said so." That sounded good enough for me. He went on and on about cold spring water, brook trout and chickens "that roosted with the screech-owls." It was getting dark now, and he turned the headlights on. He chuckled as he drove and I could see his face in the light from the dash. "No town sounds out there," he said. "Just wind and rain and running water."

SHAZAM!

It all started last summer the day after school was out. Granny was setting on the porch with her sister Tildy talking to beat the band. Granny loves to gossip and Tildy knows more bad stuff than anybody, although Aunt Elsie, Papaw's sister, runs her a close second. Tildy tells Granny terrible stories about death, sickness and heartless children. Sometimes, she manages to get all three in the same story. Granny loves it. When Papaw sees Aunt Tildy coming up the road, he tries to hide. This time, he went to the barn.

"Uh-oh," he said, "Here comes Death and Destruction." That's what he called Aunt Tildy, "Death and Destruction."

"Don't start, Arthur," said Granny. "Tildy's had a hard row to hoe."

"Yes, well," said Papaw, "I'll be at the barn." That's where he went to shell corn, maybe fork some hay into the barn loft. I was out in the road playing marbles with Boover and Tom Ed, but I could hear Granny and Aunt Tildy talking real well.

"Things have been bad and they are gonna get worse," said Aunt Tildy.

"Ain't it the truth!" said Granny.

"Maudie Birch has got a goiter as big as a mush-melon," said Tildy. "I seen her at the Shepherd reunion. I tried not to stare, of course, but it was awful, hanging there under her chin."

"You don't mean it!" said Granny. "A goiter!"

"You remember what a pretty thing she was when we was growing up on Big Ridge. All the boys running after her. Went to her head I think, all that attention."

"Married a Gibson, didn't she?" said Granny.

"Maybe it's a judgment," said Aunt Tildy. "The goiter, I mean. Maybe God's teaching her humility." Aunt Tildy sounded pleased.

Granny stood and stared at Tom Ed, Boover and me out in the road. Each of us had a cigar-box full of marbles and we was playing for keeps.

"Harley, you'uns be careful out there," she hollered. "It's dangerous to play in the road."

"O.K., Granny," I said. It wasn't really a road, anyway. A dirt trail would be more like it. Mostly, you just seen people walking, or maybe driving cows to and from the big pasture on top of the ridge. I knowed that Granny wasn't worried about cars. She was worried about Jedro Tolley. Well, sure enough, a few minutes later, we heard him. We always heard him before we seen him.

At first, it sounded like the tannery whistle.

"Eeeeeeeeeeeeeeeeee..."

Then, the sound dropped 'til it sounded like the big saw at the lumber-mill in Tannery Flats.

"Haaaaaaaaaaaaaaaaaaaaaaaaaaa.....!

Today, Boover heard him first. He was hunkered over aiming at one of my blue crackle-glass marbles in the pot, when he raised his head.

"I think it's him," he said. We all listened. For a minute, there was nothing but them marbles and jar flies rattling in the broom sedge. Then, we seen him at the top of the hill.

"Oh, lord, " said Boover. "Here he comes!"

Topping the rise at the head of the holler, Jedro Tolley stuck his chin over the warped handlebars of his fire-engine red Belknap, his skinny butt raised like the stinger of a mad hornet. Then, here he come, down the part of the trail that is as steep as a roller-coaster track, swooping like a buzzard. The pile of comic books in the handlebar-basket boiled and fluttered; Jedro's overalls whipped and cracked; his spiky, red hair bent, flattened, then streamed like a flag.

"EeeeeeeEEEEEEEEEEEEE HAAAAAAAAAAAAAAA!"

That crazy yell was as long in space as it was in time. Sometimes, we heard it before he appeared, and it echoed in the distance long after Jedro had vanished down a funnel of dust, barking dogs and cackling chickens.

"Fool's gonna kill hisself," said Granny.

"Bound to happen," said Aunt Tildy.

"That youngun's not right."

"Like his grand-daddy."

The two sisters discussed Jedro's worthless daddy and grand-daddy doomed from birth; watched the dust settle in the kudzu vines along the road; moved their chairs to the shaded end of the porch where they rocked and gazed at the cloudless, summer day. A quarter of a mile away, a faint drum roll announced Jedro's passage over the Mooney Creek Bridge. I always liked to imagine what happened then, 'cause that is where Roosevelt Wilson Hall lives. Under the bridge. I can see him setting in the cool darkness beneath them vibrating planks. Not many things crossed that bridge on the average day. And what did, Roosevelt could hear coming for ten minutes before it got there. Except for Jedro. I imagine Roosevelt staring upward in alarm as thunder shakes his roof; dust and grit sifts down into his hair and eyes and his bottle of Mickey's Big Mouth Beer or his vanilla extract cocktail.

"Jedro, you damned fool!" That's what he always hollers.

I can see Roosevelt blinking and shaking his fist at the thrumming ceiling. Beyond the bridge, Jedro pedals up Keener Hill listening to the clack and grind of his rusty sprocket chain. Then he is over the top and from there on, everything is downhill.

I guess I always knowed that Jedro was a little crazy, but to Tom Ed, Boover and me, hunkered in the dusty road with a cigar-box full of crackle-glass marbles, that lightning descent had all the excitement of an Apache raid at the Saturday matinee. The first wild screech would send us scrambling for cover, leaving marbles, sling-shots and drop-boxes.

"Eeeeeeeeeeee....."

"Here he comes!"

"eeeeEEEEEEEEEEE!"

Boover Henson, Tom Ed Passmore and me, plowing through saw-briars, broom-sedge and kudzu like victims of an air-raid.

"HAAAAAAAAAAAAAaaaaaaaaaaaaaaaaaa...aaa."

"Golleeeey!" marveled Boover.

"Hot Damn!" said Tom Ed. "He even pedals downhill!"

Everybody in the holler agreed that in addition to being "tetched" and doomed, Jedro was worthless. He had all the symptoms of corrupted youth: He swapped "funny-books," smoked cigarettes, went to the movies and hung out in the pool-room.

"Ain't nothing he can do about it," said Granny with stoic pessimism. "It's bad blood, the sins of the fathers and the chickens coming home to roost."

"Hark to my word," said Aunt Tildy. "He's bound for reform school, the chain-gang or worse."

In school, Jedro was something of a celebrity. He had failed the third grade four times, and as Boover once reverently observed, "Ain't nobody ever done that bad!" He sat in the back of the room, his chin resting on his folded arms, his green pinwheel eyes staring at the words that was carved in the surface of his under-sized desk.

During class, he would slowly remove a collection of objects from his big pockets and place them on the desk. Jedro picked up each item, stared at it for a while, placed it carefully on his desk, and then stared at it some more. Each object seemed a part of some mysterious secret ritual: a buckeye, a rabbit's foot, a hairball taken from the stomach of a six-point buck; an unpolished garnet, an Indian-head penny and a Captain Marvel Secret Decoder Ring.

When the recess bell rang, Jedro crammed everything into his pockets and left. Stoop-shouldered and pigeon-toed, he would shuffle down the hall, out of the building and across the playground to the jack-pine thicket. There, burrowing in pine needle dunes, we waited.

"How about 'Wonder Woman Meets the Moon Wizard,'" said Tom Ed.

"I'd rather hear a Tarzan story," said Boover.

"Or a Submarine," I offered.

Jedro, sitting propped against a pine tree, would just grin at the treetops, the flying birds, and the drifting clouds.

"I seen 'Roy Rogers in Shadow Canyon' yesterday," he said.

"Hey, great!"

"Tell it, Jedro!"

"Well, then," he said, burrowing his brogans into the pine needles and closing his eyes. When he started speaking, when he opened his eyes again, he spoke in a kind of sing-song voice. Those green eyes brightened, his face relaxed, and his hands began to move.

"It's night and way up on this lonesome ole hill, this wolf is howling. *'Ah-wooooooo. Ah-wooooo.'* You can see his shape against this big, full moon. The wind is blowin' and that wolf and the wind together, they sound kind of empty and scary. Then, all of a sudden, this black shape rises up! For a minute, you can't tell what it is, but then you see that it is a man on a horse. He starts riding....riding down towards this bunkhouse, and you know by the way that he is sneaking along, that he is up to no good. Then, you see inside the bunkhouse and there sets Roy and Dale singing 'Blue Shadows on the Trail.' Then, Roy, he stops singing and he says, 'Did you hear something, Dale?'"

Like I said, all of this started last summer, and went on through the fall of my ninth year. While dust devils spun across the playground, Boover, Tom Ed and me, buried in pine needles, candy wrappers, and popsicle sticks, listened to Jedro Tolley's magic stories. As the days grew shorter, and the autumn leaves flew through the jack pine thicket, the clamor of the play-ground faded as the four of us traveled to the moon, defeated gravity, restored planets to their orbits, and descended into the depths of the earth.

"Oh, help me, great white queen! Don't let me die!"

Jedro, buried in pine needles up to his chin was acting out a scene from last Saturday's continued serial, "Sheena, Queen of the Jungle." We crept cautiously near the seething pit of quicksand, where Ungawi, the evil witch doctor, begged Sheena for mercy. Jedro's head vanished, his uplifted hands jerked dramatically, and then he sank beneath the shifting pine needles. Then, his muffled voice said, "And then, Sheena, she just looked down from her tree limb above the quick-sand pit and said, 'I cannot save you. You have sinned against the jungle, evil one. Now, the jungle has punished you. So be it!'" Jedro rose from Ungawi's burial mound, brushing pine needles from his overalls and concluded, "Then, she just swung off on a grape-vine."

Batmobiles, kryptonite, the Shadow's spooky laugh, Tarzan's elephant call and the frightening revenge of the Heap - all were recreated at recess beneath Jedro's tree.

"Out of all them funny-book people, which one is your favorite, Jedro?" It was Boover that asked the question. He asked it earnestly, as though his future happiness depended on the answer.

"Oh, thet's easy. Captain Marvel!" said Jedro. His fingers poked through his pockets, removing an elderberry pop-gun, pennies and marbles, until he found it: The Captain Marvel Secret Decoder Ring. "He has one just like this. You see, he is just a ordinary feller, but when he puts this ring on, and he holds it up........." Our eyes followed the clenched fist and the gleaming ring, "When he says, 'Shazam!' why, then nobody can hurt him. Not bullets or bombs or nothing."

And then the fall passed into winter. Jedro spun yarns at mid-day and swooped on his bicycle in the afternoon. Down in the jack-pine thicket, as the weather grew colder, we stared regretfully at our chapped hands, the barren elms flanking the water fountain and the deserted schoolyard.

"Gonna be too cold to come out here before long, " said Boover.

"Guess we'll have to start staying inside," said Tom Ed.

We burrowed deeper into the pine needles, and put our hands in our armpits as Jedro described life on Krypton.

We didn't hear Jedro go by anymore in the afternoon. We had given up roadbed marbles for indoor Monopoly. It was about the last of October when Jedro got killed. Boover had just sold me his hotels on Park Place when Tom Ed opened the door, all white-faced and breathless.

"Jedro just hit Oley Barnes' Grapette truck," he said.

It had happened right in the middle of the Mooney Creek Bridge. Long before we got there, we could see how bad it was. Jedro's bike was stuck in the truck's grill. A big sunburst of blood stained the shattered windshield. Roosevelt Wilson Hall was standing near the edge of the bridge, staring at a soggy wad of comic books in the creek and around the bridge. He held a bottle of vanilla extract in one hand and a bottle of Scalf's Indian River Medicine in the other.

"Jest mixing my afternoon cocktail," he said, "when it come like a clap of thunder." He pointed at the wet comics. "Them things just rained down! Kept falling!"

Beyond the bridge Mooney Creek was filled with bright colors. Tarzan, the Heap and Sheena clung together in the muddy water. Nearby, Oley Barnes sat on the bank talking to the patrolman.

"Wasn't no missing him," Oley said. "As God is my witness, he come like a bullet down that hill, screaming all the way. Oh, Lordy," he said, wringing his hands, "That poor boy."

Boover found Jedro. On the side of the road behind the patrol car, a grey blanket fluttered in the wind. Someone had placed rocks on each of the four corners.

"That's a special blanket," said Boover. "Patrolmen carry them in the trunk....just in case."

"In case of what?" said Tom Ed.

"In case they have to cover up a dead person, stupid." We watched the fluttering blanket for a while, the shape beneath it, mysterious except for the pale hand protruding from one corner.

"Probably tore his head off," whispered Tom Ed.

"Oh, bull! What do you know about it?" said Boover.

"I heard them talking," said Tom Ed.

Boover looked unconvinced. "We don't even know for certain if that's him under there," he said.

"It's him, all right," said Tom Ed. "Look." He pointed to the pale hand, the gleaming ring.

On the bridge, Roosevelt dropped a bundle of comics into the creek. The wail of a siren grew in volume, and then the ambulance came down Keener Hill.

After the funeral, the three of us huddled against the white, clapboard wall of the Lovesdale Methodist Church and watched the gravediggers. The shovels gleamed and winked in the red dirt. On the steps of the church, Granny and Aunt Tildy turned their backs to the cold wind and commented on the poor attendance.

"Ah, well," said Granny, "His mother died when he was a baby, and his daddy went traipsing off somewheres."

"Nobody left to raise the poor youngun, 'cept that worthless uncle," said Tildy. She paused a moment and said, "Now, didn't I say something like this would happen?"

Aunt Tildy looked over her shoulder and then said, "Did you hear about Sally Fouts?"

"No, what?" said Granny.

"Died in church last night."

"They, hush your mouth!"

"Settin' there dead as a doornail with her false teeth in her lap."

"You don't mean it!"

"While they was passing the plate. That's how they knowed, when she didn't take the plate."

The two sisters shook their heads, and then went off to see if "the weeds had took over Papa's grave." The gravediggers was gone now, but still, we waited. Then, Jedro's uncle stumbled past us, his lips moving in a silent monologue.

Boover stepped forward. "Mr. Tolley, sir," he said.

The old man turned in alarm, his vague, watery eyes finally finding Boover.

"Mr. Tolley, sir. Will Jedro have a grave stone?" For a moment, the old man struggled to understand Boover. Then he smiled, fleetingly.

31

"Lord, no, child. I ain't got that kind of money." He turned back, looking at the mound of raw, red earth. Then, he shook his head.

"He were a strange boy," he said. "Never meant nobody harm, though." Then, he walked on toward the road.

"There now! Didn't I tell you," said Tom Ed.

"Yeah, well, I just wanted to be sure." He turned to me. "Let's see it, Harley."

I drew the sheet of Blue Horse notebook paper from my pocket and smoothed it out. Boover looked at the writing and shook his head doubtfully.

"It don't look much like what is on the others," he said "They got things like 'In His Bosom' and 'Eternal Life.'"

"We agreed," said Tom Ed. "Do it."

"Okay."

Boover handed me a sharpened stick, and I forced it through the bottom and top of the ragged paper. I held my breath a moment, and then, I ran across the graveyard to Jedro, and forced the stick into the earth. The paper, already damp with mud, fluttered in the wind, but when I stood, I could read it.

JEDRO TOLLEY
January 20, 1935
October 29, 1949

Across the bottom, in red crayon, we had written:

SHAZAM!

I ran back to where the others were waiting for me.

BABBY

Once a month, we go to see Babby, Papaw's mother, in Macon County. We always go on a Sunday. Papaw drives down to Dillsboro, and buys gas from Cap Weaver. Cap looks like Popeye and he is deaf as a rock. When Papaw drives into his station, Cap's "Bermuda bell" rings and out he comes. Most people can hear Cap's bell for a couple of miles, and he gets a lot of complaints at night from folks living in Dillsboro who say they can't get to sleep until Cap closes. Cap always gives me a balloon and a box of "Guess Whats." "Guess Whats" are little pieces of candy that are wrapped up with a surprise, like maybe a tiny whistle or a plastic ring. He also "gooses" me unless I stay well out of his reach. "Goosing" is when somebody tickles your ribs with his fingers and makes you laugh. Cap gooses too hard, and one time, I peed on myself, so I'm not going to give him another chance.

Babby lives in Cowee near Leatherman Gap. The little creek where she lives has been named after her and there is a little sign that says "Aunt Nancy Teester Creek." She is Papaw's mother, and her nick-name is Babby. Nobody knows why. Babby is the oldest person I have ever seen so far. She has wild, white hair that floats around her head. She is almost as deaf as Cap Weaver, and her eyesight is going. She can't walk and spends most of her time propped up in a big feather bed in the living room.

Sometimes, on Sunday, Babby's children carry her out on the porch where she sits in a big upholstered chair and watches people come and go. In the summer, dinner is served outside on big wooden tables that stretch across the yard. There are always a dozen bowls of potato salad, fried chicken, platters of deviled eggs, pork, greenbeans, corn and lots of pies and cakes. Papaw's brother, Hoyt, is usually there. Aunt Elsie and her daughter, Irene, live with Babby, and Uncle Ardell lives nearby. There are usually fifteen or twenty people that I don't know who are related to Babby.

After dinner, all the grandchildren are "introduced" to Babby. We all line up on the porch in front of Babby's chair, and then Aunt Elsie drags us forward, one at a time.

"THIS IS TOMMY" shouts Aunt Elsie.

"TOMMY?" Babby shouts back.

"ALVA'S BOY!" hollers Elsie.

'ALVA?" yells Babby.

"ARTHUR'S DAUGHTER!" screams Elsie.

"Oh, yes! That one." says Babby. Then, she hugs Tommy. Then Tommy hollers. We have been told that there is no reason to be afraid of Babby, but some of us are scared the first couple of times we get hugged. Then we get used to it. After we get hugged, we go off to throw rocks in the creek and look for snakes or inspect the outhouse that is built over the creek.

Babby's house used to be the schoolhouse, and her husband, Papaw's daddy, was the teacher, teaching all the subjects and all the grades. He had turned his house into a school because there wasn't one. His name was William and he was also a photographer who developed pictures by laying them out in the sunlight.

One Sunday, I found myself alone in the house with Babby. Papaw, Uncle Hoyt and Aunt Elsie had organized a trip to the graveyard while I was still wading in the creek. When I came in the house, Babby reached over from the bed and caught me.

"Which one are ye?" she said.

"I'm Harley."

"Well, Harley, reach under the bed and haul that trunk out."

I did.

"Open it."

It smelled like leather and snuff and the big top drawer was filled with little compartments covered with faded cushions. Underneath were tintypes and old photographs on stiff black cardboard. All of the pictures seemed to be of grim people - men who stood stiffly behind seated women, one hand grasping a coat lapel, the other resting on the woman's shoulder. The women wore huge bonnets that made their faces look like flowers surrounded by big petals. Babby took one of the photographs from my hand and peered at it for a moment; then, she shook her head in frustration and gave it back.

"Does that man have on a string tie?"

"Yes'm."

"Then, that's William and me on our wedding day."

I looked at the man's dour face. "He looks mad about something." Babby almost smiled. "Don't guess I heard William laugh a dozen times in fifty years."

"How come?"

The prolonged silence made me think the old woman hadn't heard me.

"I guess it was what happened to his daddy," she finally said.

"What happened to his daddy?"

"His name was Bryan," she said, "Your great-great-granddaddy. He was kilt."

"In the Civil War?"

"Not exactly." She pulled the curtain aside and looked out the window as though she were confirming something.

"He was in the war, though. Joined up in Clayton, Georgia and got sent up to Virginny." She prodded me in the side and pointed at a pasteboard box in the trunk. "Open that," she said.

The box contained a single letter, two pages that were brown with age. When I unfolded it, I saw letters in blue ink, but they weren't like any letters I had ever seen. Flowers and vines twined around the words; letters became birds flying.

"Pretty, ain't it? He writ a beautiful hand, Bryan did." Again, her fingers prodded me. "Read me them last few lines."

It was kind of slow going at first, but I got the hang of it. "Tomorrow, we move to Falls Church, and from there to Pennsylvania. It is summer here and the cornfields make me sick for home and your face. I must stop now, as it is beginning to rain."

Babby laughed. "That's the part! The rain! Now, look at that letter close." When I turned the letter toward the light, I saw that some of the letters were blotched and running. Raindrops.

"Two days after he writ that, he was shot in some trifling little skirmish in Pennsylvania. Captured, too. Lost his right arm. They sawed the broken bone off and seared the stump with a red-hot wagon bolt. He near died of infection in that Yankee hospital. Finally got traded in a prisoner exchange and ended up in a Confederate hospital where he stayed 'til the spring of '63 when they let him come home."

35

The old woman looked at me as though she had forgotten who I was. Then she went on. "William was 'bout your age when his daddy come home. Terrible wasted, he was. Set for weeks before the fire and tried to tell them what had happened. It wasn't just the arm he lost. He had seen things that made him feel different 'bout the world. But he mended. Come spring, he set about trying to farm. Fixed his plow so he could handle it with one arm, and he plowed and planted twenty acres of cornfield. William saw him trying to write with his left hand, and after a time, he begin to talk 'bout teaching school. That's what he always wanted to do.

"Them men that come to Bryan's farm, they called themselves 'Kirk's Raiders.' They were foraging, you see. That's what they called it. Foraging." Babby stared at the wall. "They robbed and stoled, burned homes and shot innocent people. Most wore Union colors and but a lot of them didn't have a uniform at all."

Babby's voice had changed. Now, the words sounded like sharp, hurled stones. "Bryan was in the field when they come. He knowed better than to resist. He just stood there and watched them trample his corn down. They took his horse and the mule. Killed the pig and hauled it away. What they couldn't take, they ruined. Killed the chickens and poured water in the bee gums.

"Killing Bryan seemed to be an afterthought. William said they was leaving, whooping and hollering, when Kirk stopped and rode back to where Bryan was standing. He took his sword out and sorta flicked Bryan's coat. It was his Confederate coat; pretty ragged with one sleeve pinned up. Kirk smiled at Bryan and said, 'You, sir, wear the colors of the enemy.' Then he shot him in the face. Two men hauled the body to the house and throwed it up on the porch. Bryan's wife waited 'til they were gone, and then she hit out for the nearest neighbors. Back then, that was about fifteen miles away. She left William on the porch with his daddy's corpse.

"She was gone all night. Next morning, when she got back, she couldn't find William. Called him, but there was no answer. Finally, the neighbor found him hid in the chimney corner...that little shelf behind the chimney. William wouldn't talk. Over a year before he started talking again.

"Like you said, Harley, he always looked like he was mad 'bout something." Babby laughed, but it sounded strange. "He was, I guess. The older he got, the madder he got. Wasn't just what Kirk did to his daddy. He was mad 'bout the difference between Bryan's handwriting and his. Used to say that he lost more than a daddy. He lost them roses that twined around the words in his daddy's letter."

When Papaw got back from Mount Gilead, Babby was asleep. I was throwing rocks in the creek when he came to say we were going home.

"Is Bryan buried at Mount Gilead?" I said.

"Bryan? Momma been telling you 'bout Bryan?" I nodded.

"No, he's buried somewheres else. They come once and moved him to a Confederate graveyard. Might be down in Swain County."

"How come you don't know for sure?"

"Oh, law, Harley, that was a long time ago. 'Course, Momma, she's still mad 'bout it, 'n it weren't even her kin." He shook his head and laughed. "Still mad."

I threw another rock. "Me, too," I said. "Me, too."

SHOOT-OUT AT THE RITZ

One spring, a couple of years ago, Uncle Albert took me to my first Saturday matinee at the Ritz. Well, he didn't exactly take me. He let me out in front of the theatre and gave me a dollar. He told me that this was a Lash LaRue double feature, and it was a "religious event." Said I should watch it twice, or until he came back. It was a good show. I loved to watch Lash pop that whip. The only movies I had ever seen before Lash was stuff that Aunt Ruby took me to see - stuff like "Mrs. Miniver" and "White Cliffs of Dover," which was okay, I guess, but nobody popped any whips or stopped any run-away stage coaches.

Albert didn't come back until late that night, just before the Owl show started. The Owl show is always a scary picture like "Cat People" or "The Mummy's Revenge." When I came out in the lobby to get my third Nehi and Baby Ruth, there he was flirting with Blicka Dee Passmore, the ticket-taker. His hair was brilliantined and roached in little waves along the sides and he had been eating Sen-Sen, which made his breath smell like candy.

I had a pretty good idea why he had left me at the Ritz anyway. He had driven his little roadster (with the little glass knob on the steering wheel so he could drive with one hand) up and down main street for thirty minutes, tooting his horn at the girls standing in front of Kress's Five and Dime. I may have been just a little kid, but I knew what he was up to. Well, sorta. With me in the Ritz, he could take girls like JayNelle Frady and Bennie Sue Carnes to Maple Springs where they would dance in that big, dark backroom. I knew because I had been to Maple Springs with him. I sat at a little table in the dark with a Dr. Pepper and a Moon Pie and watched. The only kind of dancing that Albert did was hugging up and sliding around on that slick, polished floor while Hank Williams whined about how lonesome he was. I don't pretend to understand Albert's idea of a good time, but I figure I could have seen a dozen Durango Kids and Sunset Carsons with the nickels and dimes he put in that jukebox.

"Don't tell Momma," he said on the way home. That is what he said that first night after the Lash LaRue double feature. "If you are a smart boy, I just might buy you some funny books at Velts Cafe."

"What's a smart boy?" I said.

"One that tells Momma when she asks you what we did tonight, that we went out to Love's Chapel Church to the big revival."

I did that. I know a good deal when I see one. Each week, he let me out at the Ritz, and each week we made up a story. Quartets, library visits, talks by missionaries while all the time I was at the Ritz watching bank robberies, runaway stage coaches and trick riding. Albert? He was dancing in the dark at Maple Springs to Hank Snow and Roy Acuff. I got the best deal! For almost a year now, I've seen cowboys like Sunset Carson, Durango Kid, Don "Red" Berry and Johnny "Mack" Brown shoot, ride, fistfight, and crack whips.

One night, he was late. The Owl show had already started, and I was standing under the big neon marquee watching for Albert's little roadster. The Ritz was next to a tombstone shop and the dark hillside was covered with sad angels and praying hands. I was a little spooked, I guess, and when Albert finally pulled up; I was staring at the hillside.

When I got in, Albert said, "That is where they bury them, you know."

"Bury who?"

"The cowboys that get killed on Saturday."

I didn't say anything. Albert was always funning. Then he said, "Not all of them, of course. Some are make-believe. But, now and then, the shootings are real. Mostly, the Lash LaRue."

I give him my 'you-think-I-believe-that' look.

Albert pointed to the dark hillside. See that big door up there in the back of the theatre? That's where they drag the bodies out. They wait until 2 or 3 in the morning, and they drag them out and bury them in one grave."

You gotta remember, I was a little kid. I mean, I'm ten now, and there is no way I would believe something like that. But, then, with Albert looking all serious and whispering, I begin to wonder.

"I've been down at the bus station on Saturday morning when they came in on the Knoxville bus."

"Who?"

"Why, the gunslingers in the movies! See, most of them are murderers waiting to be executed, so they give them this chance, see? If they can survive a Lash LaRue movie, they let them go."

"But it is a movie!"

Albert smiled. "Looks like a movie," he said, "but if you will watch real close, you can tell when it becomes real." He wiggled his eyebrows, raced the motor and pulled away.

The next day, I told Charlie Kay about it. He had been my best friend since the 3rd grade. "Goolleee!" he said. Charlie decided it "made sense." At recess, he told a dozen kids about it. Charlie organized us into a squad and said that we should all meet at the Ritz the next Saturday. "We'll all sit on the front row," he said. "When the time comes, when the movie stops and the real shooting begins, that is when we will strike!"

I realize now that I never should have told Charlie Kay. He had more funny books than anybody in the world, and he already had most of us convinced that a werewolf lived under the Sylva Elementary behind the coal furnace, and that the man who ran the ice-house was a vampire. I liked having Charlie Kay for a friend, though. He was a lot of fun.

The movie was "Shootout in Tulsa." There were eight of us on the front row. Me and Charlie were armed with cap-pistols, and we were all pretty nervous. I didn't see the change from movie to real, but Charlie did. When he pointed it out to the rest of us, we saw it, too. The gunfighters were all in the street outside the Mad Dog Saloon when Charlie said, "Now!" and we charged through the little door by the screen. We ended up in some kind of storage room and Charlie was trying to open another door when the guy with the flashlight caught us.

It was a mess. They kept us in the manager's office until the police came, and then we each got a ride home. It didn't make much sense when we explained what we were doing behind the screen. When it was all over, Granny was hopping mad. But, when she talked about it to other folks, I was just an "innocent child" who had been misused by Albert, who didn't have the sense

"God gave a grasshopper." When she cornered Albert, he said he couldn't resist the temptation. "When I tell Harley a lie, his eyes get big and his mouth drops open. It is fun to watch that," he said.

My 4th grade teacher came to the house and talked to Granny about my "overly active imagination." She had said the same thing when I was in the second grade. She said that Charlie Kay was a bad influence and that I should not be allowed to talk to him.

Well, the movies are sure less interesting without Charlie Kay and we don't buddy around together at school. I'm eleven years old now, and almost everyone has forgotten about what happened at the Ritz. I still go home with Charlie and we read his funny books for hours. I just don't tell where I've been. Charlie asked me last week if I saw what was behind the door that he had just got open when the man with the flashlight showed up. "Dead gunslingers," said Charlie. "Stacked like cordwood in that storeroom! Didn't you see them?" I didn't at the time, but now that I think about it, maybe Charlie got that door open and for a moment I could see what was in that room....all of them cowboy boots stacked on top of each other. But, then maybe I'm imagining it.

GETTING CLEAN AWAY

"Who is that, Papaw?" I had been watching the figure for a couple of minutes, as it wavered in the summer heat. Black as the crows on Painter Knob, it trudged, paused, faded, reappeared and trudged again, its progress reminding me of my old wind-up Popeye when it was running down. Papaw looked up from The Grit, watched for a minute and then, gave a heart-felt sigh.

"Oh, Gawd, it's Dony." He got up from his rocker and called into the house. "Agnes, Dony is coming."

From where I stood, peering between Granny's begonias that lined the porch banisters, I suddenly felt uneasy. Even at this distance, the figure looked unwelcome, a dark shadow shimmering in the heat.

Granny came to the door with flour on her hands and looked down the road. "Maybe she is going on up the Cove. The Ridley baby died last week." Papaw looked surprised.

"Ah, no! What killed it?" said Papaw, returning to his rocker.

"The croup, I reckon." Granny went back to the kitchen.

"The Ridleys seem to have a full plate of bad luck. First, the boy with polio, and now this."

Arnie Ridley was in the fifth grade, too, and I traded comic books with him, my Captain Marvels for his Green Hornets.

"Why does she walk that way?" I asked.

Papaw folded The Grit and stuck it between two of Granny's flower buckets that said "Crisco Lard" on the side.

"Well, Harley, that old woman has had two strokes plus she got hit by a car a few years back. She's bad to walk in the middle of the road. Got metal pins in her hip."

I finally realized that she was carrying something; it was bulky and black like the long dress. She gripped it the way Papaw gripped the big slate rocks that he dug out of the cornfield and carried to the sled, moving in a stooped and stiff-legged stagger.

"What is she carrying?" Papaw gave another weary sigh.

"That is the Memory Book." He laughed and shook his head. "She has the obituary and the picture of every man, woman and child that has died in this county since about 1920."

"How come?"

"Oh, sweet Jesus, please!" Papaw whispered. He hadn't heard my question because he was watching Dony. He pleaded in a soft whisper as the old woman halted by the mail box, swaying like a wind-racked tree. "Let her go on, let her go on," he chanted. After a bit, she turned in the trail that ran behind the springhouse to our front porch. Papaw finally stood and reluctantly called out.

"Come on in, Dony, and take a load off your feet." He gave me a sharp nudge, "Go get the water bucket and the dipper." Then, he went down the steps and took the Memory Book from the old woman. "Here, give me that. You got no business lugging this thing up Rhodes Cove on a hot day like this." He laid the book in the seat of a cane-bottomed chair, looking at it the same way he looked at dead snakes.

Dony was old beyond my experience, her skin hanging in great wattles from her neck and arms. Sweat coursed down her face, dripped from her nose and mingled with the snuff stains in the corners of her mouth. Her black brocaded dress drooped like a wet sack.

"Harley, mind your manners." I closed my mouth. "I told you to bring Dony a dipper of cold water."

"Yes, sir." So I did, returning from the back porch with a galvanized bucket filled with cold spring water. I held the tin dipper out to Dony.

She stared at me for a moment.

"John Lyndon's boy," she croaked, taking the dipper and rinsing her mouth out. She spit into one of Granny's flower buckets and then, drank, like Mandy the cow, with long, noisy droughts. "I've got your daddy in here." A finger that looked like a brown, sun-baked mud-dabber's home, thin and fluted, tapped the book. She opened it.

How could that be? I thought of my smiling, dead father trapped in that book. "Yessiree," she said with relish, "Happy Teester is in here."

There were hundreds of pages that smelled of paste and dried flowers. As she turned the stiff leaves, I saw yellowed newspaper print, condolence cards, pressed roses, faded ribbons and ancient photographs.

"Here!" The newspaper caption read, "Happy Teester Murdered at Service Station." There was also an account of the funeral at Love's Chapel, and the trial of the poor drunk who stopped my daddy's heart with a rusty pistol. Dony removed a picture and held it towards me.

"Agnes give me this!" It was a tinted photograph of "Happy" Teester with a guitar, all pink-cheeked and blue-eyed, his foot propped on the bumper of an A-model. "Don't he look just like his name! So alive...but in the midst of life we are in death!" She carefully replaced the picture in the little black holders that gripped its four corners.

Papaw rose and walked to the end of the porch where he stood staring at the Balsam Mountains.

"So, you must be Harley," said Dony, "See, your name is here, too." She traced the words on the obituary. "How old are you, Harley?"

"Eleven," I said. My grandmother opened the screen door, wiping her hands on her apron. "Well, now! It's Dony Wikle." Her smile was strained. "What brings you to the Cove, Dony?"

"Eileen Ridley." Dony displayed a page captioned, "Eileen Ridley, one year and four months, April 14, 1947."

"That is a long walk," said Granny. "Clear up to the top of the ridge."

"I'll make it before dark. It has been a week now, and I try to wait a while before I visit, 'til the grieving is over."

Granny looked at Papaw's back. "Sometimes it's never over," she said.

"True enough," said Dony. "Man cometh up like a flower and is cut down." Dony's head wobbled in a mix of palsy and conviction. "We stumble at noon as in the twilight," she was getting louder now, and her voice became a chant, "We look for justice but there is none." Dony smiled as though the things she said pleased her; smiled in a way that made me think of the way a burlap sack collapsed into itself when it was empty.

44

"Won't you stay for supper?" Granny twisted her apron in her hands and looked again at Papaw's back.

"No rest for the weary," said Dony clambering to her feet. "Of course, we will all rest *over there*." We watched as her hands scrabbled for a grip on the huge book.

"Maybe..." Granny looked nervously at Papaw. "Maybe Harley could carry the book. Arthur?" Papaw nodded his head without turning.

I managed to get both hands under it, finding that it wasn't all that heavy. I had thought it would weigh as much as one of Papaw's field rocks. Dony regarded me for a moment, and hobbled down the steps. She didn't seem especially pleased to be gaining a helper. I followed, holding the book against my chest, much like I carried a half-dozen sticks of split oak to the wood-box in the kitchen.

"Can you manage it, Harley?"

"Sure, Granny. It ain't all that heavy."

"You might feel differently by the time you get to the Ridleys." I followed Dony up the trail, forcing myself to walk slowly behind her. "Come straight back," called Granny.

My arms were tired before we got out of sight. When I sat down on a rock by Jamison's pasture, Dony retraced her steps and stood patiently until I was ready to go on.

"Why do you do this? Keep all of this stuff?" I knew I was asking a question that Papaw wouldn't approve of, but he wasn't there.

"I've been appointed," said Dony.

"What does that mean?"

"I've been called, child." I thought of the way Granny would stand on the porch at twilight and call me from play. "Come home, Harley! It's supper-time." I asked who had called her.

"It were a angel." She removed a jar of snuff from the folds of that black dress, and with a little birch twig, began to scour her gums with the brown powder. She stared into the pasture where two cows watched us.

"I had the dipthery when I were a girl. Fifteen I was, and I liked to have died. That's when she come, the angel. I woke one night to find her setting on the edge of my bed. She made a sign like this," Dony held a finger against her lips, "meaning for me to be quiet. Then, she told me about the book."

As Dony talked, I opened the book, turning the pages until a familiar face appeared. Gene "Cotton" Shuler who had died of lockjaw last year. He had been my age and had a mop of white, curly hair. Then, I found Leon Bumgarner who used to drive the Grapette truck and was a friend of Papaw's, Joe Dockery who had been killed by a falling tree while working timber, and three-year-old Drussie Passmore who ate the tips off a whole box of Fire Chief matches.

"The angel said I was to keep the record for Judgment Day when I will stand by God's throne. At God's command, I will open the book and begin to read the names."

The cows had come to the fence and poked their noses between the locust poles. Dony scratched behind their ears and chuckled. "Suuuu, Bossie, suuuuuu," she said softly, the birch brush clenched between her toothless gums. She looked at me and said, "I miss my old cow."

"What happens when you call the names?"

"They come, Harley. They rise from the grave and ascend to God's throne. And they come in the fullness of their flesh."

"Does that mean that they are fat?"

Dony laughed. "That means they appear healthy and whole. All will be restored. Youth, lost arms and legs, missing eyes. You see, if I call their names, they can enter the kingdom of God." I thought about Ila Bryson's three-legged dog, Binky, but decided not to mention him.

"Everybody gets in?"

"I didn't say that. I said *if I call their names.*"

"What happens if you don't call their names?" Dony found a wrinkled crab apple in the grass and fed it to one of the cows.

"They are lost, Harley. Forever lost, trapped in their graves."

"Why would you not call their names?"

"Call the names of drunkards? Fornicators? Blasphemers? No." She walked up the trail, and I followed. We stopped a half-dozen times, I guess and through it all, Dony talked. She told me she knew that some people hated to see her coming.

"Warfield Birch died last week, and when I made the hard trip to his house, the door was locked and the house was dark." Dony's face grew rigid. "Seen me coming, they did. So, I put a mark on Warfield in my book. There are others, too." Dony smiled that strange sack-smile.

The sun was setting when we got to the Ridley place. Arnie had seen us coming and met us on the trail, swinging on his aluminum crutches with a quickness that always surprised me.

"I got a stack of Black Hawks and a Submarine."

"Hey, Arnie. I didn't bring my funny books. I'm just carrying this Memory Book."

"What's in it?"

"You are in it, for one, Arnie Ridley," said Dony.

"Everybody that ever died in the whole world is in here," I said. Of course it seemed that way to me.

Arnie laughed. "But I ain't dead."

"Well, you was so close, I put your name down." Dony fumbled with the pages and then showed a page, blank except for Arnie's name at the top.

"I've got a place for you. I'll fill it in sooner or later."

"You got other people in there that are still alive?" I asked.

Dony didn't answer. She turned and began the long climb to the Ridley porch. It was so still for a minute, I didn't notice Arnie's parents. They sat quietly, watching Dony struggle toward them. Why did no one help her? Papaw had done the same thing, sat watching Dony climb. Then it came to me. She didn't want help. The way that people acted was because they knew this.

"You know why I've come," she said. Mrs. Ridley held out a picture. Dony took it and pressed it into the book. "I need to ask some questions." The Ridleys looked at each other but said nothing as Dony began to write.

"I gotta go, Arnie. Granny said for me to come straight back." I bounded down the steps and Arnie followed me to the trail.

"I'll be back Saturday and bring my funny books."

"Okay." He swung up close to me. "Everybody in that book is dead, right?" I nodded. "But me," he said.

"No, I think there are others." I told him about Dony and the angel.

"Do you believe it?"

"I'm not sure. I need to ask Papaw and maybe Uncle Albert."

"Well, I don't like her looks," said Arnie, "and I don't like being in her book." From the porch came the soft mumble of talk. The sun was down now and Arnie's face was dim and shadowed as I turned to go.

47

"See you Saturday," I said and ran, ran as only an eleven-year-old boy can run downhill, a wild, careening descent, weaving and turning, imagining the posse close behind as I made for my hideout. I took a bullet in the shoulder but kept riding and by the time I passed the two cows, I had lost them. My palomino galloped through the cornfield, swerved around the pigpen, and finally I saw the safety of the porch and Papaw waiting in the dim light.

"Slow down! You are gonna break your neck." He had lit a kerosene lamp, and sat with his Old French harp, huffing a hymn. I recognized it. "I'll Meet You in the Morning." He always played it when he was thinking about my daddy.

"Who was you running from?"

"Pat Garrett. He winged me with a lucky shot."

"Did, huh? So where are you now?" He started on "Red River Valley."

"In Mexico. I'll be safe here."

"All them movies and funny books are making you crazy."

I laughed. "I'm just pretending, Papaw."

"But sometimes, it becomes real, don't it!"

"That's when it is the most fun."

Papaw laughed. "So, you left the dark angel at the Ridleys?"

I nodded. "She's got people in that book that ain't dead yet."

"Yeah, I know. She tell you about the marks?"

"Yeah! I seen some of them. She draws a black star on their face."

"I expect I'll get one before long."

I sat for a while, listening to Papaw play, and then I asked him.

"Are people afraid of her?"

"She makes people nervous. She just makes me unhappy." Papaw laughed and shook his head. "She's crazy, I reckon. Had a fever when she was a child and it sorta pickled her brain." Papaw started on "The Waltz of the Wind." Granny opened the screen door and stood for a moment, listening to Papaw play.

"I need to set a minute, catch my breath," she said. "Then we'll eat."

The moon was up now, and I could see mica glittering in the trail. Papaw quit playing and stared into the darkness. We heard the shuffle and drag of Dony's feet on her way back down the trail. For a moment, we could see her, a darker darkness in the night as she passed. The rain-crows mourned on Painter Knob; the wind stirred the leaves, and when they were still, she was gone.

After supper, I went to my bedroom and listened to "The Squeaking Door." As I lay in the dim light of the pink radio, I finally reached behind the bib of my overalls and took out the picture. My daddy smiled at me.

"Thanks for getting me out of there," he said. He smelled faintly of roses and glue.

"We got clean away," I told him. "We're in Mexico now." I propped the picture against the radio and stared at the pink ceiling as Tommy Tucker and the Champagne orchestra began to play "South of the Border." In a few minutes, Happy and me were in a Mexican cantina drinking Grapettes and playing Chinese checkers.

DARCY COMES HOME

We was setting on the porch last night when Otis Bumgarner come walking up the trail from the barn. Everybody got a little nervous right off on account of Otis being the local sheriff. When Otis comes to see you, it's usually bad news. Since the road stops at the barn, Otis had left his car there and walked up the trail through the cornfield to the house. As it turned out, he was just delivering a message.

He was breathing hard when he got to the porch, and stood a while in the yard with his hands on his knees waiting for his wind to come back.

"Hook up the phone, Arthur. Darcy is gonna call you at ten o'clock tonight." Darcy is Papaw's brother that nobody talks about.

"Ah, God," said Papaw, walking to the end of the porch and staring off at the Balsam mountains. Granny excused herself and went to get the phone. She kept it in the bureau drawer with the hot-water bottle and Papaw's truss. She come back in a minute and asked Albert to hook it up.

"Life would be a damn sight simpler for me if you can see your way to just leaving the phone hooked up like everybody else," said Otis. He went on to say that this was the third time this month that he had been to the house to tell Papaw that somebody was trying to call him.

"As much as I hate to inconvenience you, Otis, I just can't stand the damned thing. It always rings just as we set down to eat or just as we cut the light out to go to bed." Otis sighed and nodded. He knew the story about Papaw tearing the phone out of the wall and heaving it into the cornfield. Granny sent me to find it the next morning. It was in a patch of Big Boy tomatoes, and it was banged up pretty good. After that, when we would hook it up, it never sounded right. The little bell would "ting" a few times like it was afraid to ring real loud.

Uncle Albert convinced Papaw that he needed to keep the phone.

"People get sick, die or get throwed in jail all the time," said Albert. "How are they going to call you if you keep tearing the phone out of the wall?"

"Seems like ever time it rings, it's bad news or foolishness. Ain't never heard nothing on a phone that brightened my day," said Papaw. But he finally agreed to let Granny keep it in the bureau.

Otis said that he would wait 'til the call come in, and set down on the steps. Later, I wondered about that. Maybe Otis already knew why Darcy was calling. The rest of us gathered in the living room and waited for the phone to ring. When it did, it said "tick, tick, ting! tick, tick, ting!" We waited for Papaw to answer it. He took his time, picking it up on the fifth "ting."

"What? No, I don't want no subscription to the Grit. I already got one! Who is this? Suzie who? Are you Ralph Woodard's girl? Raising money for the senior trip! Well, there's bound to be a better way to do it!" Papaw slammed the phone down and stared at Granny.

"Maybe I ought to call Hoyt," said Granny.

"Not yet," said Papaw. "Wait 'til we hear from Darcy."

"Maybe he's already called Hoyt."

"No," said Papaw. "Let's wait."

When the phone tinged again, Papaw didn't move. "Answer it, Agnes," he said. Granny said hello, and then she just listened a long time. When she put the phone down, she didn't say goodbye or anything.

"That was about Darcy," she said. "He wants you to come and get him." She waited a minute and then she said, "He's dying."

"Ah, God," said Papaw, "I knowed it. Was that him talking?"

"No, that was his doctor, but Darcy was there. Said Darcy wanted to die at home. Said that he couldn't come home alone and wanted to know if you could bring a ambulance or at least something that would let Darcy lay down." Papaw put his head in his hands. "Ambulance! What do you reckon something like that would cost?"

Papaw went out on the porch and we could hear him talking to Otis. When he come back, he looked better. Through the window,

I saw Otis walking back down the trail. Fireflies was rising in the corn.

"Polly Pratt's flower truck," he said. "It's got a big middle seat in it, and Darcy could lay on that. Hoyt can go with me."

"How far is it to Morganton?" said Granny.

"At least 150 miles," said Papaw. "It's been twenty years since we took him down there, but I remember every mile." He looked at Granny and smiled. "Go ahead and call Hoyt and then call Polly. If everything works out, we'll go Saturday morning."

"There's something else," said Granny. "He has a list of people he wants to see."

"Ah, God!" said Papaw.

"He wants to see Judy Quinn."

"Jesus, save us," said Papaw. "She's married and got four grown children."

"I don't guess that matters," said Granny.

"So, we drive around to these people's homes, and they come out and.....and say goodbye to Darcy. Is that it?"

"That's what he wants," said Granny.

Papaw shook his head and looked at the ceiling. I'd never seen him cry before. "He only give me four names on the phone. Four people he wants to say goodbye to. Your sister wasn't one of them."

"He never forgave her for signing the papers," said Papaw. "I ain't ever forgive her either."

"Is he in the hospital?" I said. They both looked at me like they didn't know who I was. Then Papaw laughed, but it was a sad laugh.

"Yes, Harley, your Uncle Darcy has been in the hospital for twenty years."

"How come I never heard about him before?" I said. Nobody said anything. Then, I understood. "He's crazy, ain't he?"

"I never thought so," said Granny. "Peculiar, maybe, but not crazy." She smiled at Papaw. "And he looks just like Arthur. I remember the first time I saw them together. Looked like twins."

I tried to imagine two Papaws and couldn't. "What did he do that made people think he was crazy?"

Granny laughed. "He liked to travel," she said.

Papaw got up and went back to the porch. I started to follow him, but Granny said, "Leave him be. He wants to be alone." I could see him out the window. He was looking at the Balsams.

When he come back, he said, "We can fix him a pallet in the back of that flower truck. Maybe put Harley's cot in there."

Albert said, "You want me to call Polly Pratt, Daddy?"

"If you don't mind." Papaw stared at the phone. Granny went in the kitchen, and I followed her. She was washing dishes.

"What's wrong with Uncle Darcy?"

"He's what you call quare," said Granny.

"Does it hurt?"

"I don't think it does. Most quare people seem pretty happy."

"Is it catching?"

"Well, yes, I believe it is. Most of the Teesters got a touch of it." Granny put down her dishrag and smiled at me. "Some of us got a big dose. You got a double dose."

"How come?"

"Cause your daddy was a Teester and your momma was a Extine." The corners of her mouth twitched, so I thought she was funning.

"Is this like the bad blood you and Papaw keep talking about?"

"That's right."

"I thought my bad blood was all from the Extines," I said.

"No, not all. You know what that teacher said about you and Charlie Kay."

Papaw come and the kitchen and said it was all settled. "Albert's calling Hoyt now. If it all works out, we'll go in the morning." He said Albert was going too, and that Hoyt could ride in the back with Darcy on the way home. "I need Albert to ride up front with me," he said.

They left before daylight. Albert wore his dress pants 'n his striped shirt and vest. He had "roached" his hair and he was eating Sen-Sen.

"You're not going on a date," said Papaw.

"Never can tell who you might meet." Albert winked at me.

The flower truck was black with "Polly's Flowers" on the side in yellow letters. When Albert and Papaw put the cot in the back, I crawled in and laid down. I could smell tulips, roses, lilies and carnations. The truck smelled of old weddings, funerals, Easters and Christmases past.

"Get out, Harley. We've got to go." I opened my eyes and climbed out. I wanted to go with them, but knew better than to ask.

All three got in the front. "Ah, me! Poor Darcy," said Uncle Hoyt. He was rocking back and forth, shaking his head and crying. "He was the best of the lot if the truth be told."

Papaw looked at Albert and sighed. "It's gonna be a long trip." Me and Granny stood in the road by the barn and waved. "We'll be home before dark," said Albert, combing his hair again.

That was the day I found out about Uncle Darcy, for as we waited, Granny talked.

"When he was in his teens, he took to leaving home. He would just get up and start walking. Went hundreds of miles sometimes. He might be gone a week and then he would come home or someone would bring him, and then he would set and say the names of the places he'd been. I seen him for the first time right after I had married Arthur. He was settin' on the porch at Babby's, your great-grandmother.

"Arthur introduced us. 'Darcy, this is Agnes,' and he took my hand and said, 'Goshen, Standing Indian, Winding Stairs, Nantahala and Cold Water Gap.' Well, I didn't know what to say. Arthur told me that Darcy was telling me the names of places he'd been. Darcy smiled and asked if I would like to hear more. I said I didn't mind if I did, so he went on. 'Willets, Addie, and Dark Horse Cove. Balsam Gap, Saunooke and Utah Mountain.' He went on like that 'til Babby told him to go get some firewood. He smiled at her and said, 'Yes, Momma,' like a child, and he was gone to the woodpile.

'He'll say them names all day if you let him,' Babbie said."

We were back in the kitchen and Granny was finishing the dishes. She pulled the plug and watched the soapy water gurgle away. She stood for a minute like she was making up her mind about something. "Let's go set on the porch," she said.

"Well, I don't see what is wrong with him," I said. "What is wrong with going places and saying names?"

"Nothing is wrong with it, Harley."

"Then why did they send him to Morganton?"

"Well, there were other things."

"Like what?"

"Darcy met people in the woods. Indians and wolves in places where nothing like that had been seen in a hundred years. Then, there were the women."

"What women?"

"The ones that Darcy met in Blaze Creek. At first, they frightened him. He would come home, pale as a sheet and tell the family about dogs that glowed in the dark, and old Indians with fire in their hair. He claimed he saw the women one summer night when he walked up to a place where Blaze Creek runs through them deep pools in Callie's Cove. He said he learned to wait until twilight when the first fireflies started rising above the creek. That is when they would come. Darcy said the women had stars for eyes and waded down the creek into them deep pools. Then, they would call his name. He said that some of them had wings."

"Like angels?"

"I guess so."

"Golleeee! Did you ever see them?"

"No, Harley. If I had, I would be in Morganton, too. Nobody ever saw them but Darcy."

"But, if he said he seen them....,"

"Some people see things that ain't there. Some people get 'til they can't tell the difference between what is real and what ain't." Granny gave me a hard look. "Like that teacher said about you."

"Charlie Kay sees things that ain't there," I said. "Sometimes, when he sees them, I do, too."

"Charlie is pretending, and so are you. Now, hush before you get me upset again."

They got back right after the nine o'clock whistle blew at the tannery. The truck stopped at the barn, but the headlights stayed on. I figured that was so we could see to get to the barn, so I ran down the trail toward the lights. When I got there, I could see that Albert was driving. Papaw said, "Tell Agnes to come and speak to Darcy." I ran back up the trail. When we got back, Albert had opened the door, and there was Darcy propped up in the cot.

There was another smell now, like something sweet and wet. Darcy was breathing fast, and his eyes were real bright, like Toby, my feist dog that went mad. He did look like Papaw!

"Hello, Uncle Darcy."

"I don't believe I know who you are."

"No. I wasn't even born when you went away."

"He's John Lyndon's boy," said Papaw.

"Do you remember me, Darcy?" asked Granny, leaning into the truck.

"Of course, I do, Agnes. Come hug me goodbye."

"He wants to go to Leatherman, and we need to get there," said Papaw.

"Leatherman?"

"That's where Judy Quinn lives. He's determined to see her tonight." Granny hugged Darcy and backed away. We watched the truck til it was out of sight. Granny looked up at the moon, and I could see the tears in her eyes. We watched the fireflies for a while, and I remembered that she once told me when I was real little that they were baby stars on their way to the sky.

"Who's Judy Quinn?"

"That's Darcy's true love," Granny said softly. "All these years when anyone went to see him in Morganton, he always asked about Judy."

"Is she still his girlfriend?"

"Well, she is married and has grandchildren, but some things never change."

"They don't?"

"You'll probably find that out yourself."

The moon had gone down when Papaw and Albert got home. When they got to the porch, Albert said that he would take the flower truck back to Polly Pratt's shop, and maybe stop in at Velt's Cafe for a cup of coffee.

"Don't lay out all night," said Granny. Albert grinned, and vanished, whistling down the trail. Papaw come up the steps with a paper sack.

"Is that what I think it is?" said Granny.

"I'm not a drinking man," said Papaw, "but tonight, I've seen more than I can stand."

"Well, I never thought I'd live to see the day. Where did you get it?"

"Where the woodbine twineth."

"Where is Darcy now?"

"He's in Babby's bed. When we carried him in the house, she said for us to put him in her bed. She said that was where he come into the world and that was where he would go out."

"Did he see Judy?"

Papaw took a quart Mason jar out of the bag and held it up to starlight and fireflies. He unscrewed the lid and took a big swallow. Then he coughed for a while.

"Never was no good at this."

"Tell me about Judy."

"Ah, God. Judy, poor woman. She didn't know we were coming. Her husband, Walter, he was a mite put off at first, but when he understood that Darcy was dying, he went in the house and left them alone. Hoyt started crying and talking, so me and Albert got him and walked to the barn." Papaw took another swallow and shivered. "I had opened the door for her, and as we walked away, I could hear Darcy saying her name. She crawled in that truck with him. That 52-year-old woman crawled in there in spite of the smell, and she put his head in her lap. She hadn't seen him in thirty years."

Papaw got up and walked to the end of the porch. "I was afraid that she wouldn't know who he was. I was afraid that when we knocked on the door and told her why we were there, she would say, Darcy who? But when I told her...when I said, Darcy is outside and he has come home to die, she didn't ask me another thing. She run down the steps and straight to that truck."

"She still loved him, then," said Granny.

"I reckon," said Papaw. He took another drink and sat down in Granny's rocker. "He won't live 'til morning, but he is back where most of us would like to die. In our mother's arms." Papaw hiccuped and started to cry.

"Hush, Arthur. Stop talking, now. Look at Harley's mouth."

It was hanging open, I guess. Papaw laughed. I shore don't understand grownups sometimes, laughing and crying all in the same breath.

UNCLE HOYT

About five years ago, Uncle Hoyt started calling us every day. When the phone rang at 4:30, I knew that it was Uncle Hoyt. That's when he always calls, you see. After he retired from his job in the green hide room at the tannery, he spent a lot of time on the phone.

When I said hello, Uncle Hoyt would just start talking.

"Harley, it's 4:30 here," he says. "What time is it there?"

"It's 4:30 over here, too," I says.

"O.K." he says, and then he hangs up.

If it comes a rain, Uncle Hoyt calls back.

"Harley, it's raining here. Is it raining there?"

"Yep, Uncle Hoyt, it's raining here, too."

"O.K.." Then he would hang up.

I'm just twelve years old, and there is lots of things that I don't understand. Uncle Hoyt's phone calls is one of them. Granny told me that Uncle Hoyt is lonesome. "Time hangs heavy on that poor man," she said. "Ever since he quit the green hide room, he don't know what to do with hisself."

Uncle Hoyt is Papaw's brother. He has a wife named Beulah Mae, but she won't speak to him. She quit talking to him ten years ago on Christmas morning in 1940, and nobody knows why. Now, she spends all her time putting together jigsaw puzzles. She does the kind that has a couple of thousand pieces, and when she finishes one, she glues it together. She buys picture-hanging kits from Kathy Kay's Kreative Kraft and hangs them puzzles on the wall. The last time I was there, she had framed a big one of Donald Duck, Huey, Dewey and Louie, and Uncle Scrooge in a hot-air balloon over the Empire State Building. It was hanging above the big Silvertone radio.

Uncle Hoyt's retarded son, Hoyt Junior, hates him, and sometimes when Uncle Hoyt calls, I can hear Hoyt Junior talking to his daddy. He hollers things like, "You damned old bald-headed son-of-a-bitch. Come out in the yard and I'll stomp a mud-hole in your ass." Uncle Hoyt don't pay any attention as far as I can tell. Granny said he's used to it, said Hoyt Junior has been talking to his daddy like that for the last ten years.

Sometimes Uncle Hoyt will ask if my granddaddy is home. "Is Arthur there?" If I say no, he says, "All right," and hangs up. If I say yes and then ask if he wants to talk to Papaw, he says, "No," and then he'll hang up. He's just killing time according to Granny. She asked me what I would do if I lived with a woman who wouldn't speak, and even fixes her own meals in her room, and a dimwitted son that carried a baseball bat.

"The green hide room at the tannery was a blessing," says Granny. "At least that job got him away from home."

Once I asked Granny what a green hide was.

"It's a cow hide that still has green, rotten flesh on it," says Granny. "I've been told that men that went in that room for the first time usually puked. You get used to it, though. Your Uncle Hoyt did. Your granddaddy said that your Uncle Hoyt was happy in the green hide room. Smiled and cut up. He used to sing hymns in there with all them green flies buzzing around his head while he stripped them hides."

When Uncle Hoyt used to visit us, he smelled real bad. Granny told me to act like I didn't notice. She said if you worked in green hides, you finally got to smelling that way. Boots, my feist dog, he gets one whiff, and he crawls under the house. He stays there 'til Uncle Hoyt leaves. The cats love him though. Sometimes they foller him when he leaves and I have to go catch them and bring them back.

When I see Uncle Hoyt with my Papaw, I always notice that they don't look anything alike. Papaw is tall with black, curly hair and looks like the picture of Stonewall Jackson in the school library. Uncle Hoyt is skinny and bald-headed. He has a dent in the top of his head where Hoyt Junior hit him once, and I was told not to stare at it. He has a big yo-yo Adam's apple, and he always stands with his hips in front of him and his hands on his hips. His favorite expression is, "Shoooooo, I reckon!"

59

Papaw and Uncle Hoyt talk a lot about the good old days in Macon County. They growed up there in a place called Leatherman's Gap, and it must have been sort of like the Garden of Eden. Papaw says things like, "Hoyt, do you remember that gritted cornbread Momma used to make? You remember that sorghum sop and saw-mill gravy?"

"Shooooooo, I reckon," says Uncle Hoyt.

"Remember that little spring on Blaze Creek that come out from under that big rock, and it was so cold it would make your teeth hurt?"

"Shoooooo, I reckon," says Uncle Hoyt.

Papaw would laugh when he remembered growing up in Macon County, but sometimes Uncle Hoyt would cry. Granny says that Uncle Hoyt is emotional. She says he cries at everybody's funeral and sometimes weeps in church when they sing hymns. "Don't make fun of him, Harley," she says. "He can't help it. His mother was a Sizemore." She says the Sizemores are all "high passioned." I found out later that "high passioned" covered more territory than just crying at funerals.

People still talk about Uncle Hoyt and the hospital. Papaw's daughter, Aunt Elda who sings in the choir at the big Methodist church in town, said she is ashamed for people to know that Uncle Hoyt is related to her. Papaw don't say anything, but I think that the stories about Uncle Hoyt at C.A. Parrish Memorial Hospital embarrassed him, too.

What happened was Uncle Hoyt started going to the hospital every day and staying 'til dark. He would sit in the visiting room and talk to people. Sometimes he would wander up and down the hall and peep into rooms. When he saw somebody he recognized, he would go in and visit. Lots of folks in the hospital was glad to see him, like if they had been there for months and they was bored, Uncle Hoyt was a welcome change. But some of the patients' relatives didn't see it that way.

Uncle Hoyt went into Freida May Coolidge's room just before she died. She was in an oxygen tent, and the whole family was in the room. Uncle Hoyt went over and looked through that plastic sheet and said, "Hey, Freida Mae! Knowed you right off! Knowed your daddy, Bennie that lived on Larka." Uncle Hoyt set down by the bed and started talking. Didn't seem to notice the Reverend Varner there, holding Freida May's hand. Uncle Hoyt asked if Freida May didn't have a sister that married a Jacobs over in Dellwood. Nobody said anything but Freida Mae's daughter went and got a nurse.

The nurse took Uncle Hoyt back to the visiting room. She told him that the family didn't want any visitors (Didn't he see the sign on the door?) She also told him there had been other complaints. Was it true that he sometimes ate the patients' meals? Well, yes, Uncle Hoyt said, but it was only when it seemed that the patient didn't intend to eat it, and he hated to see good food go to waste. Was it true that he had eaten a five-pound box of candy in Willie Cowan's room? Attorney Cowan, who was recovering from hemorrhoid surgery, said that when he regained consciousness, he found the empty box on the bedside table. Well, not at one setting, said Uncle Hoyt. It took several trips. "I didn't eat all of it," says Uncle Hoyt. "I left the ones with the jelly centers."

For a while, Uncle Hoyt stayed out of rooms. He wasn't banned from the building until the big wreck. The headlines of the local paper said TRIPLE TRAIN-TRACK TRAGEDY! Three football players was killed and four cheerleaders got tore up real bad. They was struck by a southbound train and the car was dragged for half a mile. Everybody in the county heard the sirens. Me and Papaw stood on the porch in Rhodes' Cove and watched them red lights coming down the Waynesville road. The ambulances took all seven to the emergency room where all of the doctors got busy separating the living, the dead and the near dead. Joretta Gibbs that lives up in the cove above us, her daughter, Pricella, is a nurse, and she said it was awful. She said people was screaming and crying and the blood was dripping on the floor. Joretta told Granny all about it sitting in the living room eating a piece of Granny's stack cake. She said, "Ah, Lord, Agnes! There was one poor boy..." She looked at me, and then leaned toward Granny and whispered. I heard most of it anyway. I said, "The train tore his head off?" Granny give me a hard look. Then, she told me to go out on the porch. "We're talking," she said.

Out on the porch, I found I could still hear Joretta. She said that Dr. John Jacobs had put one of them football players' leg back on, and had just turned to speak to her when he saw Uncle Hoyt. She said that Uncle Hoyt was standing by the operating table, and he sorta stood out since he was the only one in there who didn't have on them gowns and gloves and stuff. She said that Uncle Hoyt was chewing tobacco.

"Do you think he will live?" said Uncle Hoyt.

"How did this man get in here?" shouts Dr. Jacobs.

"Does that head over there by itself belong to Johnny Ledford's boy, Woodrow?"

"Get him out of here!" hollered Dr. Jacobs.

"It favors Woodrow," said Uncle Hoyt. Then, he got hustled out of there by four nurses.

"Can you put his head back?" said Uncle Hoyt from the hall.

According to Granny, the story spread like wildfire. If things wasn't bad enough, Otis Balmgardner, the town policeman, brought Hoyt Junior home in the police car a week later and told Uncle Hoyt that he should keep Hoyt Junior home. Otis said Hoyt Junior had been standing in front of the Ritz theatre and staring at this picture of Debra Padget in *Broken Arrow*, which had been held over for another week. Members of the Cherokee tribe down on the reservation had been "coming in droves," according to Purvis Moody, the owner of the Ritz. Otis said that Hoyt Junior was "abusing himself" while looking at Debra. I don't have a real good handle on what that means, but it has gotta be pretty bad, judging from the way everybody acted. Granny took her sister, Tildy, out on the back porch to tell her about it, and when Papaw heard it, he went to the barn and stayed a couple of hours. I heard Granny tell her sister, "He can't help it. Sizemore blood, you know. They are high passioned."

Right after that, Blicka Dee Waldrop that works at the courthouse went up to Uncle Hoyt's one morning and told him he could put Hoyt Junior in the sheltered workshop. She said that they would come and get him every morning and bring him home every afternoon. The whole time that Blicka Dee was talking to Uncle Hoyt, she said Hoyt Junior sat on the couch and stared at her. Hoyt Junior asked Blicka Dee if she wanted to see his trouser worm, and Blicka Dee said no, she didn't.

Uncle Hoyt was kinda surprised when Hoyt Junior said he would like to go to the workshop. "Sounds better than staying home with that old bald-headed son of a bitch," he said, pointing at Uncle Hoyt, and smacking the palm of his hand with his baseball bat.

"You can't take that ball bat," said Blicka Dee.

The next morning, a little blue bus came and took Hoyt Junior away. That evening Hoyt Junior told his mother, Aunt Beulah Mae, that he liked the workshop. Uncle Hoyt heard them talking, and he told Papaw about it. They was training Hoyt Junior to put mouse traps together, and he was going to get paid just like he had a regular job. There was about a dozen other retarded people in the program, except they wasn't called retarded. They was called "Exceptional Adults." When Hoyt Junior would get excited and cuss somebody, they would take him to another building and give him some pills. After that, he would calm down and laugh a lot. Blicka Dee told Granny that the pills calmed him down, but his mouse trap production fell off. She said that maybe they would hit a "happy medium" eventually.

For a while, it looked like everything had worked. Uncle Hoyt stayed home more since Hoyt Junior was at the workshop. When the bus brought Hoyt Junior home in the evening, he would be smiling. He stopped carrying the baseball bat, and although he still cussed Uncle Hoyt, it seemed to be a habit more than anything. I seen him on the street a few times with Beulah Mae, and he was grinning like a mule eating saw-briars.

"He sure loves that workshop," said Beulah Mae. "Can't wait to get back in the morning."

Things went real well until the workshop people found out about Hoyt Junior and Suewhetta May Higgins. Suewhetta looks like a Kewpie doll with her blue eyes and blond hair that is always combed in a big curl on the front of her head. Granny said that she looked intelligent, but the truth was, she couldn't dress herself. Suewhetta took a shine to Hoyt Junior right off, and they started eating their lunch together. At first, the sheltered workshop folks thought they was "just as cute as two bugs in a rug,"

Blicka Dee Waldrop told Granny that Wendell Livingood, the director of the workshop found them in a storeroom. They was "doing it." I couldn't hear everything Blicka Dee said from the bedroom closet where I was hid, but I heard enough. Wendell said he heard a crash in the storeroom and went to investigate. Hoyt Junior and Suewhetta had knocked over a huge stack of boxed mousetraps. They were covered up by them, but they were still "doing it." "They was like animals," said Blicka Dee. She whispered that last part, but I heard it anyway.

Not long after that, we went to the Teester reunion in Macon County, and there was three hundred people and dinner on the ground. After everybody ate, they brought Great-Grandma Teester out on the porch and her children and grandchildren gathered about. I stood in line with the great-grandchildren and waited to be introduced and hugged by Great-Grandma Teester. Since she was deaf and had cataracts, it took a while. Then, her children, which was my grandpa and Uncle Hoyt, went up and talked to her.

I guess that Uncle Hoyt must have told her about his troubles cause she started shaking her head and Uncle Hoyt got down on his knees and laid his head in Great-Granny's lap and cried. Everybody got real quiet then. Great-Granny patted Uncle Hoyt's bald head just like he was a child. I noticed that one of her fingers had settled into the dent in Uncle Hoyt's head. It looked a lot like the way I have seen people at Smoky Mountain Bowl-arama hold a bowling ball.

On the way home with Papaw and Granny, I laid in the back seat and pretended to be asleep so I could listen to them talk.

"Well, Suewhetta is pregnant," said Granny.

"Tell me it ain't so," said Papaw.

"It's that Sizemore blood," said Granny, shaking her head. "Makes people slaves to passion." She glared at Papaw.

"Don't look at me," said Papaw. "I don't think I got any of it." We rode for a while and Papaw said, "I thought they put something in their food at that workshop so as they wouldn't do things like that."

"They do," said Granny, "but it don't work on people with Sizemore blood." We rode some more, and then Granny said,

"Suewhetta wants to get married."

Grandpa pulled the car off the road and stopped.

"Why don't you just tell it all at one time," he said. "I can't stand it when you dole out servings like hash in a cafe."

"Well, it looks like it's all settled," said Granny. "They are gonna live with Hoyt and keep right on going to the sheltered workshop. When that baby is born, Hoyt will be what they call a legal guardian."

"Jump down, Jesus!" said Papaw. He pulled back on the road.

Not long after that, Hoyt Junior and Suewhetta got married. The society page of the local paper said that the "newly married couple would reside with the parents of the groom." A few nights later, I heard Papaw talking to Granny on the porch.

"Well, old girl, you always know all the gossip, but this time I know something you don't," said Papaw.

"Like what?"

"Beulah Mae has started speaking to Hoyt again."

"Last Sunday morning while they was listening to Renfro Valley," said Granny. She smiled at Papaw.

"How did you know?"

"She called me." Papaw's mouth fell open like the little door in the cook-stove and stayed that way.

"Said that things was in such a mess that she decided to start talking. Said that when she seen Suewhetta and the way she was wrapping Hoyt Junior around her thumb, she said she decided to straighten things out."

After a long while, Papaw said, "I don't suppose she told you why she stopped speaking in the first place."

"As a matter fact, she did. She said that she quite speaking to Hoyt after he gave her some black stockings and a little red lace nightgown for Christmas. That was a long time ago. She said it had a card that said, 'Let's start a fire in the stove.'"

Papaw grinned. "And she ain't spoke and there ain't been a fire in the stove since that Christmas."

"That's right. She said that she might be speaking again, but she told Hoyt right off that there would be no fires."

"What did Hoyt say?"

"He said that was fine with him. Said he wasn't interested in starting fires anymore."

"Well, now, that's strange, don't you think?"

"What's strange about it?" said Granny.

"Well, what about that Sizemore blood? What about that high passion?" Papaw put his hand over his mouth. I could tell that he was trying to keep a straight face.

"Well, I don't see why Aunt Beulah Mae won't let Uncle Hoyt build a fire," I said. They both looked at me. I guess they had forgotten about me sitting at the other end of the porch pretending to read my new Captain Marvel.

"Harley, why don't you go feed the chickens." I had already fed them, but from the tone of her voice, I figured that maybe I should feed them again.

Hoyt Junior named the baby Beretta after his favorite television show. That got shortened to Bret. He told Suewhetta that she could name the next one. Uncle Hoyt said that Aunt Beulah May told Suewhetta that there wasn't going to be no next time. He said that Suewhetta giggled when Beulah said that. Uncle Hoyt said that she was always taking Hoyt Junior in the bedroom and closing the door.

Aunt Beulah told Hoyt, "I know she can't dress herself, but when she wants to watch Lawrence Welk in her birthday suit, I think she knows what she is doing."

He said that Aunt Beulah had the two of them sitting on the couch in the living room most of the time watching television like little kids. After Jack Paar went off, Suewhetta would take Hoyt Junior's hand and lead him away. "Night, night, Mamma Teester," she would say.

Uncle Hoyt said that things do seem to work out. After the baby was born, Suewhetta went back to work. The little bus comes every morning and Hoyt Junior and Suewhetta hold hands while they ride to the sheltered workshop. Uncle Hoyt told Papaw that the walls was covered with little plaques from the sheltered workshop. Hoyt Junior and Suewhetta won them for "maximum quota." He said that meant that they always made more mousetraps than anyone else. Between the jigsaw puzzles and the "maximum quota" plaques, there ain't a square inch of wall space left.

"To tell you the truth, Arthur," Uncle Hoyt told Papaw, "Life seems pretty good now. It was awful for a while, but I like the way things turned out."

Papaw stared at Uncle Hoyt. "Hey, that's fine, Hoyt. I'm happy for you."

Uncle Hoyt loves that baby. Bret is three now, and he goes to town with Uncle Hoyt. You can see them most every day standing in front of the Farmers' Federation. Bret holds onto Uncle Hoyt's pants leg while Uncle Hoyt talks to the loafers. Sometimes, they come to see us.

Uncle Hoyt still calls, but he lets Bret do most of the talking.

"It's fo' thudy oveh heah, Hah-ley," says Bret. "Whut time you got?"

"It's four-thirty here, too, Bret," I say.

"All right. Bye, bye."

NICK-NAMES

"They put old Beekus away," whispered Pooter Dills. Old Beekus was the ninth grade social studies teacher. She was a nice old lady who looked like George Washington. It was fifth period study hall, and I was reading "Red Badge of Courage" when Pooter stuck me with his pencil.

"What do you mean, 'put away'?" I said. I pictured my Granny "putting away" ironed sheets in the bureau.

"Mr. Dills, if you speak again, I will give you cause to regret it."

Silence.

"Did you hear me, Mr. Dills?"

"Yes'm."

I sneaked a look at "the Green Bitch," who was giving Pooter her killer stare. She had sharp little pointy, brown stained teeth. She was squirrelly looking, too, and she had this huge pile of hair that looked shellacked.

"That goes for you, too, Harley Teester."

"Yes'm."

A few minutes later, Pooter passed me a note. "She ben toke to the kraze farm." I could see why Pooter was flunking English. When the bell rang, me and Pooter were the first through the door with the Green Bitch watching us like one of them cobras in jungle movies, all puffed up and ready to strike. I followed Pooter to the bus yard where kids were lining up for the ride home.

"Why?"

"You ain't gonna believe it, Harley." Pooter shook his head. "I wouldn't believe it myself, but I heard Daddy tell it to Momma."

"Okay, so tell me."

"They found her in Preacher Tutt's house."

"What was she doing?"

"Eating. She pulled a chair in front of the frigerator, propped the door open, and she was eating. Been there a long time, too, 'cause the ice was melting and dripping on the floor. Daddy said that she had eat a pound of bacon raw as well as half of a chicken and a bowl of potato salad."

"You mean she broke in?"

"I reckon. Get this! That ain't the first time. She been doing this for a long time, breaking into people's houses and eating their food. Her daughter wanted to hush it up, but Tutt called the police."

"She got arrested?" I was amazed; teachers just didn't get arrested and hauled to the jail like Roosevelt Wilson Hall, the town drunk!

Pooter nodded. "That's why she ain't been teaching. She's been in jail for breaking and entering. Daddy said she broke into lawyer Higdon's house and eat two quarts of strawberry ice cream."

"I don't understand. Was she starving? Don't teachers make enough money to buy food? What you're saying don't make sense." Pooter shrugged.

We got on #18, the Rhodes Cove bus, and moved to the back where we could talk.

"She's not a bad old lady." I felt a little embarrassed to be complimenting a teacher. "If I had to pick a candidate for a padded room, I woulda picked the 'Green Bitch.'" Her real name was Greenich, but most of the 9th grade called her "Green Bitch."

"Yeah," said Pooter, "She'd be my pick, too. I think she's got it in for me."

"She's got it in for all of us. Did you hear about her going in the boys' bathroom? Whimpie Dean was smoking a cigarette and taking a leak. Hauled him out by the ear and down to the principal's office. Whimpie's pecker was still out."

"Yikes!" said Pooter, " That's as bad as what happened to me!"

Pooter had got his name on Sidney Lanier Day. We was all in the auditorium to hear the glee club sing *The Song of the Chattahoochee*, and Miss Worley had just held up that little stick, and all the singers was quiet and looking at her. That's when he did it. *Poot!* It was real loud, and Miss Worley turned and looked at us.

It still might have been ignored, but the "Green Bitch" rose and pointed at Andy.

"Mr. Dills," she said.

"Yes'm."

"Come with me."

There went poor Andy up the aisle while all of us watched. When the door closed, *The Song of the Chattahoochee* began. By the time the bus ran, Andy had become "Pooter." He is my friend, so I always call him Andy, but I think of him as Pooter, 'cause it's hard to forget that day.

"She said I did it on purpose."

I didn't say anything since that is what I thought, too. I also thought that he was right about the "Green Bitch" having it out for him. She seemed to dislike kids in general, but after Sidney Lanier Day, Pooter was singled out for special attention.

"Has Whimpie got a nick-name yet?" Pooter sounded hopeful.

"Andy, he already has one."

"Oh, yeah." Pooter sighed. "Still and all, maybe they will pay less attention to me now."

Getting a nick-name is tricky. It could be a blessing or a curse. "Rocket Reems" was lucky and they even used his nick-name on the sports page of *The Ruralite*. "Poss" Stephens and "Trigger" Young seemed like a good deal too. For a while, I was "Sack" because I sorta collapse when I sit.... like an empty sack. I would rather be "Spike" or maybe "Studs." Now and then, I've tried to drop a hint, you know.

"At home, they call me Spike."

"Oh, yeah?"

"Yeah. Spike."

It never worked though. So, I'm still Sack or just Harley. Could be worse, I guess. As we sat in the back of the bus as it chugged up Main Street on its way to Rhodes Cove, I brought the subject back to Old Beekus.

"Why do you think she does it?"

"She's crazy," said Pooter, like he was surprised I didn't see the obvious.

"But, why?"

"Why is she crazy?"

69

When I nodded, Pooter rolled his eyes, like he was getting fed up with my dimwittedness. "Harley, crazy is...... just crazy! There ain't no why! It is like grass growing or apples falling off trees. It just is!" I thought about that.

"All the same, I think I'll ask Granny."

When I got home, Granny was on the porch with her sister, Tildy. Tildy tells long, sad stories about death and sickness, and she was just finishing up on a "dead baby story."

"Eat the paint off the wall. Blue paint."

"You don't mean it!"

"Its little mouth was full of it."

"Blue paint? Imagine that!"

"Robin's Egg, was the name of it. Earleen bought it at Stump's Hardware."

"I declare!"

"Garrett's Funeral Home did a good job. I told Earleen, that little baby looked like one of them dolls down at Kress's Dime Store."

"Poor woman!"

"She said, 'I was trying to make her little bedroom cheery.' Ain't that pitiful! Lead, it was. Lead in the paint. I couldn't stay long since there was two funerals that day, Granny Watson, you know. Fell and broke her hip in February. Never mended. So I told Earleen I had to go and she followed me out in the yard. 'Do you think I killed my baby?' she said. 'Was it my fault?' Pitiful."

So, I told Granny about Old Beekus before Tildy started another story, and Granny was amazed. That is something I don't see very often. Tildy, of course, already knew about it.

"Ate two pounds of souse meat, a baked chicken and a cake of cornbread at Oscar Ridley's. They just called Jean, the daughter, and sent her home."

"Well, I can't believe what I am hearing," said Granny.

"It's true," said Tildy. She seemed pretty happy about it. "It is probably a judgment."

"I don't believe it," said Granny. "Knowed her for forty years, and there ain't nothing to judge her for."

"Worthless husband," said Tildy.

"Well, he has been gone for thirty years."

"Used to beat her."

"Left her with two children, and the boy is brain-damaged." Granny shook her head. "She is a good woman. When bad things happened, she just got up and went on."

"Don't be too sure," said Tildy. "There's always something. When we get too proud and self-sufficient, God teaches us humility."

"Bull hockey!" said Granny. Her face was getting red. "Looks to me like Mary Beekus has been humbled all of her life."

There was a long quiet spell after that, and I decided to go to the barn where Papaw was hulling walnuts.

"I thought you had decided to throw them walnuts away," I said.

"Right enough. That's what ought to be done with them." He stared at the stain on his fingers and overalls. "Won't come out. Walnut stain is worse than pokeberry. Still, I had rather hull walnuts than listen to old Doom and Gloom."

That was Aunt Tildy's *other* nick-name. Sometimes Papaw called her "Death and Destruction."

"Rather dig ditches, eat sawbriars and pick beggar-lice."

Aunt Tildy's husband "Bow-Wow" stopped his truck at the end of the road below our cornfield and tooted the horn.

"Thank you, Jesus," said Papaw. "Now I can go back to the porch." He poured the walnuts into a sack and threw them into the barn-loft.

At supper, nobody seemed inclined to answer my questions about Old Beekus. When Papaw said that he heard that the family was reluctant to sign the papers that would send her to Morganton, Granny started giving him them little frowns that meant he shouldn't talk in front of me. I didn't hear anymore until bedtime.

Papaw and Granny talk themselves to sleep. I've learned a lot just being quiet and listening. Sure enough, they talked about Old Beekus.

"Growed up real poor, you know."

"Sorghum sop and sawmill gravy," said Papaw.

"Was in the fields shocking corn for other people when she was nine. Washed clothes, cooked in restaurants."

"But she went to college."

"Yes, she told me that she worked her way through. When she got that teaching certificate, everybody was glad. She was going to have a decent life."

"I wonder when the bad stuff started. Willard drank, then, I heard that he smacked her around. When he left town with a bunch of guys going out west, I thought good riddance."

"She worked hard, I reckon, all of her life."

"Yes, but think about it. Think about forty years of teaching ninth-grade Civics, grading papers, and taking care of the boy."

"Yeah, but that is what we all do, ain't it? The daily grind? Day to day? It may not be exciting, but I like it fine."

For a while I thought they had gone to sleep, but then Granny spoke again.

"I think she has always been hungry."

"Now, what the hell does that mean?"

"I'm just trying to make sense out of the breaking in and eating food."

"Mary Beekus was well-fed, Agnes."

"There's all kinds of hungry."

For the first time I thought about Old Beekus in the classroom...how, when we took a test, I would look up from my paper to see her looking out the window. It was a look she didn't have when she was teaching. It was like waiting for the bus, watching to see the big yellow hood appear at the top of the hill. Every day I got excited when I saw it.

"Jerusalem oak seed," said Papaw. "Lespedeza, jimson weed and love lies a-bleeding. Sycamore, ironwood, boxwood and poplar."

"We are born hungry."

"Hush, Agnes. June-apple, wintergreen, wormwood and stump of the world."

The house is quiet now, except for the spring water running on the back porch and the sigh of wind in the maples. I turn my little radio on and it lights up the darkness in my bedroom. "From high atop the Roosevelt Room in downtown Chicago, we bring you Tommy Tucker Time." The sound is a whisper as I listen to champagne corks and polite applause. I begin to dream to "Apple Blossom Time." Old Beekus and I are eating June-apples and grapes in the front yard, and a Pet Ice Cream truck is backing up the trail toward us. Special order for Sack and Beekus. We are waiting for the bus.

FOXIE AND BEAR

Among the puzzles and mysteries of childhood, the most provocative are sex and death. This story is about the latter: imagined, romanticized, evaded and real.

The way I remember it, we were running. That's what we did, you see, at recess. Cold, oh Jesus, it was cold and the playground was frozen hard as a brick. No baseball or football in March. The water fountain looked like an iceberg floating in the fog, wrapped in sheets of ice, and most of the fifth grade stayed in the room, hanging over the steam radiators, their noses pressed against the window panes, just watching us run. Across the field we went, screaming like banshees, Johnny Mac and Eddie and me.

I guess we were the cavalry riding to the attack and the jack-pine thicket at the end of the playground was an Apache village. We whipped our horses by slapping our hands against our hips. Then, we would raise our invisible rifles as we galloped over the fallen braves, saying "Ka-pow! Ka-pow!" That's when Johnny Mac tackled me, and we crashed to the earth. Took the skin off my elbows and knees.

"I recognize you, white eyes," said Johnny Mac, giving me his mean, Indian-warrior look. "You are the one called Harley." Then, he cut my throat and scalped me. "Your scalp will hang on my lodge pole this night," he said. He galloped in pursuit of Eddie Mathis. Johnny Mac had seen Jeff Chandler in *Broken Arrow* six times, and it had made him dangerous. I laid on the frozen earth and watched Johnny Mac kill Eddie. Then we heard the sirens.

Everybody stopped running and then the whole make-believe world of Cochise and the "blue bellies" vanished, and in its place we saw Mutt Gibbs the sheriff and his big black and white car. It moved real slow like it does when Mutt is leading a funeral through town. It came down Freeze Hill with the siren going *waaaauuh, waaauuh* and that blue light on top whirling round and round. None of us had ever seen the police car going slow at the same time the siren was going fast. The car stopped on the Freeze Bridge across the road from the playground, and Mutt got out.

We all ran to the chain-link fence between the playground and the road and stood there with our breath fogging the air, huffing and puffing like ponies. Then, two patrol cars came from the opposite direction and parked facing Mutt. The patrolmen got out with rifles and climbed up on the bridge railing. Then Mutt opened the back door and motioned for somebody to get out. Johnny Mac recognized them first.

"It's Foxie and Bear," he said. They looked pretty pitiful when they stood up and looked about. Ragged overalls, wild hair and run-down brogans. Mutt said something to Foxie and pointed to the creek. Foxie looked at the patrolmen, and then he started down the bank. That's when we seen the chains on their hands and feet. Bear followed Foxie, and since he was big and awkward, he stumbled and fell down the bank. I shivered thinking how that cold water felt soaking through their overalls and long-handles.

Then, Johnny Mac climbed up the fence. Me and Eddie did the same, wedging our shoes and hands in the chain-links, climbing until we could see black water beneath the bridge - black because of the stuff the paper plant dumped in the creek two miles upstream. The water looked cold, and when poor old Bear stood up, he was steaming. Water poured from his clothes, and his face and arms looked red and raw. Both men were wading knee-deep in the fast water. Mutt yelled something at them and Foxie nodded. The patrolmen were smoking cigarettes now, their rifles braced on their thighs as they watched the chained men flounder and slip on the creek's slick bottom. Bear fell again.

Finally Foxie stopped and pointed at a place where the water whirled around a bridge support. He and Bear were standing with their backs together, looking back and forth between Mutt and the chill water. We couldn't hear what was said, but we could see Foxie shivering, his teeth clenched and his eyes rolling like a frightened steer. Then, both men plunged their hands and arms into the water, and started to move in a sidling circle, the water churning around their shoulders and faces. It didn't take long. First Foxie and then Bear stood holding up something hard and blunt. Sunlight glinted on wet metal and water sparkled on the swinging wrist chains.

"What is it?" I said.

"Looks like hammers," said Johnny Mac. "What they call ball-peen hammers— like them in the school shop."

"All right, boys, come down from there," said Baldy Coggins. "How many times have I told you to stay off this fence?" We all looked at the principal beneath us, his big bald head shining in the sunlight. Then, one by one, we came down. Johnny Mac was last, reporting what we could no longer see.

"They're giving the hammers to Mutt. He's leaning over the bridge taking the hammers. He's putting them in some kind of sack. Foxie and Bear are climbing up the bank."

"Get down, Johnny Mac," said Baldy.

Johnny Mac began a slow descent, but he kept talking. "They're getting back in the sheriff's car. Mutt give 'em some big blankets. Now the patrolmen are getting back in their cars."

"Johnny Mac, don't make me tell you again," said Baldy.

"No sir," said Johnny Mac. As we walked back to the school house, we heard Mutt's siren, and saw the cars disappear toward Court House Hill.

"Well, I guess the big mystery is solved," said Baldy.

"What mystery is that?" said Johnny Mac.

"Who killed Moon Mullins and his wife last night," said Baldy.

"Killed 'em with hammers?" I said.

"Looks like it. Aren't you boys supposed to be in geography?" Baldy started humming "John Henry." Then, he sang, *Die with a hammer in my hand, Lord, Lord.* Sang it real soft like maybe he didn't even know he was doing it.

Walking home with Johnny Mac after school, he told me about Moon Mullins and his wife, Tillie. "Somebody beat their brains out," he said.

"With hammers?" I was having trouble imagining the hammers rising and falling. "The ones they got out of the creek?"

"Yep."

"Yikes!" I said. "Why?"

"Robbery. That's what Daddy said. Didn't Moon ever show you his money?"

"Oh, yes," I said, "Lots of times."

And he had, too. I would be passing the poolroom on Main Street where Moon parked his taxi, and he would be sitting on the back of a bench with his feet on the seat. That's where he sat when he wasn't driving the taxi.

"Hey, kid," he would say, "Come here."

"I'm in a hurry." Moon made me nervous, always smiling like he knew something the rest of us didn't.

"You ever seen a hundred dollar bill?" Smirking because he knew that I lived in a world of nickels and dimes. Then he would bring out this big roll of money. It wasn't in a billfold or anything, just naked money with rubber bands around it. He would fan out the bills, and it looked like every one was a hundred.

"How 'bout that!" he would say. Somehow, I always felt small and worthless after Moon showed me his money. I think my Uncle Albert felt the same way.

Last summer when Albert came home from the Navy, he rode from the bus station to Rhodes Cove in Moon's taxi. Albert had on a war bonnet and carried a bow in one hand and his sea bag in the other. When he got out of Moon's taxi and fell down, I knew he was drunk. He lugged his bag up to the porch and dropped it. The feathered shafts of three arrows stuck out of the top and they looked a little ragged. Albert notched an arrow in his bow and shot at Moon's taxi and missed. While we watched Moon struggle to turn around in the dirt road, he shook his head. Then, he winked at me, and I winked back.

"Somebody's gonna kill that fool," he said. "Always showing his money. He just showed me a couple of thousand dollars." He got another arrow and took a bead on Granny's milk-bucket on the back porch. "Maybe I oughta kill him." He shot and missed. The arrow stuck in the springhouse door. It didn't stick and quiver the way arrows did in the movies. It just waggled once or twice and fell out.

"He's showed it to me, too," I said.

Albert stared at me.

"His money, I mean."

"Kinda like he's daring somebody to take it from him," said Albert. The next shot hit the bucket.

"Hot damn," I said, "You hit it!" The arrow hitting the bucket made a hell of a racket. Went through one side of the bucket, too. The bucket fell and bounced off the porch.

"Jesus, Joseph, and Mary!" said Albert.

"Granny is gonna take a fit when she sees that," I said.

"Now, why did I do that?" Albert took the war bonnet off and scratched his head. He peeked in the window. "I tell you, Harley, this has been a hell of a day."

"You been to see Helen, ain't ya?" I said. He nodded. I guess that explained why he was drunk.

"Been to Cherokee, too. Had to wait two hours for the Asheville bus." That explained the war bonnet.

"What did you bring me?" I said. Albert had spent over a year on a big ship somewhere close to Japan, and he always bought me a souvenir.

"Maybe I didn't bring you anything," he said. He laughed when I looked disappointed and knelt by his sea bag, scrounging around inside. He held out something limp and goggle-eyed.

"What?" I said.

"It's a gas mask. Jap soldiers carried these things in case they ran into a poison gas attack." He slid it on my head and tightened the straps. It had a long snout with some kind of can screwed on the end.

"Filter system," said Albert. I listened to myself breathe inside the mask. The rubber expanded and collapsed, and the little glass windows fogged.

"Reckon it has ever been used?" I asked. Albert laughed.

"We didn't use any poison gas on the Japs," he said. "Old Moon tried to buy it from me."

"He did?"

"Oh, yeah. You know how he is. He'll use any excuse to get his money out and wave it around in front of you." Albert grabbed me and gave me a knuckle-rub. "Told him it wasn't for sale." He jumped off the porch and threw the bow and the one raggedy-assed arrow by the springhouse door under the porch. He removed the war bonnet, folded it into a square, and sailed it after the bow.

"Keep your mouth shut, and we'll go see Lash LaRue tonight," he said. He drifted to the end of the porch and gazed at the sun-struck mountains. It occurred to me that Granny didn't even know he was home.

Ten minutes later, I was crawling through the barn loft with my Daisy air rifle, braving the deadly fumes from the metal canisters that the Japanese had hurled into my hideout. "Come and get me, yellow peril," I said. Then, I pretended that a bullet had shattered the filter system, and deadly gas was seeping into my lungs. Rushing from my hideout, I stood like Brian Donlevey, in a hail of enemy fire. I emptied my rifle, one b.b. at a time, and clutched my throat as the poison brought me down. Alarmed chickens fled, cackling as I laid twitching in the barnyard.

"Harley?" Granny stuck her shoe under my shoulder and flipped me over. I pulled the gas mask off and squinted at her.

"Hey, Granny."

"Would you know anything about this?" She held out the milk bucket with the arrow in it.

"Yikes!" I said. "How did that happen?" I tried to sound pretty amazed. Then Granny saw Albert standing on the porch staring at the Balsam Mountains.

"Hey, Babe," she said. She dropped the bucket and went up the porch steps. She called him Babe because he was the youngest. He was also her favorite. You wouldn't know it though. She didn't holler and hug him. Nothing like that. She just walked up real close to him and stared at him for a minute. "Come in, and I'll fix you something to eat."

Albert picked up his sea bag and followed her.

Helen had divorced Albert while he was overseas. Granny said that Helen had broke Albert's heart. Each time that he got a furlough, he stopped in Bryson City and asked Helen if she had changed her mind. She hadn't; in fact, she was getting married again. This time, the new husband-to-be had answered the door. That's why Albert was drunk.

"The guy is a 4-F," said Albert. He was sitting at the kitchen table drinking coffee while Granny admired her Japanese teapot. It was white and blue and the little porcelain cups looked thin as eggshells.

"I ain't ever had any tea," she said. "Do you think I'd like it?"

"She met the son-of-a-bitch at one of them Red Cross things. Don't that beat all!" He got up and poured more coffee.

"My sister Helen drinks tea," said Granny. "She raises peppermint."

"I'll tell you one thing," said Albert, pouring sugar in his coffee, "She ain't gonna get the car. It ain't worth a damn, but I'm going down to the Mooney Creek store and call her. Damn car's mine."

We didn't have a telephone since Papaw tore it out of the wall and threw it into the garden again.

"Don't go right this minute," said Granny. "Eat something first."

I was sitting across from Albert with his sailor hat on. "Have you got an extra one of these?" I said. Albert stared at me for a minute.

"You look like your daddy, Harley," he said. "You look like John Lyndon."

Granny put the teacups down and looked at me. "Yes, he does," she said. She didn't look happy about it.

Albert winked at me. "*Shootout at Durango*," he said "Lash LaRue takes on the Hole-in-the-Wall gang. Lash and Sunset Carson."

"They're in a movie together?" I said. Albert shook his head.

"Double-feature. The other one is called *Oregon Trail*."

I was speechless with excitement.

Life went on from summer to fall. A new continued serial, *Nyoka,Queen of the Jungle*, came to the Ritz, moved through twelve episodes and was replaced by *Space Cadets*. Winter came, the creeks froze over and Foxie and Bear killed Moon Mullins and his wife.

Johnny Mac was the first to see the picture at Donninger's Studio.

"It's taped to the glass inside the door," he said. "And it's...well, it's hard to look at." It was a picture of Moon and his wife.

So, every day for a week, we walked up Main Street after school, and sat on the steps that went up two flights to the studio. I never made it up the steps. The closer I got, the less I wanted to see it, so I waited for Johnny Mac and Eddie Mathis. Eddie came back first. "His eyes are hanging out and the top of her head is gone," he said. Each time he gave the same report. "Don't you want to see?"

"I guess not." I tried to imagine the broken faces, but couldn't.

Albert came home during the trial, stopping in Bryson City to reclaim his belongings; Helen had packed them in the trunk of his car. The battery was dead and the tires were flat. When he finally drove into the driveway in an oily cloud, he was angry and frustrated. "I think the motor block is cracked," he said. He said he was afraid to cut the engine off because it might not start again. The car smoked and popped as he unloaded his clothes. I told him about the murder.

"Yeah, I heard," he said. "I'm not surprised." The next morning, one of the tires was flat again. After changing it, Albert turned the ignition and listened to the weakened battery strain, whine and die. He had skinned his hand changing the tire, and he sat for a while with a bloody knuckle in his mouth, staring at the car. Looking at his face, I decided that I shouldn't give my opinion. Then, he went to the woodpile and came back with the axe. After shattering the windshield and the headlights, he left the axe embedded in the radiator.

Granny was on the porch watching, and she said, "I'd give it a couple of more licks if I was you. I think it's still alive." Then, she come down the steps to Albert and said so soft I could barely hear her, "Babe, if anybody saw you now, they would probably take you to the asylum in Morganton." Albert sat for a while with his head in his hands.

"Momma," he said, "Be glad that it is just a *car* I killed."

The murder trial was pretty short. After relatives of Moon and his wife asked Donninger's Studio to remove the picture, Johnny Mac and me migrated to the courthouse. Climbing the stairs to the balcony, we listened to the lawyers refer to "the accused, Johnson Dills and Willard Merkin." That was Foxie and Bear's real names. It was a surprise to not hear them referred to as "Foxie and Bear," the names that we had given them.

The year before the murder, all of the students at Sylva Elementary got to go to the Ritz for *Song of the South*. We were herded from the school to the theatre by all twelve teachers and Baldy Coggins, where we sat enthralled by singing crows and comic animals. When Uncle Remus started talking about Br'er Bear and Br'er Fox and we saw the nervous, chattering fox accompanied by the huge, slowwitted bear, Johnny Mac turned to me and said, "Dead-ringers for the guys down at the poolroom!" And they were! In fact, Dills and Merkin had been a familiar sight on the street and throughout the county for years where they worked as day laborers. The contrast between the two men was remarkable. Dills, small and clever, seemed to dance along, maintaining a steady, confiding discourse in the huge, shambling Merkin's ear.

After the movie, as we returned to the school, walking single-file down Main Street, we saw Dills and Merkin sitting with Moon Mullins on the bench in front of the poolroom. "Br'er Fox and Br'er Bear!" said Johnny Mac, and his pronouncement raced down the line of students, jumping from class to class as we repeated the words.

"Look! It's them!" I guess they never knew that we had named them. That day, Dills stopped talking for a moment, puzzled by the laughing children and Merkin raised his morose head, staring at us in a remarkable mime of his cartoon counterpart.

Eventually, the names were shortened to Foxie and Bear and they became familiar objects to us. "There are Foxie and Bear," we would say when we saw the two men trudging the roadsides, weeding gardens or sitting with Moon Mullins in front of the poolroom. We would stop to watch, waiting for them to mimic their movie counterparts, Foxie, dancing about the sluggish Bear, wheedling, whispering, suggesting. Sometimes, we would shout out our favorite Br'er Bear speech - the one he gave when he was finally goaded to anger; "Ah'm gonna...knock..your head..clean off!" That was before the murder, of course...before the hammers.

Merkin confessed, telling how Dills had convinced him that "no one would ever know." At the trial, Johnny Mac, Charlie Kay and I sat in the balcony and stared through the honey-colored afternoon sunlight at Merkin as he told "the plan." With the hammers concealed in the bib of their overalls, they waited in the dark below the Jordan farm, knowing that Moon and Tillie visited her parents each Saturday night. When they saw the lights of the taxi approaching, the two men rose and began walking, knowing that Moon would stop. After all, he sat each day with them in front of the poolroom. Dills struck the first blow, he said. The taxi rolled to a stop in the ditch and Merkin killed Tillie. "We couldn't seem to stop," he said. "Kept hitting them long after they was dead." Both were sentenced to die in the gas chamber in Raleigh the following summer.

They never found the money. When questioned about the fat roll of bills, both men became silent. For years, Johnny Mac and I looked for it.

"They built that rock wall at the Gibsons," said Johnny Mac.

"What about the swimming pool?" I said. "They helped pour the concrete." Then, there was a waterline and all the junk cars where the two men were known to sometimes sleep and the beer joint at Maple Springs where they drank together.

The editor of the local paper traveled to Raleigh for the execution and gave a two-page account. He had sat in a dark room with a glass wall and watched the two men die. Papaw read it aloud on the porch while Granny shelled peas. "Merkin proved to be uncommonly vigorous and continued to struggle for over twenty minutes. Throughout the ordeal, his frightened eyes sought the faces of the witnesses. When death finally came and the restraining straps were removed, a massive congestion of blood had gathered beneath the bonds, forming a huge, black cross on Merkin's chest."

"I don't want to hear anymore," said Granny.

"I do," I said. "We ain't heard about Foxie."

"Well, you are not going to. It's not healthy, Harley. Makes me wonder about you."

"It's them funny books and movies. That stuff is bound to make you strange," said Papaw. "It's time you went to bed anyway."

That summer, *The Sands of Iwo Jima* came to the Ritz. Uncle Albert moved to Brevard and married again. He invited me over for a couple of weekends and bought me enough funny books to last me the summer. Johnny Mac and I found a place in the pasture where we could recreate John Wayne's final charge. We would spend hours crawling through the sawbriars and leading suicide charges before Granny called me home for supper.

In the fall, an escaped convict was killed as he fled from a work crew across a pasture. On the way home from school the next evening, Johnny Mac and I stopped at the funeral home and asked if we could see him.

"You want to see the dead convict?" said Mr. John.

"Yessir."

He led us to a room where a sheeted figure lay face down on a table. Pulling the sheet back, he pointed to a blue dot on the man's back. I had seen dead people before, but they had been relatives in caskets. This was my first time to see somebody killed by a bullet.

"That little hole killed him?" said Johnny Mac.

"It isn't so little on the other side," said Mr. John.

The man's eyes were open and we spent a while looking at them.

"How come they are different?"

"Death makes a lot of things different," said Mr. John. "Do you want to touch him?" Johnnie Mac and I looked at each other. "It's okay," said Mr. John. "Go ahead." We both gave the man's arm a poke. He was cold, of course, but that doesn't describe the way he felt. He was more than just cold.

Mr. John's wife came in and got very upset because we were there.

"For Heaven's sake, James, what are you doing? These children shouldn't be here!" She nudged us toward the door.

"They are just curious, Ellen. I was the same at their age. No harm done."

Out on the street, we stood for a while thinking about the blue hole, the dead eyes and the cold flesh.

"Being dead is different than what I thought," said Johnny Mac.

"Yeah," he turned toward home.

"You going to the movies tonight?" I said. *"The Damned Don't Cry."*

"Maybe. I'm not sure." I watched him vanish down the street towards Keener Hill. I felt it, too. Everything was different now - the street beneath my feet, people's faces, and the way the light fell on the distant mountains. It was like a new color had been added to the spectrum. I walked faster, eager to get home.

THE SIRENS OF MOONY CREEK

Then, there is that other mystery......

Harley crept out the back door and dropped into a crouch by the springhouse. Then, gripping his Red Ryder Daisy, he made a dash for the big oak in the front yard. Halfway there, he dived behind Granny's bed of Love Lies Bleeding and crawled the rest of the way. So far, so good. Now, he would have to cross some open space before he gained the shelter of the woodpile. He made a dash for it.

"Harley!" Harley stopped, and managed to convert the dash into a casual walk.

"Where do you think you are going?" Granny stood on the porch staring at the eleven-year-old who had stopped and was sitting on the chopping block.

"You were supposed to clean out the chicken house."

"I did, I did." He had spent the better part of an hour hauling wheel- barrow loads of manure to the garden, his eyes burning from the acid stench, despite the Japanese gas mask that Uncle Albert had brought him from Okinawa. He had made a lame attempt to convert the whole experience into an attack on a Nippon base that manufactured poison gas, but the fogged goggles and the thunderous sound of his own breathing inside the mask defeated him.

"Well, all right." Granny peered at the manure pile in the garden. "Where are you going?"

"Painter Knob." Harley sensed that Granny had given him permission, and he raced toward the woods barely hearing her "You come when I call you." Within seconds, he was deep within the cool, shadowed trees where pine needles, rotting leaves, and rhododendron covered the ground.

Harley knew that Audie was waiting for him at the top.

They had met each day for two weeks now, he and Audie Murphy. Together, they had dug fox-holes, reconnoitered Jap installations, and had made lightning-quick attacks on hill-side pillboxes where the last remnants of a crazed and suicidal force of the sons of Nippon fought until the death. Now, as Harley sprinted from tree to tree, he kept his eyes on the crest of Painter Knob where the sky and the loblolly pines met.

Audie rose from the foxhole that the two had dug with Harley's Boy Scout shovel. Audie slung his rifle over his shoulder and smiled his lop-sided smile. "Hey, Harley. You ready to go to hell and back?"

"I'm ready, Audie." Audie tilted his helmet back with one finger and pointed down the back side of the hill.

"There is a machine-gun nest at the bottom of this hill near that little creek."

"Mooney Creek," said Harley. "I know it like the back of my hand."

"Good! Your familiarity with the terrain will be a definite advantage here. Let's not waste time, Private Teester. We will move parallel to each other down the slope." Audie racked a shell into his rifle and Harley pumped a deadly b.b. into the chamber of the Red Ryder.

"I'll follow your lead, here, Teester." Audie moved like a shadow into the woods, halted and then returned.

"One final thing, Teester. You handled yourself with remarkable valor yesterday when we rushed that pill-box in the old mica mine. I owe my life to your quick thinking when you dispatched that crazed spawn of Nippon that was about to bayonet me."

"Thank you, sir."

"Let's move out."

Audie vanished into the laurel and rhododendron and the two began their stealthy descent. Moving with the experience gleaned from two weeks of combat (since the day that school had broke for the summer) Harley quickly gained the creek bank. With the Red Ryder balanced in the crook of his arms, Harley crawled through a patch of broom sage and blackberry vines until he heard the soft murmur of water and the loud cries of the red-winged blackbirds that flocked to the vine-choked banks of Mooney Creek. Pulling his compass from the chain around his neck, Harley checked his bearings. If his instincts were correct, he was slightly upstream from the old bridge - possibly the location of the yellow peril. He crept forward, breaking through a blanket of vines, and found himself looking down into the creek. Immediately, he noted that the normally clear waters were dark with mud.

So, some activity is taking place up-stream. He thought about establishing contact with Murphy, telling him that he had located the enemy, but he decided not to risk speaking - even in the terse whisper that he used to communicate with his friend. Carefully, he moved down stream until he encountered the rock masonry that supported the old abandoned bridge and crept across the warped and rotting floor. From this point, he could see 50 yards up the creek.

The stream flowed through a tunnel of vines and kudzu-choked trees, a dim passage laced with shafts of sunlight. Here, in a deep pool, Harley sighted the enemy. Two figures stood waist-deep in the dark waters, naked and limned in pale light.

Hell's Bells and Hot Damn!

It was Katie Sue Carnes and Jackie Dehart, both in his fifth-grade class this past year and both stark, raving naked! The two girls splashed each other, their laughter pealing like bells. Harley leaned his rifle against the railing. These were the first unclad females that he had ever seen and the effects were startling. He began to breathe in shallow, quick gasps as he leaned across the railing. Even as he watched, the two figures rose from the water, and danced about, flinging rainbow-tinted cascades of water into the sunlight. When Katie Sue climbed up the trunk of an ancient oak that had fallen across the stream, vertigo seized Harley and he fell to the floor of the old bridge. Rolling over on his back, he stared at a blue, summer sky and tried to understand.

When he raised his head again, Katie Sue was standing atop the tree trunk, straining to reach a tangled mass of grapevines. Jackie sat astride the tree, combing her hair. Harley's heart thundered and his vision blurred like an unfocused telescope. What was happening to him? He grasped the rusty railing of the bridge and pulled himself up, straining to see, to memorize, to fix this image forever. Nubile and sleek as the bodies of mountain trout, the two girls flickered in the dim light; yet they filled Harley with a wild and desperate yearning. He could see goose flesh on Katie Sue's arms and the water drops suspended in Jackie's red hair, but he somehow could not see enough. Straining forward, his hands fumbled on the railing and the Red Ryder clattered to the bridge. Both girls turned, wild-eyed, mouths agape and Harley dropped out of sight. Moments later, when he peeped again, the girls were gone!

"Harley Teester!" Yikes, he thought, they know who I am!

"Harley Teester, we see you!" He peeped again and saw their heads bobbing in the pool. He decided that they must be kneeling on the bottom.

"We are going to tell on you, Harley Teester." The boy's mind raced. What did that mean? What would Granny or the Sheriff do to you for looking at naked girls? It had to be at least a prison sentence, maybe worse.

"You get away from that bridge!"

Harley picked up his Red Ryder and started a strategic withdrawal as he thought about what Katie Sue had just said. Why "Get away from the bridge"? Why not just "Go Away!" Then, he saw them. Two summer dresses, one blue and one yellow, faded from many washings, and two pairs of panties hanging on a metal strut beneath the bridge. The boy stood for a moment grappling with alien factors and new knowledge. Shame at what he was doing warred with a new, stubborn resolve to stay where he was.

"You better go away if you know what is good for you!"

He waited.

"We need our clothes!"

"Well, come and get them, then."

Two hours later, the sun was going down and Harley knew that if need be, he would wait until winter came and Mooney Creek froze over. He had found a strange, new deity and he was prepared to die in its service. He heard the two girls whispering together and then suddenly, they stood.

"Okay, we are coming for our clothes."

As they waded down the creek and away from the pool, the waters dropped below their knees. Harley's throat became dry as he gripped the railing of the bridge watching with a fervor that was strange and frightening. Arms behind their backs, their teeth chattering in cold air, Katie Sue and Jackie advanced as though they were approaching a firing squad. As he looked at their grim faces, Harley had misgivings. He was probably in deep trouble, but he also sensed that he did not regret his decision to stay....to see.

Then, the girls raised their hands and hurled handfuls of Mooney Creek mud at Harley's face. He fought to dig the grit from his eyes, but by the time his vision returned, both girls were beneath the bridge, whispering as they struggled into their clothing. Night fog was moving down Mooney Creek, and the slopes of Painter Knob were becoming indistinct in the fading light.

Harley retraced his steps. Near the crest of Painter Knob, Audie was waiting.

"Well, Private Teester, we seem to have encountered a different test of valor today," Audie smiled and tilted his helmet. "Or at least, you did."

"Yes sir."

"Given the circumstances, you handled yourself pretty well. Of course, you gave up your advantage too quickly."

"I've got a lot of questions, Sergeant Murphy."

"I'm afraid I can't help you much, kid. I can tell you how to move soundlessly in the dark and cut the throat of the enemy sentries, but in situations like the one you just encountered, I'm afraid you are on your own." Audie gave an apologetic shrug.

"I guess I'm in trouble."

"Oh, definitely, Private Teester."

Harley started down the slope of Painter Knob. In the distance, he heard Granny calling him. There was an edge in her voice that suggested that she had been calling a long time.

"I don't guess I'll see you tomorrow," said Audie.

"No, I guess not."

"Ah, well, what the hell. We had fun for a while, right?"

"Right." Harley turned and Audie was gone. He broke into a run through the dark woods.

"So there you are, mister." Granny stood on the porch with her hands on her hips. When she said, "mister" she was mad. Two kerosene lamps cast a flickering light across the porch. Their glow had served as beacons when Harley had foundered in the darkness of Painter Knob.

"I was down at Mooney Creek," Harley said. "Couldn't hear you."

"That is no excuse." Harley dropped the Red Ryder on the porch.

"No, I guess not."

"That is no way to treat your air rifle either." Granny peered closely at his face. "What is all over your face and shirt?"

"Mud," said Harley. He brushed the grit from his hair and scraped muck from his eyebrows.

"Fall in the creek?"

"Not exactly."

"You are acting strange, young man. What's wrong with you?" Harley looked at Painter Knob where a moon was rising, a great melon of a moon that filled him with joy and pain.

"I wish I knew," he said.

DANCING IN THE DARK

When I remember Jackie, I always see him dancing at the Ritz. He is wearing a pair of powder-blue slacks, a pink shirt and a dark blue, sleeveless sweater. His hair glitters with pomade as he taps across the narrow strip of flooring before the movie screen. In the summer of my sophomore year in Sylva High, he always danced on Saturday nights just before the Owl show - the Ritz did the zombie and spook films then. In the fifteen-minute intermission before the werewolves and vampires appeared, Jackie would do what he called "dance medleys." He would move effortlessly from Charleston to tango to mountain "buck and wing," the taps on his shoes making sharp, satisfying clickety-clacks that carried clear out to the lobby. The audience loved it, and they would throw pocket change on the stage. Sometimes, he was still picking up quarters when the lights went out and the movie began.

Two years older than me, Jackie moved through the halls at school with little shuffles and twirls, like he was still dancing at the Ritz. I guess I was awed by him, and I yearned to move through life like Jackie did. I worked at the Ritz - popped the popcorn, swept the theater, and put the big letters on the marquee. Jackie came almost every night, and when business was slow, he would stand in the lobby and talk to me. We both loved movies, and since the Ritz only showed two each week, plus the western and the Owl show on Saturday, we both saw them over and over. I remembered them, but Jackie *memorized* them.

Sometimes, in the lobby, after Doris, the ticket-taker, had gone, Jackie would dance, mug and sing. Sometimes, we played the game, the wonderful game.

"Harley, who is this?" Jackie would turn up the collar of his blue blazer, hang a Winston in the corner of his mouth, squinch his eyes in a parody of sadness and wrinkle his brow.

"Jimmy Dean!" He would smile, pleased by my quick response. Then maybe he would lurch about the lobby, grasping the walls for support, his breath hissing through clenched teeth. Grasping his stomach, and giving me a stricken grimace. "I'm a hundred dollar a day newspaperman...." Sinking to his knees, he said, "You can have me for nothing." Then he fell on his face.

"Kirk Douglas in *The Big Carnival*." Then he would do Cagney and Glenn Ford, or dance like Astaire and Gene Kelley. He was the best of all the movies I had ever seen. He was magic.

"Are you going to be an actor, Jackie? Are you going to be in movies?" I guess I asked that a dozen times that last summer before Jackie vanished.

"Not likely, Harley. Gotta take care of Mom."

I knew about old lady Campbell, the lush who sat in Velt's late at night, drinking black coffee, her cheeks rouged like a Christmas Santa. Sometimes, Jackie would do a parody of her, his eyes unfocused, his mouth agape, just the way she looked sometimes in Velt's.

"Jackie, have I been to the bathroom, or am I going?" he would say in a nasal whine. But, he would add with a smile, "She's a drunk, but I love her."

His father had left town with a carnival when Jackie was six. He had been back a few times, a big man who talked too loud and too much; but mostly Jackie got postcards. From Winter Park, Florida; Palm Springs; Tia Juana. "Maybe next time he comes back, he will take me with him. I could do stuff in the carnival."

"But your Mom..."

"Maybe he will take us both."

Usually, when I cut the lights and the big red and white neon tubes in the marquee bled to black, Jackie would be standing out front, shuffling back and forth in front of the ticket booth snapping his fingers, his taps doing little staccato riffs as he stared up and down the street. Sometimes, a car would pass, horn blaring - usually college students from Western Carolina University cruising our lone street with its single, pulsing caution light. Sometimes, Jackie waved.

"You want to come down to Velt's?"

91

"No, thanks, Harley."

"They've changed the records on the juke-box. *Blue Tango*! Louis Armstrong's *Story of Love*."

"Oh, yeah?" He did a slow-slow-quick-quick-quick step and twirled like Jose Greco. "See you tomorrow."

"Are you going to stay here? Why?"

"I'm meeting someone."

"Oh. Well, see you!" I would leave him there, dancing in the dark.

Sometimes, as I sat in the back booth at Velt's, pumping nickels into the jukebox and talking to Gentry, the short-order cook, I would see Jackie pass the window. His mother was usually sitting at a nearby table drinking coffee and staring at the empty street. She never knew that her son had passed, and he never came in.

Then the college guys beat him up.

The morning after it happened, everyone was talking about it. Griff Middleton, the sheriff, had found him in a ditch two miles out of town. Charlie Kay, my best friend at school, said he overheard "Baldy" Coggins, the principal, talking to the sheriff.

"He was unconscious," said Charlie, "and he was ...naked!"

When I got to the hospital that afternoon, and found Jackie's room, I thought I was in the wrong place. This couldn't be Jackie, livid with bruises and his eyes blood-shot and swollen. The blond hair was mostly gone, his head laced with stitches. I sat for a moment, wondering if he knew I was there. Then he said, "If you think I'm going to squeal, copper, you're wrong." It was Cagney, and it was Jackie! He laughed and tried to smile at me.

"So, what happened, Jackie?" He turned his face away.

"Heard it was some college creeps."

"Yeah, well, I'm not going to press charges. Nobody saw them."

"You did, though!" I waited. "Right?" He shook his head.

"Some farmer milking his cows said he saw the car and the college jackets, but nothing positive."

"So, what happened?"

After a while, he said, "Maybe I'll tell you someday."

But Gentry told me. That night when I sat in Velt's, Gentry said, "Three football players. They are probably going to get away with it, too."

"Why?"

"Well, the fact that Jackie's queer, you know."

I'd heard the word, of course. I guess I had some vague idea of what it meant. There was the local pharmacist, a fat man that prowled the Ritz on Saturdays. Some of the boys told stories about him, but even so, I didn't know. What did he do? Exactly what did queers do?

Gentry told me in graphic detail. And he told me that Jackie had been standing under the dark marquee at the Ritz for over a year, waiting to be "picked up."

"Things like that get around," he said. "The Ritz is Jackie's hang-out," said Gentry, "Didn't you know that?"

I thought of the nights when I had locked the doors and found Jackie beneath the marquee, shifting and turning, dancing in the dark.

"I'm waiting for someone," he had said ...

"I don't believe it."

"Yeah, well, sorry to disillusion you, old son. Maybe I shouldn't have told you." He gave my head a gentle knuckle-rub and smiled. "There are worse things. Willard Tolley, the mechanic down at the Texaco station? He got romantically involved with a little heifer."

"No," I said, shaking my head, "You're making that up."

Gentry grinned. "Let's talk about something else, Harley. How are you doing in English?"

Jackie didn't come back to school. I was relieved because I didn't know how I would react. I was repelled by what Gentry had told me, and I knew it would show in my face. But, a night came when he returned to the Ritz, mounting the steps slowly like an old man. There were no powder-blue slacks, no pink shirt; that night it was T-shirt and jeans. He stopped by the popcorn machine and smiled. "Ah, sure, and it's a fine night, but me bones are achin' 'n I shouldn't be here a'tall, a'tall." Barry Fitzgerald. We looked at each other.

"So, now you know." I nodded. "I see it makes a difference, and I am sorry for that. I'm going to miss you, Harley." He turned away.

"Why do you do it?" I blurted. Jackie turned back then. "Do what?"

"Why do you wait out there in the dark? ....and do what they say you do when people....." I was having trouble concluding, "...people pick you up?"

"It's like the movies," he said.

"Well, I don't see..."

"Each time is different. Like sitting in the movies when the lights dim and not knowing what is going to happen, but willing to go with the story....see where it takes you. Getting in somebody's car can be like that." Then he said, "Gotta be going, Harley."

"Where to? You just gonna leave?"

He did a John Wayne, then. "A man's gotta do what a man's gotta do." Then, he winked and he went cautiously down the steps. For a while, I could see him beneath the marquee, looking up and down the street, and then he was gone.

I think he came that last time to the Ritz to tell me that. I never saw him again for forty years. His mother continued to sit in Velt's and although I wanted to ask her about Jackie, I didn't. Sometimes, I wondered if she knew he was gone. She died two years ago.

Last month, I heard that Jackie was back. Gentry told me, of course.

"Tested HIV positive," he said. "Came home to die."

"Have you seen him?"

"Oh, sure! Stopped one night and talked a bit. He sits on the porch and reads, plays old records." Then, after a moment, he continued, "You should go see him, Harley. You will regret it if you don't."

And so I went. I found him sitting in the dark, listening to Frankie Lane. *My heart knows what the wild goose knows.....* The streetlight touched his face, and he smiled.

"Ah, Pud," he said. For a moment I thought he didn't know me, but then, he continued. "I've got Death up in that apple tree, and he can't come down until I say." He was doing a beautiful Lionel Barrymore imitation.

"*On Borrowed Time,*" I said

"Right you are!" He took my hand, and I saw how sick he was, his damp, cool fingers barely managing a grip. I told him about teaching school, the childless marriage and the divorce.

"And where have you been?" I asked.

"Been to see the elephant!" I laughed at the old expression that meant you had seen things that shocked and amazed you.

"I take it that you are glad that you did."

"Oh, yes! It has been a good life."

"Did you find a career in acting?"

Jackie laughed. "In a way. Ended up in a carnival, like my father. I think that is where us mediocre talents go."

We talked a bit more, but Jackie was visibly tiring. As I rose to go, I said, "I would like to ask you something."

"Well, now is the time."

"When you used to stand in the dark outside the Ritz, what were you waiting for?"

"You mean besides those beefy lads with beer on their breath? There is always something besides the obvious, of course." He thought a moment. "I was waiting for someone with travel on his mind and a full tank of gas."

"That was all?"

"Pretty much. I could make it more poetic and talk about finding myself, but no, that's it. I needed to escape." He rose and came forward. "Thank you for coming, Harley."

"Do you need anything?"

"Got all that I need." He indicated the apple tree. "And it's time for him to come down." Lionel Barrymore. He even had the little chuckle down pat.

When I got to the car, I turned to wave goodbye, but I couldn't make him out. I heard music and saw what might have been a wavering figure on the dark porch.

TINY'S CURVE

"Get out of the road, Tiny. You know you ain't supposed to be out there." Tiny grinned at her husband, Robinson, and crept into the dusty weeds.

"You know what the law said. If they have to come back again, they just might put you in jail." Tiny laughed, shook her head and covered her mouth with her hand.

"Can't do a damn thing with her, Harley. After the last time, when the woman from Floridy knocked her in the ditch, they come up here and laid down the law."

"Talked mean to me," said Tiny.

"Told her that a 80-year-old woman with a broke back ain't got no business standing in the road. Told me to see to it, but I can't do nothing with her. I mean, hell, I been laid up myself."

Tiny didn't get a broken back by standing in the road. Robinson said it was a childhood injury. He once told me that "it happened in Georgia," and then gave me one of those looks that implied secret causes and mysterious powers. "Georgia," he repeated with an affirming nod.

Robinson had just removed his shoe to show me where the copperhead bit him forty years ago. I strained to see two pale indentations under the anklebone. "Don't look like much, but I ain't been able to work since." Robinson leaned closer, speaking in a whisper. "Can't lift nothing." Then, he nodded his head sagely. "Took my spunk, it did."

"I spy a blue car at the Painters," said Tiny. "Who you reckon that is?"

"Might be that daughter in from Atlanta," I said, " the one that is in nursing school." Tiny nodded. Then, with her hand aslant her forehead like a sailor in a crow's nest, she peered the other way.

"Old black dog," she said, giving a melodramatic shiver. Tiny didn't like dogs, since she kept over a dozen cats.

"Car coming," warned Robinson. A big van, its tires whining, swept around the steep curve by Tiny and Robinson's shack, the van's windows full of gaping children and a yapping spaniel. The driver braked for Tiny who rushed to a patch of gravel and began to pelt the van with sand and rocks. "Tiny! Stop it, now!" said Robinson.

The astonished driver stared at Tiny's little capering figure as she continued to scoop sand and pebbles from the roadside and fling them opened-handed at the van. Finally, turning his head, he stared open-mouthed at Robinson sitting on the porch.

"Sorry!" shouted Robinson. "She ain't got a lick of sense." Then, he laughed and spat a great dollop of tobacco into the dusty kudzu. The van proceeded cautiously and we watched it vanish toward town.

"Come in, now, old woman. You've done enough damage for one day." Tiny clapped her hands and then crept slowly down through clumps of daffodils that grew along the bank.

"That was fun," she said.

At one time, Tiny and Robinson had lived in pastoral isolation in a little shack that leaned askew in a protected cove amid water oaks, giant poplars and laurel thickets. But then, the little trail by the door became a path, and when summer homes began to appear like toadstools atop the ridges above the shack, the bulldozers came. Gravel became pavement and finally, a smooth two-lane road of oily asphalt coiled around the porch.

"Time was, the only thing that come up that road was cows," said Robinson. "You could set here all day and not see a soul, except maybe somebody going to milk their cow in Wilkes' pasture."

"Watkins man used to come," said Tiny, clapping her hands. "Sold pie mix and cocoa." Robinson laughed. "Tiny used to eat it out of the can. Set there and eat a whole can of pie mix with a spoon."

"Yum, yum," said Tiny, stooping to pick up one of her cats and sitting on the edge of the porch. "You want a good cat?"

"I got three, Tiny."

"They might be lonesome. You need a few more."

"Quiet, it was, too," said Robinson. No sound in this holler but rain crows and hoot-owls." A car rushed into the curve, braked and sped away with a thunder of drumbeats. The cats vanished beneath the house. "College boys," said Robinson. "Got them damn boomboxes." He shook his head. "That's what we got now, instead of rain-crows." Another car passed and dust drifted through the laurel hedge.

"Twenty years ago, I knowed the name of every family on that ridge. Gibsons, Middletons, Brysons and the Hoyles family." Robinson stood and walked to the edge of the porch, pointing at a glint of mobile homes on the ridge line. "Now, it is all summer folks and college boys. I'm a stranger in a holler where I lived for seventy years."

"Well, there must be some advantages to that road, besides the Watkins man," I said. The mail-truck went by. "What about the mail?"

Robinson snorted. "Never get nothing I want." He pointed at the rusty box, almost concealed in a tangle honeysuckle, its mouth agape as though slowly strangling. "Bills, catalogues and tax-notices."

"Town water?"

"Nope. Got a spring, or at least, had one 'til that road ruined it." Tiny rushed to the bank and pointed at a patch of dry sand encircled by rock. "Used to be there," she said. An old gourd dipper still hung from a broken laurel limb.

"Carry it now," said Tiny, and she mimed lugging a bucketful of spring water.

"Up the hill a piece," said Robinson, "and the neighbors don't mind. No 'lectricity, either. Got three kerosene lamps."

I knew about the lamps. Coming home late, I sometimes saw them glowing through the thickets. On summer nights, the light was hardly distinguishable from the fireflies.

"Know what used to be there where that road is? A thicket of jack-in-the-pulpits and three dogwood trees."

"Purty," said Tiny, her little gimlet eyes brightening.

"Bull-dozer wiped 'em out." A yellow school bus passed. Tiny waved.

"I wish me and Tiny was in some forgotten cove if there is such a thing as that anymore. No roads, no cars, no noise."

"No dogs," said Tiny.

"How about no cats?" Robinson winked at me.

Tiny shook her head in solemn disagreement. "Lots of cats," she said, stroking an old calico as she stared down the road.

"Red car," said Tiny. She dropped the cat and scrambled up the bank to the pavement. "It turned off by the creek. Stopped at

Patti Flowers' house." She peered for a moment and announced. " A man and a woman. She's got on a blue dress."

"Get out of the road, Tiny."

"Wait. Wait. I want to see if they go in. They did."

"She is driving me crazy, Harley." Robinson laughed. Tiny laughed, too, clapping her hands.

Two months later, Robinson was dead. A social worker found him in his chair on the front porch with his shoes in his lap. Tiny, of course, was in the road watching a work crew cut limbs that threatened the power lines that served the trailers and summer homes on the ridge. The social worker noted that the old man was still warm and had probably been dead less than an hour. Things moved pretty quick after that. Tiny was told that she was being taken to a nursing home and to be packed immediately. I found her one morning standing in my driveway like a forlorn question mark.

"My cats," she said. "Feed my cats."

I tried, but with the old woman gone, the cats soon vanished, some victims of the road, and others taken in by neighbors. It was amazing how quickly the undergrowth moved in, and by the year's end, kudzu had completely covered the house. Within a few months, Tiny followed Robinson. A nurse at Hemlock Nursing Home told me that she just "withered away."

"She was already small," she noted, "but she actually became more so. Atrophied, I guess."

Within two years, the roof of the little shack collapsed and kudzu wound through the shattered windows. A decade later, the County has "condemned" the little plot of earth, stating that it didn't meet zoning standards for water and sewer service and couldn't be used as a future building site. The little constricted piece of pavement around the vanished shack is still known locally as "Tiny's curve," but few people know the source of the name.

Last week, I came around the curve to find two cars - one in the ditch and one in the road. Two well-dressed ladies stood nearby, shouting at each other. I was told that one lady had stopped in the road and climbed down the bank to uproot the "wild daffodils" growing in profusion there. The second car had back-ended her. Both were summer-home residents. I left them there, edging by their expensive cars and hoping that maybe, back in the shadows of the roadside, a tiny figure was gamboling in delight.

A STONE, A LEAF, A DOOR

Strictly speaking, this is not a "Harley story," but it is also true that there is autobiographical content in all the stories about a young boy who lives in Rhodes Cove with his grandparents. Like Harley, I listened to "The Squeaking Door" ("The Inner Sanctum"), read comics and had teachers who were concerned because I loved "fantasy more than reality."

I did throw my grandmother's Mason jars into a flooded branch and I bade farewell to Audie Murphy one summer day when the excitement of imaginary combat lost its appeal when compared to a newly discovered part of "the real world."

Even though I am the narrator of "A Stone, A Leaf, A Door," and a part of me is Harley, this speaker is also someone else.

When I was a senior in high school, we lost our English teacher in the middle of the school year. Well into her seventies, Miss Boggs became increasingly distracted in class and sometimes seemed to forget that we were there. She would look up from the grammar book, smile sweetly and say something like, "Oh, the infinite mysteries of the comma!" Then, she would diagram some intricate sentence, filling the blackboard with jungles of compound sentences and dependent clauses. She once diagrammed the first sentence of Paradise Lost and it filled two blackboards. We were required to list each word in that astonishing invocation and label it according to the "parts of speech." Milton made a bad first impression on us.

One day Miss Boggs went to the office for a box of chalk and never returned. The principal told us that she had been "called away on personal business," and that we would have a substitute teacher for the remainder of the year. That is when Miss Boobies came. Her real name was Judy Briggs, but Bobbie Lee Haskett named her Miss Boobies the first day she taught. We all loved her at first sight (all the boys, that is), and when she told us that there would be no more diagramming and grammar, and that she intended to teach literature, we were ecstatic. Each day she read, pacing up and down the aisle, leaning in the window, sitting on the corner of her desk as her wondrous breasts heaved and shifted like sacked and sleeping cats.

Sometimes, she was moved by what she read, and her eyes would fill with tears. She read a poem about being one and twenty and another about cherry blossoms and snow, and we, too, wanted to weep. One day she read Thomas Wolfe, first telling us that he had been born less than fifty miles from where we sat. "He writes about loneliness and loss," she said, and then she read passages from "Look Homeward, Angel" and "You Can't Go Home Again." I didn't understand a word of it, but it was beautiful, the words booming like the organ at First Methodist. I found myself responding to the sound rather than the meaning. "Lost! Lost!"

"Who of us is not forever prison-pent," she said in a tearful whisper. "Who of us is not forever alone?" My mouth gaped and I turned to see my two best friends, Darryl and Ed, gaping too, like baby birds. Those magnificent breasts heaved and strained threatening to burst their flimsy restraints, and my horny little adolescent mind struggled and failed to distinguish between the beauty of Wolfe's words and my reverence for those awesome mammaries. It was all one.

Later, in the cafeteria, Ed said, "What did it mean?" I admitted that I didn't know. Darryl shook his head, implying that he knew, but he didn't want to talk about it. We went to the library and checked out the novels, and we began to memorize the passages that Miss Boobies had read us - passages that thundered and echoed like Old Testament verse.

When Darryl got his driver's license, we took to riding around at night, drinking beer, and proclaiming Housman, Byron ...and Wolfe. I guess we perceived ourselves as awesomely gifted but totally unappreciated young men who were lost and lonely. After Troy's, the local drive-in cafe closed, when the jukebox was unplugged and Johnny Ray's tearful whine was finally silenced, we rode through the dark mountain coves of Jackson County proclaiming poetry. On Monteith Branch, curious cows came to the fence to listen to Darryl assure them that we would go no more a-roving so late into the night.

Driving through Moody Bottom under a full moon with the headlights out, we talked about being one and twenty (which none of us were) and harmonized on "The Great Speckled Bird."

Each night, we would halt atop Freeze Hill under a graveyard oak and watch Sylva's only traffic light pulse like an amber beacon on Main Street. Darryl would turn on the radio, and we would wait for "Moon River." (No, not that one! This was long before Andy Williams.) A man named Franklin McCormack, with a voice like warm molasses, would quote poems about loneliness and heartbreak while discreet violins whispered in the background. We would sit rapt and breathless as Franklin quoted the title poem, "Down the valley of a thousand yesterdays flow the bright, cool waters of Moon River...on and down, carrying you to....." Franklin's voice was like Miss Boobie's straining blouse, and when it was all too painfully beautiful for us to stand any longer, Darryl would quote our favorite passage in "You Can't Go Home Again." It was the letter to "Dear Fox, old friend..."

Darryl's deep, moaning bass sounded like a lorn and love-sick bull bellowing in the dark pasture on Monteith Branch.

"A voice has come to me in the night, telling me I shall die, I know not where...."

Then, Ed, who had a fluting falsetto, would say, "To give up the friends I know for greater knowing...."

And finally, I would chime in with my pronounced nasal whine, "A place more kind than earth, more dear than home;" and then we would all three harmonize on the ending, "A wind is rising, the rivers flow." Oh, it was wonderful! We were wonderful! Lost, sensitive, and misunderstood. Like Wolfe, we were searching for a father, and we rode through the night, keening and shouting, in love with our tragic beauty.

After high school, Darryl went off to Chapel Hill and Ed and I went to Western Carolina Teachers College. Within a year, Ed decided to become a dentist and transferred to UNC, leaving me to wind my way through an English and drama major. Occasionally, I saw my friends when they came in for holidays, but we were drawing apart. We talked less about loneliness and loss and more and more about employment and economics. I went off to north Georgia to teach, Darryl moved to Charlotte and Ed opened an office in a nearby town. I became a casualty of departmental politics, lost a job, got divorced and went to graduate school. Darryl found a home in corporate law; Ed discovered politics and became a mayor. Winds blew, rivers flowed, and thirty years passed.

One October, I found myself alone and unemployed in my grand-parents' old farm. I had just survived another departmental pogrom and my second divorce, and had fled to the bleak but certain shelter of an abandoned house. As I sat before the fireplace, listening to my internal timbers creak and shift in empathy with the quaking roof, the phone rang, abrupt and impertinent. It was Darryl. "I saw a light in the old house," he said, and told me he was in to visit his mother. Then, he added, "Listen, guess who is here!" He meant Ed, of course. He had picked him up an hour ago. "You want to go for a cup of coffee?"

It could have been 1955 and we might have been on our way to the Ritz to see James Dean in *East of Eden*. I banked the fire, locked the door and waited on the porch. It was blowing snow when his BMW came purring to a stop in the driveway. I got in the back, and they both turned to greet me, two overweight men, ruddy and full of good will. "Can't go to Troy's," said Darryl. "It is a real estate office now. There's a new place, though." So we went there. It was filled with college kids and incomprehensible music. We talked as best we could. Darryl said he was being treated for stress "and other complications." Ed had suffered a minor heart attack and worried about high blood pressure. I said little since my ailments were harder to define. How do you talk about vague fears, nightmares and a sense of aimlessness? For a while they talked about torts, writs, implants and crowns, but gradually we stopped talking.

On the way back, we lapsed into silence. The engine purred and Vivaldi whispered from an FM station. It was cozy there and I thought of the drafty old house and the coming night with regret. When the car stopped at the driveway, I suddenly knew what I wanted to say.

"*Something has spoken to me in the night, burning the tapers of the waning years, and told me I shall die, I know not where*," I said. I guess it sounded a little abrupt, and for a moment, I was certain that the two gentle bears in the front seat would interpret what I had said as a confession of failing health. But, as I reached for the door-handle, Darryl finally spoke. "*To…to lose the earth you know for greater knowing; to lose the life you have for greater life…*"

And finally Ed, hesitant and piping, *"To leave the friends you loved for greater loving, to find a land more kind than home, more large than earth."*

And then the three of us spoke together, *"Whereon the pillars of the earth are founded, toward which the conscious of the world is tending - a wind is rising and the rivers flow."* And it was quiet for a moment, except for the wind. I watched the snow and leaves that raced through the beams of the headlights, and then Darryl laughed. Then Ed and I joined him. We laughed like we had heard the greatest punch line in the world - a punch line that had been 30 years in coming.

And so, I got out of the car and watched Darryl and Ed whisper away into the darkness. I thought about Wolfe and the business of being denied the return home; and the old Greek who would have known what Wolfe meant. "You can't step in the same river twice," said Heraclitus. That is true, you can't, but sometimes your foot may find a familiar stone beneath the water. I knew that I would probably never see Ed and Darryl again, but for a fleeting moment, we were there, riding through the dark, shouting and singing.

I looked at the sky and the cold, bright stars. There was smoke coming from the chimney, and I was glad that I had left a fire.

HARLEY'S DREAM

I dreamed last night that I heard Papaw walk barefoot through the house to the back porch. Water was running in the old trough and fireflies pulsed in the dark. I heard him take the gourd dipper from the rusty nail and fill it with cold spring water. "Ah, boyz," he said, after a long drink. "Ahhh, boyz." I rose in the dark, fumbled with my jeans; then crept through the kitchen to the back door where I could see him, standing in his long underwear, staring at the moon.

"Harley," he said in his noncommittal way, and nodded at me.

"Ain't you dead?"

"I guess." He smiled at me and turned back to the moon. I moved to stand by him. I could smell leather and hair tonic. "How you been?" he said.

"Pretty good, I reckon." I stared at my young hands. Clenched my fist and felt strength in my fingers.

"I'm sixty-five years-old, Papaw. How come I'm standing here with you like I was twenty and you are still alive."

"This is a dream, Harley; a dream of how it used to be."

"So, you aren't real, then?"

"Just passing through."

"That trough is dry as a bone and full of beer cans. The spring dried up twenty years ago. I moved back here after the divorce." Papaw splashed water on his face and ran his wet fingers through his hair.

"Is that right?" He smiled at me.

"I been thinking about fixing it, making the water run again."

"Why would you want to do that?"

"Well, I used to love that trough. Used to be full of milk and butter. I even kept a trout in here one summer. Killed hisself trying to catch fireflies one night."

"Ain't you got one of them frigadaires?" I nodded. "I treasure the past, I guess."

"Well, Harley, the past is just like this dream. You are molding it, shaping it; not looking at it true."

"What do you mean?"

"I ain't here, Harley. What's left of me is out in the Love's Chapel graveyard. And this spring water..." He dipped his fingers in the trough and flicked my face with water..."it ain't real, either." Then, I heard the music. Papaw heard it too, and smiled. We could see the dark shape beneath the old oak, and the moonlight touching the strings of the guitar.

"Is that..."

"I reckon."

"My father. Can I...?"

"No, Harley, you can't speak to him."

I tried anyway, but as I approached the dim shape, it turned to night fog and drifted away.

"Why can't I see his face?"

"Because you have no memory of it." Papaw touched my face the way he did long ago. "How can you see what you can't remember? You were only two when he was killed."

"Granny told me how he used to sit there under that tree playing on summer nights..."

"That is real as he is gonna be for you, I reckon."

"I wonder what he would think of me?" When I turned back to the dark porch, Papaw was gone, and there was nothing but the churn of cold spring water. Then that, too, was gone, dissolved into fog and the parched trough was filled with winking beer cans.

What am I doing standing out here?

Over the years, I have written stories that didn't fit in the world where Harley Teester lives. A few of them are "what if" stories. What if Harley's father had not died when he was two and his mother had not vanished? What if his grandmother had been an enthralling storyteller, but what if she dipped snuff, drank apple brandy and had a streak of the perverse? What if her personality changed with the seasons? What if Harley had had a little sister? This is how the "Granny Stories" came into being.

All of Granny's stories have roots in folklore and some of you may recognize traces of the Wandering Jew, Irish tales of the supernatural with fragments of Chaucer, the Decameron, and the Ozark stories of Vance Randolph. Combining these elements was fun. So, I recast some ancient stories in an Appalachian setting and created a "dark Granny," one who would qualify as a Jungian "other".

So, here is a Granny who is a little wicked. Despite the fact that she tipples in the winter, occasionally becomes downright ornery, dislikes churches, has a tendency to "stretch the blanket" (distort the fact a bit), and loves to provoke her daughter-in-law, she can always tell a good story. In fact, with a little brandy and a stormy night, she can speak like an Irish bard. I think she loves her grandson, especially when he listens with his mouth slightly ajar.

If you have the occasion, please read these stories aloud.

G.C.

TOASTED SPIDERS

To tell you the truth, I don't like Granny in the fall. I guess that's a terrible thing to say about a feeble old creature, but when I see her sitting in the chimney-corner on an October night, stirring the ashes with that black walnut stick of hers, she just plain gives me the willies. Oh, it's easy to forget what she's like during the day when she sleeps in her chair on the porch, just a sweet white-haired lady, chuckling and nodding to herself. But on cold, windy nights! When the temperature falls, Granny changes.

Like when the wind is hooting in the eaves and the trees are thrashing their arms about, something happens to Granny. There she sits in the glow of that fireplace, her old eyes glimmering like sparks. Wide awake! Just when the rest of us are thinking about crawling into bed and pulling pillows over our heads to shut out the sound of the wind, Granny gets sharp and alert. Sleeps all day and talks all night. She looks at us kids and snickers. She don't laugh; she snickers. She's thinking of ways to give us bad dreams. I'm twelve now, but she can still make me sit up half the night in my bed with my back to the wall, listening to the house creak. Granny's a wicked old woman, but she can tell a good story.

Last night, she said, "It were a night like this when they hanged Solomon Hardy."

Even when we know that we will regret it, we always rise to the bait. "Who was Solomon Hardy?" says my sister, Frankie Jean. She is five and sleeps with Momma when she has nightmares.

Granny gets a dip of snuff. Using her little white birch brush, she scrubs the snuff on her gums, snorts a bit of it up her nose, blinks her eyes and starts.

"Oh, he were a demon, that Solomon." She shakes her head and snickers. "Killed six women in the hollers and coves of Hintuga.

What he done to them is too terrible to tell. According to what Solomon said when they caught him, every one of them begged to die before he was through. Why, I heard that he..."

Momma cleared her throat. "Let's not frighten the children, Mother Teester," she said. Granny turned and looked at Momma where she sat by the lamp, mending our ragged clothes. The needle hung suspended in the yellow light as the two women measured each other.

Daddy was sharpening an old mowing blade, and pretending not to hear. Granny irritated the coals with her stick and hummed something gay and strange.

She had us hooked, though. I finally said, "What happened at the hanging?"

Granny noticed a spider that had been foolish enough to build a web in the chimney corner. She wound the spider, web and all, around the tip of her stick and then shoved it into the coals. We watched the spider shrivel, smoke and burst into a blue flame. Granny peered hopefully at the oak planked ceiling, looking for another victim. Disappointed, she settled back into her chair.

"What happened?" I asked again.

"Not much," said Granny. "Just the usual. Another botched job. Wasn't a proper hanging anyway," she said with regret. "Just put him on the back of a borrowed mule, give it a kick in the ribs, and whoops! Old Solomon goes sliding off the mule's rump!" Granny wheezed with glee and slapped her skinny shanks.

"Did you see it, Granny?" I said.

"Indeed I did, Harley!" Granny's eyes twinkled merrily. "Wore my new frock, I did. I was a sweet thing of sixteen, just beginning to spark your granddaddy. We climbed to the top of a rail fence to see better." Granny looked at us and grinned. "Now what was I talking about? Solomon! Yes, well he did a little dance, then, he did!" Granny giggled and jiggled her feet. "Looked like he was trying to climb the air. Couldn't get a foothold, though. Just hung there and choked to death, face turned black. Took a long time. Fourteen minutes, I believe."

Momma cleared her throat again. "Martha, leave it be," said Daddy. "It won't do the kids any harm to hear what happens to men like Hardy. Besides," he added, "it was a long time ago." Momma sighed.

"At any rate," said Granny, speaking a bit louder now that Papa had give her leave, "It was what happened later that was interesting." She gave me and Frankie Jean one of them bright little looks of hers. She winked and waited.

"What happened after the hanging?" said Frankie Jean, sounding like she wasn't sure she wanted to know.

"Well, actually, it was five nights after the hanging," said Granny. "Cold October night it was. One of the long nights...the nights when this world and that other world sorta get mixed up. They had left Solomon hanging from a dead locust tree in front of the old shack they called the Dark Corners courthouse then. I believe they said they'd let him hang for a week as an example...in case there was other men that was thinking about butchering and torturing women. The buzzards started gathering in the locust on the third day. The ugly varmints left at night, but each morning brought a few more. Your granddaddy come home each night talking about them.

'Solomon's got a tree full of angels,' he said. "They are eager to carry him away.' Oh, your granddaddy had a wicked wit, he did." Granny wheezed and chuckled. "And he was a wondrous mimic. Many's the night he come from the tavern and kept me laughing 'til daylight, imitating the regulars. Sounded like half a dozen people talking.

"Well, old Jacob Rash, that lapsed Catholic that used to work on the railroad, he come through Dark Corners the fifth night and seen old Solomon swinging like a pendulum in the moonlight. The wind was moaning like all the damned souls of the world was keening and sighing. Jacob didn't drag his feet although he did get a good look at old Solomon 'keeping sheep by moonlight.' That's what they say about a hanged man in the old country. 'He's keeping sheep by moonlight,' they say. *Heeee.*

"Jacob, he went on out the old post road that runs from Dark Corners to his farm in Tick Town. He decided to stop at Verlin Haskett's old tavern that used to be out there by the corn-mill.

"There was a good crowd of drunks and loafers in Verlin's place, including your granddaddy, and when Rash come in, he told them about seeing Solomon tick-tocking in the cold wind." Granny got up from her chair and did a fair imitation of Solomon, mouth agape with his eyes rolled back in his head. Frankie Jean's eyes got big and her mouth turned into an O. Granny snickered and winked at her.

"'Did it make ye narvous, Jake,' said Hanky Dobbs, the barkeep, 'Seeing Solomon in the moonlight?' Your granddaddy had Hanky down pat with that old country brogue. Hee, 'narvous' he says. Jake allowed as how it did. Said the buzzards had been at Solomon, and he had lost both ears and most of his nose. Jack allowed as how it give him a turn, and that he was surprised to see that nobody had took Solomon's shoes. Then, he downed his greasy glass of whiskey and blinked. A lively discussion started. When your granddaddy repeated it for me, it was just like I was standing next to Jacob listening to them talk.

'Don't surprise me none,' said Hanky Dobbs. 'Most folks 'round here wouldn't touch a hanged man.'

'Especially this close to the long nights,' said Skank Elmore.

'What long nights?' said Rash.

'The longest nights of the year,' said Skank. 'When the dead come visiting.'

'Don't put no truck in superstition,' said Rash.

'And you a Catholic! But you didn't bide your time with Solomon,' sneered Skank. 'And you look a bit pale around the gills when you come through the door.'

"So I did,' admitted Rash, 'but it was more from the smell of the man than the fear of spooks.'

"Stuff like that don't bother me none,' said Larkin James. 'I was at Antietam.'

"Sure you was,' said Lindsay Sizemore, who got a little surly after three or four drinks. 'God knows, we've all heard about it.'

"Well, I was. Walked in blood up to my ankles.'

"I'll buy you a drink if you'll hush,' said Sizemore.

"Fair enough,' said Larkin, handing his glass to Hanky. Everybody laughed.

Granny was up and moving now, acting out the parts. It was strange listening to her shift from Hanky's Irish whine to Shank's angry wheeze. Maybe Papaw was a good mimic, but Granny wasn't bad herself.

"Now, according to your grandfather, that's when Verlin Haskett spoke up. He was standing at the end of the bar clacking these five dollar gold pieces together. Verlin was bad to show off when he was flush, and he was just back from Charleston where he had sold a dozen horses and fifty hogs.

"Tell me, Larkin,' said Verlin, winking at the others, 'would ye go down to Dark Corners and fetch me Solomon's shoes?' Rush said it got real quiet then except for the thumping of the shutters in the wind. Verlin stacked a dozen coins on the bar and slid them next to Larkin's glass.

"I know you would do it for nothing, being a war hero and all, but it seems only fair to give you a little incentive.' Everybody was watching Larkin. He downed his drink and looked around. I guess he thought that the moment would pass. People would laugh, start talking again, and eventually, he would buy Verlin a drink, and the night would wear away like it always did. That's not what happened, though. Everybody was waiting for Larkin to say something.

"Hell, Verlin,' he said, 'For that kind of money I'll bring you Solomon.' Verlin said that just the shoes will be fine and picked up the stack of coins and handed them to the barkeep. Told Larkin that if he left now he could be back in thirty minutes, smiling all the while at the loafers."

Granny laughed and shook her head.

"That's how Larkin James came to find hisself out in the road, his coat cracking and popping in the wind. Your granddaddy always said that the poor devil had trapped hisself. All them years of bragging about killing Yankees and wading in blood had caught up with him. Did he do it for the money?" Granny laughed. "Your granddaddy said not likely. Oh, he could have used it for sure, for Larkin James was dirt poor, living in that shack out on the Tick Town road, eating sow belly and sawmill gravy. But, the truth is, when he looked at the faces of them drunks and loafers, he saw the meanness in their eyes. He knew that if he didn't go back down the Dark Corners road to where old Solomon twisted in the wind, he would live with that look the rest of his life."

Granny cackled. "The poor fool," she said. "Standing in Haskett's tavern in a ragged coat that he had pinned so the holes and the missing buttons didn't show; poor Larkin with a borrowed dollar in his pocket and no food in the house — poor Larkin was proud! All them eyes judging and weighing his pitiful worth. So, what did he do? He pitched his only dollar on the bar, walked to the door, turned and gave a little bow to the room. 'Back directly, fellows,' he said.

"Now, little sprouts," said Granny, "From here on, we just have Larkin's word for what happened. He come back all right, but

112

it was four hours before he showed up. Came stumbling through the door with Solomon Hardy's shoes in one hand and a broken shovel in the other, his hair all mare's tails, a face as pale as clabbered milk."

Granny pitched a piece of split oak in the fire, took another dip of snuff and listened to the wind. "Sometimes I think I can hear voices out there," she said. "*OOOOOooooooooo.*" Frankie Jean got up and moved closer to Momma. Granny snickered and stirred the coals with her stick. Then, she peered at the pieces of oak stacked by the chimney, and quick as a wink, she poked her stick between the logs and brought out another spider - a mean looking bugger with red dots on his back. Granny bundled him up in his own web and held him over the coals where he popped and blazed like a pine-knot. Granny sighed, took a bit of snuff, and winked at me.

"Years later, Larkin admitted to your granddaddy that he was sorely tempted to go home that night. Figured he would just quit Haskett's place. If he needed a drink and some sociable folk, he could go over to the Starved Dog Tavern in Widdy Branch. But then, word would probably spread and any place he went, there would be some wag that would ask him about Solomon's shoes. So, he went. Head down, the wind ripping his hair, he stumped and stumbled to Dark Corners.

"He could smell Solomon long before he saw him."

"Larkin said he sat for a while on the steps of the courthouse. Said he needed to work his courage up. When he finally crossed the road to Solomon, he raised his hand and stopped the dead man like you might stop a shutter that was banging in the wind. The feet hung about even with Larkin's belt, and when he took one of the brogues in his hand, he saw that the leather strings were untied. All he had to do was pull the shoes off. He grabbed both feet, ready to twist the shoes off and back away. But, then they...moved."

Granny slowly wrapped her skinny arms around her own waist to show how Solomon's legs moved.

"Larkin said it was like he sprung a trap when he touched the dead man's shoes... like old Solomon was hanging there waiting, and then, "Whoops!" Granny snickered when me and Frankie Jean jumped. "He said it was like Solomon woke up! And then, Larkin, he found hisself hoisted, his own feet losing touch with the earth.

"There they hung, the dead man and the living, Larkin kicking and screaming, his feet paddling the air just like old Solomon when he went off the mule's back. Finally, the locust limb cracked and they

113

came crashing down... Poor Larkin! Laying with the corpse of Solomon Hardy on his back, he felt them dead legs tightening about his waist and the arms wrapping about his neck. Solomon's head settled on Larkin's shoulder, the dead lips touching his ear, and he said....."

Granny winked at us.

"What do you think the dead man said, chaps?"

Neither of us spoke.

"*Waa-terr*," whispered Granny. "That's what he said, and his legs tightened even more, causing poor Larkin to holler."

"*Waa-terr*," Granny croaked again.

Frankie Jean covered her ears, but Granny went right on.

"I guess panic took Larkin then. I can see him thrashing and struggling, trying to rid hisself of his awful burden. Struggling to his feet, he crashed into the locust. Solomon seemed to have become a part of him, and each effort merely caused them legs to tighten. Solomon's arm swung, falling across Larkin's shoulder stiff as a stick, a black finger pointing."

Granny pointed her bony finger at me and Frankie Jean.

"*There*," she rasped in the voice of the dead man.

"He was pointing across the road. There was a spring near the courthouse. Well, poor old Larkin tottered across the moonlit road toward the spring; fell to his knees, his head striking the thin skin of ice on the water; and then he collapsed into it. Before he could drag himself upright again, he heard Solomon drink, an awful, sucking sound. With each swallow, Larkin said he felt the dead flesh tremble.

"Then, the dead man laughed. His teeth clicked and the lifeless lungs took air. I've never forgot what Larkin told your granddaddy. He said that Solomon's body seemed reluctant to live again, but live it did. When the surface of the spring grew still, Larkin could see the moon reflected in it. The moon and Solomon's face. It was still the slack face of a dead man – a face a bit worse for wear. Shrouds of flesh hung from the ruined cheeks, bone showing through where the buzzards had fed, but there was a glint of life in the eyes."

Granny stood with her back to the fire, her back humped as though she carried Solomon Hardy who spoke through her.

'Better,' said Solomon in a hoarse whisper. 'Now, I can speak better.'

'You can't be alive,' said Larkin.

114

'Fool!' said Solomon, 'You touched my flesh on one of the Long Nights. Now, you are mine until daybreak. You will be my horse tonight.'

'What do you want of me?' said Larkin.

"Solomon drove his heels into Larkin's ribs. 'Gittup,' he said."

"And so they moved down the moonlit road, between the waving limbs of trees, the dead man and the living. When Larkin's pace slowed, the heels drummed on his ribs. When he stopped at a fork in the road, a dead finger pointed the way. Where were they going? Larkin didn't know. Between the frantic beating of his heart and the failing of his legs, the poor man could think of nothing but the moment. But when he saw the crumbling wall, the broken fence, and the field of barren stone, Larkin knew where he was.

"Black Rock Kirk,' he said.

"Right you are, Dobbin,' whispered Solomon Hardy.

"Whatever makes sacred ground, Black Rock had either lost it or never had it. Nobody remembers a church, and nobody claims kin in the graveyard - if it is a graveyard. The big rock that gave the place its name is covered with strange marks. There ain't nothing you can read - just snaky loops and lines. Some folks think that whatever sleeps in that rocky, barren soil has little in common with Christian folks. The ruined wall could have been anything - maybe it was an Indian burial ground, maybe something even older.

"Standing in the pale light of a moon that hung above Larkin and his rider like a blind eye, the living man stared about him. Nothing else lived there. No trees, no grass, no night birds. Only the wind and barren stone. One of Solomon's hands closed on Larkin's throat, the other pointed at the earth.

"There!' said Solomon. A shovel with a broken shaft lay half-buried among the rocks. Larkin fell to his knees. 'Dig!'

"Can you picture it, Harley?" said Granny. "Can you see the man digging a grave with a dead man on his back?" Granny grinned and spit into the fire. "Hard work, that! Like digging in water. Each time he lifted a shovel full of stones, the hole filled rocks and sand. But, little by little, Larkin made a hole. Finally, when he was standing shoulder-deep in that stony pit, he felt Solomon's grip loosen and the dead man slid into the pit. Solomon's blackened fingers still grasped Larkin's ankles.

"Take the shoes,' said the dead man.

115

"As Larkin raised the brogues in the dim light and set them on the edge of the grave, he felt the fingers loosen and fall away.

"Then, he saw them. It was as though a great shadow crept down the hill, crept into the grave with Solomon Hardy. Spiders. As Larkin watched, they covered Solomon's face, wrapped his dead flesh like a winding sheet.

"He filled the grave, of course, knowing that was part of his work. The stones seemed to rush to hide Solomon. Then, with the shovel in one hand and the shoes in the other, Larkin retraced his steps.

"Oh, would that I had been there, chaps! I'd have given a pretty penny to see Larkin come through the door of Haskett's tavern. Better yet, to have seen the faces of Hanky Dobbs, Skank Elmore, Lindsay Sizemore, Verlin Haskett and your granddaddy! Jacob Rash had gone home, of course, but the rest had decided to drink pop-skull until either they fell down or daylight came. Oh, many's the witty insult that had been said about Larkin James! As the hours reeled by, they jeered and sang, knowing that poor Larkin had gone skulking home. But, here he was, staggering through the door with a broken shovel in one hand and Solomon Hardy's shoes in the other.

"I asked your granddaddy, 'Rush,' I said, 'How do you know that Larkin didn't go home and get a pair of his own shoes?'

'Ah, no, now Nance,' he said, 'If you had seen the man with his hair trying to jump off his head and his eyes bugged out like a pole-axed steer, you would not doubt his word. Skank Elmore took one look at him and bought him a drink. Long before he finished his tale, Verlin Haskett told Hanky Dobbs to give Larkin his money.' Granny stared into the fire and shook her head like the whole thing still amazed her.

"What happened to the shoes?" I said.

My question caused Granny to go off into some kind of snickering fit. "Oh, Harley, you're a caution," she said. "That is the last thing I expected you to say." She loaded her lower lip with snuff.

"They are still over at Hasketts," she said. "Verlin tied the strings together and hung them on a nail. Sometimes folks come in and ask to touch them. Heeee! Ain't that something! Supposed to bring them good luck, I guess."

"What happened to Larkin James?" I said.

"Oh, now, your Pap could tell you that as well as me. Quite a prosperous man. Took Verlin's money and bought two steers.

Turned that farm around, he did! Bought more land and prospered. He is sort of a solitary fellow, though. Not much for socializing. Never showed up at Haskett's place again."

I looked at Daddy, and he nodded. "He never mentioned Antietam again either," he said. "Still lives out on the Tick Town road, but he is a quiet man. Withdrawn, I guess you could say."

It was time to go to bed. Frankie Jean was asleep with her head in Momma's lap. Momma got up and carried her to the bedroom. Papa was checking to see if the doors were latched. Granny was still sitting by the fire.

"Is that why you hate spiders?" I said. "Because of Solomon Hardy?"

"You mean why do I fry them in the fire? Well, Harley, there's an old superstition about spiders. They are supposed to be the souls of poor devils that committed unforgivable sins. They are doomed to forever creep about in darkness, eating flies and spinning webs. I've always been partial to that belief. My Granny told me that when you toasted a spider, you hastened that doomed sinner on his way. 'Course it never ends. The sinner just comes back as another spider." Granny punched the back log and sent a shower of sparks up the chimney.

"Just think, Harley," she said brightly, "I may have toasted Solomon Hardy tonight."

Granny was still laughing when I climbed the ladder to my bed in the loft. Laying under the feather tick, I watched firelight flicker on the ceiling. I wasn't very sleepy, to tell the truth.

OLD HOSS

Granny was bored. Sitting in her black oak rocker, she peered through the window at the rain mixed with sleet that lashed the house in fits and starts. Holding Momma's lace curtain aside, she glared at the cold, wet world. Sleet tapped on the tin roof and ticked on the windowpanes.

Momma was home from Knoxville. After Daddy went to Oregon to work in a lumber camp, she left me and Frankie Jean with Granny and enrolled in a business school. She was gone most of the time, only coming home on school "breaks." When she was home, she always did all the cooking, telling Granny to "sit by the fire and rest." Granny hated it. Now, Papaw was gone, too, and Momma fretted about leaving us with Granny.

Last night, she said, "Maybe I ought to quit the school and come home."

"No, no," said Granny. "You just lack a year. Then, you can get a job at the courthouse or some lawyer's office. I can take care of these younguns."

"Well, it's not just that," said Momma. "I know you don't mean any harm, Momma Teester, but you're filling Harley's head with all of this foolishness. Old stories and superstitions." Momma had took to talking that way after she went to Knoxville. Granny would just smile and wink at me. But, she hated sitting still.

"Bah!" said Granny. "I hate February. Always did. Nothing to recommend it. Miserable coming and going, and dead on both ends."

Granny dropped the curtain and looked at me. "It'd be a good month for hell! What do you think, Harley? Instead of fire and brimstone, eternal February! That ought to scare the bejesus out of the Baptists. *Heeeeeee.*" Granny was always pondering ways to improve hell.

I allowed as how it had been bad last year, too. "February is always bad, little chap. It's a mean, miserable month." Granny stared fretfully around the room. Wet wood smoldered in the fireplace and Frankie Jean sat at the table coloring horses, cows and pigs in her "Old MacDonald Coloring Book." The pigs was green, the horses, blue and the trees, pink. In the kitchen, Momma was singing "I'll Meet You In the Morning" as she cooked supper. Granny grabbed the poker and whacked the logs in the fireplace until a puny flame caught.

"February makes me think of the time me and your granddaddy moved to the coal mines in West Virginia. Lived in this one-eyed, blinking little settlement called Rough Butt. Terrible place." Granny looked at Frankie Jean who was doing purple ducks, now. I got my Barlow knife and started working on a peach seed ring.

"That's where we met the man that couldn't die."

Me and Frankie Jean looked at Granny who was pretending like she was already thinking about something else. She hummed a bit, then glanced at me and winked.

"What do you mean, he couldn't die?" I said.

"Just that, Harley."

"Well, that would be a good thing, wouldn't it?"

"Not when you yearn to die. Not when the beating of your heart is a misery and each breath, a torment."

I tried to imagine wanting to die, but I couldn't. I closed my knife and laid it on the table, and Frankie Jean put her crayon down.

"All right, now, you're joshing me, ain't you?" I said.

Granny just looked at me, her eyes as bright as the ones on Buddy Dalton's pet crow.

"Is Granny going to tell a story?" said Frankie Jean. It sounded like she wasn't sure that she was pleased since Granny had scared her pretty bad last Halloween.

"Oh, no, honey. You don't have to listen to poor old Granny tell one of her old tales. Go on with what you was doing. You, too, Harley." She stirred the coals in the grate and fed some pine chips to the fire.

"How old was he?" I asked. Granny smirked.

"Older than Methuselah," she said.

"Who is that?" said Frankie Jean, coming to sit on the stool by Granny's chair.

"A man that lived for more than nine hundred years," I said.

"That's right, Harley," said Granny. "You're a scholar. Been studying your Bible, have you?" She grinned at me.

"Just Sunday school," I said, remembering that Granny never went to church. "God blessed him with long life."

Granny cackled. "Now, there you have it, chaps," she said. "Long life is a blessing! Old Ahasuerus, though, he didn't see it that way."

"That's his name?" I said.

Granny looked at me and Frankie Jean like she was trying to decide if we was worth the trouble of a tale.

Then, she said, "Go tell your Momma to let me have a dram of that apple brandy in the jug behind the churn." In the kitchen, Momma quit singing. "Tell her I got a bit of a sore throat and it hurts me to talk." I did as I was told.

Momma stepped to the kitchen door and said, "Frankie Jean, bring your coloring book and come in the kitchen." My little sister dragged her feet and whined. Momma poured the brandy in a jelly glass and handed it to me. I could tell that she was less than pleased.

"It was the winter of '29 when your granddaddy and me moved to Rough Butt," said Granny, setting the jelly glass on the window sill. "After the mills closed in Gastonia, things got desperate. Rush heard that there was somebody hiring in the coal mines in West Virginia. Didn't know nothing about that kind of work, but we went. Drove for two days through them fog-filled hollers, past tipples and railroad tracks between grim little shacks with big-eyed younguns standing on the porch." Granny sipped the brandy and laughed.

"O, Harley, I was home-sick! I told Rush that we ought to go home, but he wouldn't hear of it. On we went 'til the car broke down in Rough Butt. We stayed three months in a company shack while your granddaddy worked the mines. Made not quite enough to buy flour and spuds at the company store. Took the check plus a little credit. Stayed in debt, we did.

"Jacob Rash, that lapsed Catholic, he explained purgatory to me once. About how you had to stay there after you died - stayed 'til your earthly sins was forgiven. Well, that was Rough Butt. We was neither dead or alive, but just waiting to be one or the other. Everybody talked about leaving, but nobody did. No one seemed to make friends or fix up them sorry shacks because everybody thought that Rough Butt was temporary, so they waited. I remember there was a dead dog in that muddy road in front of the company store, and nobody buried it. It just laid there and slowly rotted. Its bones was still there when we finally loaded the car and drove away three months later. Heeee!" Granny laughed without meaning it. "That sums the place up, I guess, that dead dog."

"I'd set by the window and watch for Rush, like I'm setting by this window now. It was a strange thing to see the men walk up the holler. That mournful whistle would blow, *OOOOOOooooooooo*, and then you would see them coming out of the fog, slack-jawed and covered with coal dust. Most wore them goggles around their necks. The skin around their eyes where the goggles had been, it was white. Looked like they had white masks on. Nobody laughed or talked; they just walked on up the holler.

"It's like working on the chain gang," said Rush, who knew something about chain gangs, "except most of them act like they are lifers. Oh, they talk about leaving, but it's just talk. Most likely, they'll stay here 'til they're carried out of the hole on a shingle."

"When Rush tried to tell a joke or josh a bit, which he was want to do, them men just stood about and looked at him like lost sheep. They wasn't unfriendly - just not given to humor."

Granny took a swig of brandy and swished it about in her mouth. She gulped, shivered and blinked. "*Wooooeee*," she said, "Them apple parings do brighten an old woman's outlook. Where was I? Oh, yes! Them people in Rough Butt.

"I guess we'd been there a month when he came. I was sitting in the window watching for your granddaddy when I seen the ragged man trudging up the holler. There wasn't much wind and the snow was drifting down in big slow flakes, but the ragged man seemed to be walking in a whirlwind. Bits of paper, leaves and grit spun about him, and his pitiful clothes flapped and fluttered like rags on a fence in a high gale. He was carrying a feed-sack on his shoulder, and I just knew that what few earthly possessions that man owned was in that sack."

Granny stopped talking and peered out the window, watching the dying sunlight in the leafless trees. For a moment, she seemed to have lost the thread of her story. Through the window, we could see a flock of birds crowding the barren branches of the big oak in the front yard.

121

"Ah, Harley," she said it a tired voice, "I'm an old woman, and I have seen peculiar things. Seen it snow in the middle of summer, and I once seen a night sky turn into red and pink flames. I remember when your granddaddy brought home a two-headed snake, and once in a church in Arkansas I heard a hundred people speak to each other in an unknown tongue while blue fire flickered in their hair. But Harley, I ain't never seen nothing like Ahasuerus.

"He stopped in front of our shack and stared at the number above the door. Ah, God, it chilled me to see that man, kicked and slapped by the wind, staring at me through the window. He trudged up the steps and knocked. When I opened the door, he said that the company had hired him and that he was to stay with us. Seems we had a 'family house' and since there was just the two of us, they felt we could take a 'boarder' in the back room. There wasn't much I could say.

"I had a terrible time with his name.

"'Ahasuerus,' he said. Said it several times. Then, he said the company men had nick-named him 'Old Hoss,' which sounded a bit like the first of his name. Some wag in the company office said it seemed to fit him, too, since Ahasuerus had the look of an old workhorse, sway-backed, spavined and weary.

"He asked if he could put that tow-sack down, and I offered him a chair. Any resentment I had about him being a 'boarder' sorta dried up when I looked at him. Don't think I ever seen a man so tired."

"Looks like you come a long way," I said. He seemed to find that funny. He smiled and said, 'So I have, so I have.'"

Granny drained her glass and sent me off to the kitchen for a refill. Momma's mouth got all pinched, and she come to the kitchen door and stared at Granny. "I'd just as soon you didn't get in your cups before supper," said Momma.

"Leave it be, Martha," said Granny. "It's not as though I make a practice of it. Ain't been in the brandy since Thanksgiving. There's not many vices left for an old widow-lady; just telling lies, dipping snuff and tippling in February." Momma poured the brandy and I took it back to Granny.

Frankie Jean appeared in the doorway and watched Granny take a sip. "Frankie Jean, you can help Momma make biscuits," said Momma.

"Granny's telling a story," said Frankie Jean.

"I know she is, honey," said Momma, "but you don't need to hear it."

"Harley's listening to it," whined Frankie Jean.

"Harley's a boy," said Momma. I was glad to know it counted for something. Granny winked at me and continued.

"When Rush got home, he took it better than I expected."

'You'll have to help with chores," he said. 'Cooking, firewood and that.'

"All right.'

"We could do with a change, anyway. Where you from?'

"Hard to say. No where and everywhere, I guess.'

"The way you talk, you sound *fureign*, maybe across the water. Maybe Ireland or Scotland.'

"Been there,' said Old Hoss. 'Been there.'

"When supper-time come, our new boarder made a stew out of just about nothing. A little bit of pork, fatback, beans and onions.

"Where did you learn to make that?' I asked.

"Germany, during the war,' he said.

"He didn't say which war. In fact, later I realized that he didn't exactly answer questions. He would say something, but it wasn't exactly an answer. He washed the dishes and tidied up. When he finally set by the fire, he reached in that old sack and brought out this strange little flute, asking if we minded if he played it. 'Course we didn't. Hadn't heard nothing but the company whistle since we came to Rough Butt. The music was beautiful and sad. Like the sun rising in a land without people. After a half-dozen mournful ditties, Rush finally asked him if he knew some "jigs" and happy songs.

"No, I don't know any,' he said. He seemed sorry that he couldn't please Rush, and said, 'I guess it just ain't my nature.' When we went to bed, I laid in the dark staring at the cold winter moon and cried, and didn't know why."

"He was gone to work the next morning when we got up. He'd already had his coffee and had washed the cup.

"Rush said he was a good worker and the straw boss was pleased. 'Wish I had a hundred like him,' he said. Old Hoss worked slow and steady and never spoke 'til he was spoken to. Rush said he fit right in."

"A week later, when a rotten timber broke and buried him under half a ton of shale and coal, Rush said they took their time digging him out. They figured he had to be dead, you see. Would have killed any normal human being. But, when they found his legs and dragged him out, Old Hoss opened his eyes and stared at them. After they had stood him up and beat the coal dust out of his hair and clothes, Rush told him that he was supposed to be dead. "You was buried for two hours,' he said. 'That should have killed you.'

"No such luck,' said Old Hoss. He scrabbled around in the dirt until he found his pick, and then he went back to work. The other miners got a little uneasy then. They are a superstitious lot, you know. Won't light three cigarettes on the same match or allow women to come in the mine.

"It didn't help none when a new man named Radley Mathis arrived in Rough Butt a few days later and went to work on the second shift. Rush happened to be standing by him during a shift change and seen what happened. Rush said Radley dropped his Prince Albert can and stared at Old Hoss as he came trudging up out of the hole. He punched Old Hoss on the shoulder, more like you would touch something to see if it was real than to get a man's attention.

"I thought you was dead!' he said.

"Where you from?' said Old Hoss.

"Bloody Rock Mine in Harlan,' said Radley. 'Thought you was killed with six others over there.'

"In a coal-dust explosion,' said Old Hoss, as though he had just remembered it. 'Three years ago.'

"But nobody survived,' said Mathis.

"Just me,' said Old Hoss, 'Just me.' He nodded at Radley and then he trudged on up the street towards the company store.

"Now, if that don't beat all,' said Radley. He turned and looked at Rush, and then he sorta whispered, 'Them guys was cinders, Teester! I seen 'em. Not enough left to tell who was who.'

"Must have been somebody else,' said Rush.

"Hell, you heard 'im. He was there.'

"Rush come on home then. Left Radley standing there gawking up the street. He come in and set his lunch box on the table and said, 'Nance, there's something a bit strange about Old Hoss.' Well, that was no surprise. Then, he went on.

"He told me what Radley said, and we talked about the cave-in that should have killed Old Hoss. Then, there was that nasty little whirlwind that we sometimes seen around Old Hoss's head as he went to and from the mine, and the darkness in his face like he carried his own shade.

"Do you think he is dangerous?" asked Rush.

"Not to us,' I said. I don't know why, but I knew that was true.

"That night, I decided to talk to him. There he was sitting by the fire, stirring the ashes and humming some strange little ditty while I talked about the cave-in and the fire in Kentucky. When I got through, he just looked at me and smiled. 'Ah, well,' he said regretfully, 'time to be moving on.'

"Some of the men are afraid of you,' said Rush. 'I heard one man quoting scripture. Said you are a omen.' Old Hoss smiled.

"True enough,' he said, 'but not the way they think.'

"I asked him who he was.

"Had lots of names,' he said. 'Lots of names.' Then, he covered his face with his hands and set for a while. I knew better than to speak and I motioned to your granddaddy to hold his peace. Finally, Old Hoss gave a long shuddering sigh and said, 'I'll be gone by daylight.' Then, he said a strange thing. 'Do you like stories?' he said. 'Old stories?'

"Well, I dearly love a good yarn, as you well know, Harley. Love to tell them; love to hear them, so I told Old Hoss as much. He said that we had been kind to him, so he wanted to tell us a story. 'Something you can ponder and think on in the years ahead.' I believe he said 'a little something to ease our journey.' Then, he turned his face to the fire, and it was as though he was reading the words he spoke in the dying embers.

On the day that Christ died, the streets were filled with merchants and peddlers, children and dogs. When we read about that day now, we perceive Christ's death as the central event. All else becomes unimportant and petty. But that was not the way it was. On that day, when merchants bartered and the people of that town set forth on business, the fate of a minor criminal was of little interest. The people had grown accustomed to seeing the bloody bodies of thieves and murderers crawling toward Golgotha.

Consider this. Here is a man newly arrived in town. Let us call him Tobias. He is a cobbler and he has come to barter and trade for leather and lambs, spices and cloth. As he moves from booth to booth on the crowded street, he sees the jeering mob and asks what is happening.

'Three petty criminals are being executed,' some said.

Tobias has finished his business. He has gifts for his wife and children, and he is pleased. He joins the crowd and sees one of the doomed men falter beneath the lash of the soldiers; the weight of the cross.

'What did he do?' asks Tobias.

'He is an inciter,' says someone. Then, the criminal falls. As he lies panting on the bloodstained street, Tobias prods him with his foot.

'Get on with you,' he says.

"Old Hoss stopped talking. His mouth moved a bit, as though he were struggling to speak. Then, he gave a sigh like none other I have heard in this life. Rush moved as though he meant to touch Old Hoss' shoulder, but then, he went on.

It is then that the fallen man turns his agonized face to Tobias and says, 'I shall go, but you shall stay.' Rising beneath the stinging lash, he looks at Tobias and says, "Until I return.'

As he watches the man stagger on towards Golgotha, a terrible dread falls on Tobias. Even the sun seems to have darkened, and when Tobias turns his steps towards home, the world about him is a dark and empty place. Trees, flowers, all the natural world seems to be a painted veil stretched before a great darkness. At home, his wife rushes to greet him and his children gather about him. Tobias is sickened by their touch. He takes no joy in food and his sleep is troubled by the face of the man who cursed him.

When he awakens the following morning, it is to death in life. Unable to bear the presence of his family, he becomes a wanderer. As he travels from village to village, he walks in a whirling wind, a storm filled with nettles, sand, and stinging flies.

Nor can he cease from living. Ropes will not stop his breath nor poisons halt his heart. He is doomed to wander down the centuries through a thousand doomed cities. The rest of human kind quicken to love, wither and die, but Tobias abides. Worlds pass like fevered dreams; days become minutes. Tombs, monuments and temples rise and crumble away. Only Tobias is untouched, a doomed wanderer through the sad temporal gardens of the world.

126

"When Old Hoss stopped talking, we sat for a while, me and Rush, afraid to break the silence. Finally, I said, 'Now, that is some story.' Old Hoss smiled and watched the fire.

"Don't seem fair to me,' I said, 'the curse, I mean. You didn't..' I corrected myself, 'Tobias didn't know who Christ was. Just happened to be in the wrong place at the wrong time.'

Old Hoss nodded.

"I mean, the story says that life or fate is blind chance, accident. It says that life isn't fair.'

"It would seem so,' said Old Hoss.

"Is this feller dangerous to other folk?' asked Rush.

"Not the way you mean,' said Old Hoss. 'He don't cause bad things to happen, but he shows up where bad things happen. He is just there to witness, to experience humanity at its worst.'

"I guess Tobias has seen a lot,' I said.

"Hastings, Constantinople, Antietam, Verdun... If I named the places, the naming would take the whole of this night. It seems likely that the worse is yet to come.'

"We went to bed, then, Rush and me. Late into the night, we heard the flute. When we woke the next morning, Old Hoss was gone, but his flute was on the fireboard. There was strange marks on it, curious words in an unknown language. Rush learned to play it, too, but it would only play sad music. He finally broke it one night when he got drunk and fell down in a tavern. I still have the broken pieces someplace.

"Not long after that, we left Rough Butt. Loaded our pitiful rags in that T-model and coasted down that muddy street past the company store where we owed money, past that dead dog. Rush didn't crank the car or turn on the lights 'til we was a half-mile down the ridge. Then, we come on home."

Granny turned in her chair and winked at me. "He's out there somewheres, Harley. I think about him sometimes standing at high noon in that Japanese city where they dropped the big bomb, or walking into the showers at one of them Nazi camps. I guess he has been to Africa and Asia several times. Seems strange that he showed up in Rough Butt. But then, maybe that's why he had to go there. Because it was petty and mean."

We heard Momma go out the back door on her way to the barn and the chicken-house. 'Come on, Frankie Jean. Let's go look at the biddies,' she said. Granny peeped out the window and watched Momma and Frankie Jean 'til they was out of sight.

"February," she said and sighed. Then, she brightened a bit and turned to me.

"Harley," she said, "Go bring me the jug."

"The jug?"

"Yes, little chap, quick before Martha gets back." I didn't want to do it.

"Harley, I have managed to make myself unhappy. Now, that don't happen often. The only cure for it is to go to bed with the jug."

I did as I was told.

THE BELLED BUZZARD

From where me and Granny set on the porch swing, we could see the buzzards. Granny was humming and chuckling to herself as she watched them fly in a circle over the jack-pine thicket above Wort Jamison's house.

"Hit may be spring, Harley, and things may be coming alive all over this mountain, but something's dead over there."

There was a cool nip in the air and Granny had one of her quilts wrapped around her shoulders. She paddled the porch floor a bit, just enough to keep the swing moving.

"What is it the Bible says? Something 'bout death in the midst of life? Well, there it is." Granny quotes the Bible a lot for somebody that never goes to church.

I watched the buzzards wheel like coffee grounds around the drain in the kitchen sink. "What do you reckon it is?"

"Could be anything." Granny cupped her chin and squinched her eyes, like she was trying to see what it was. "A still-born calf. Maybe a mad dog. Seen one yesterday staggering down the trail behind Wort's barn. 'Course, it may be something that ain't dead yet."

"Maybe we ought to go and see," I said.

Granny waved her hand at me like she was swatting a fly. "No, little chap. Sometimes you leave things be. Let 'em run their course. Me, I'm just tickled that I'm going to see another spring." Granny inhaled like she was drinking the air, a big, long gulp. "Oh, my! That's nice." She looked at the blue sky and the budding trees.

"I smell new-turned earth," she said.

"Folks is plowing all over the cove," I said.

"That they are," said Granny. "Earth turning, clouds sailing, birds singing and buzzards circling." Granny grinned and slapped her leg. "Thank you, Jesus."

"You ain't been to church in five years," said Momma. She was standing in the doorway looking at us. "You ain't got no right to be talking to Jesus." Momma's mouth was all pinched up the way it gets when she disapproves of something. Most of the time, she disapproves of Granny.

She was right. Granny quit going to church when Papaw died. "I just went to please Rush," she said after the funeral. "From here on out, I got better things to do." The day she said that, we was all standing out behind the Balm of Gilead Baptist church watching them fill in Papaw's grave.

"What could be more important than your soul's salvation?" said Momma, asking one of them questions you ain't supposed to answer.

"Sleeping late on Sunday morning," said Granny, the gleam in her eyes showing how she loved to get Momma's goat. "Then eating red-eye gravy and hot biscuits while all of you Christians are humped up on them hard pews up at Balm of Gilead while Preacher Jeeter does his best to keep you awake."

She was good as her word, too. From then on, Momma herded me and Frankie Jean and Daddy down the trail to the truck every Sunday morning. Granny slept late. When we got home a little after noon, she would be setting out on the porch in the swing and dinner would be in the warming closet of the Home Comfort.

"It's embarrassing when the preacher asks about you," Momma would say.

"Tell him I'm senile and can't go out in public," said Granny. "Tell him I wet my drawers and speak in tongues."

"Sometimes I think you're wicked, Mother Teester. Maybe there is a demon in you."

"Could be. Maybe we could tole it out with some fried parsnips and okra." Then Granny winked at me and said, "Let's eat."

I had been listening to this argument for five years. Granny always had the last word, just as she did now. Momma huffed off to the kitchen and Granny pumped the swing a little higher as she hummed something strange. Her hand began to pat time on the swing arm.

"What are you humming, Granny?" asked Frankie Jean. We hadn't seen her setting on the steps with her doll. She's my little sister and she is sneaky. Always showing up in places she shouldn't be. Five years old and still dragging that doll with the back of its head gone, along with one arm and most of its stuffing.

"Oh, that!" said Granny, looking surprised. "That's a old fiddle tune that Rush used to play. Watching them buzzards put me in mind of it." Granny hummed a bit more. "It's supposed to sound like buzzard wings, you see." She emphasized the slow up and down motion of wings. "It's called 'The Belled Buzzard.'"

I knew what was coming then. One of us was supposed to ask what a belled buzzard was. I sometimes got the feeling that Granny could play me and Frankie Jean like a French harp. Just when I thought I couldn't wait any longer, Frankie Jean said it.

"What's a belled buzzard?"

"Well, it's a buzzard that has a bell around its neck."

"Like a cow bell?"

"That's right, honey, only smaller than most cow bells."

"Who put the bell on it?"

"Well, that's a long story, Frankie Jean. It's so long, it would just bore a sweet little girl like you." Granny went back to humming and patting time with her hand. I finally gave in.

"Somebody caught the buzzard and put the bell on it?"

"That's right, Harley." Granny hummed some more.

"Why?"

"Well, if you'll go get me a glass of buttermilk and a piece of that stack-cake in the pie safe, I'll tell you."

"Frankie Jean, you come in the house," called Momma. "You don't need to hear another one of Mother Teester's godless stories."

"Thet's right, sweetness," said Granny. "Go in the house and let your mother tell you a good story. Get her to tell you about the children who laughed at Elijah's bald head." Granny laughed.

Frankie Jean looked sideways at Granny and went in the house, her doll bouncing and thumping behind her. She is only five, but she is beginning to suspect that Granny don't always say exactly what she means. I went after the buttermilk and cake.

"When me and your granddaddy was young, we traveled a lot. Like gypsies, we acted. Worked in cotton mills in Georgia and textile mills in North Carolina; coal mines in West Virginia, and sharecropping in Arkansas. Never had nothing, of course. Never stayed any place long enough." Granny took a long, slow drink of buttermilk, popped the last of the stack-cake in her mouth and dusted her hands. "I can't say that I regret it, living that way. I seen things, and a few times I done things that was mighty different from life on the side of this mountain. Labor unions and strikes in Kingsport and Gastonia, snake-handling on Sand Mountain."

"The belled buzzard," I reminded her.

"I'm getting there, Harley. That was in Arkansas near the Arkansas River. Rush had decided to try his hand at farming and raising cattle, and we was looking for an abandoned farm he had heard about. Rush's truck had been giving trouble and we had to nurse it along. I remember we come around a bend in the road, and there was that slow-moving, muddy river. These big rock cliffs dropped straight down into the water and the tops of them cliffs, as far as you could see was covered with buzzards."

"Like them buzzards over there?" I asked pointing.

"No, Harley. Arkansas buzzards are bigger. Black with red wattles. They set on the edge of them cliffs watching the river. Now and again, they would drop, come sailing down to land on floating logs. Least, we thought they was logs or dead trees at first. Turned out to be dead hogs. We went on down the road apiece and stopped at a place called Grizzard's Store, and Rush asked the loafers on the porch about the hogs.

"Well, they told us there was a cholera epidemic. Back then, hogs lived wild in the woods and farmers marked their ears to tell them apart. Them hogs traveled in droves moving from the woods where they ate mast. Then, they would go to the river where they drank and wallered. When the cholera broke out, them hogs died by the thousands on the river bank and many of them ended up floating down the river gorge. That's where the buzzards waited.

"Rush asked directions to the abandoned farm and we found it without any trouble. The former owners had loaded up and left years ago. Somebody had carved the letters GTT in this oak tree in the front yard. That was the first time I ever seen that. Rush said it meant "Gone to Texas." Lots of folks was moving west and Arkansas was full of abandoned farms. Rush found out that the bank that held the mortgage was happy to let us move in. Rush signed a note that said he could keep two-thirds of what he raised, and the bank told him if all went well, he could buy the place on time.

"Each day, we would drive to the river. That flock of buzzards was growing and it was a little unsettling to watch them. Sometimes, they would blot out the sun. They would wheel over the river like a big, black funnel. It were awful quiet out there. So quiet, you could hear them big wings paddling the air. *Flap-flap. Flap-flap.*" Granny imitated a buzzard flying.

"For a while, I got caught up in that farm, planting, cooking and cleaning. I liked that place, and I sometimes wonder what my life would have been like if we had stayed. It were a good life, but your granddaddy, you know, there was always a place he hadn't seen, a way to make a living he hadn't tried. One morning, Rush called me to come outside. There was buzzards on the ridge-pole of the house. I tell you Harley, I've seen some homely creatures in my time, but a buzzard takes the cake. They was lined up like mourners at a funeral watching our chickens. Rush throwed a rock at them and they left but they took their time. I don't guess a buzzard can be in a hurry. Don't need to. Anything that it is interested in ain't going nowhere. They just sort of slowly flew away, and we knowed they'd be back.

"The men at Grizzard's store said the buzzards was showing up everywhere, and one bunch had took to roosting on the church in Sulphur Springs ten miles away. The men told Rush they was going to have a meeting at the store that evening to decide what to do. They said that the cholera was spreading all over the county because of them buzzards. Seems that if a buzzard eats the flesh of a hog that had died of cholera, the buzzard becomes a "carrier," and when he flies other places, he takes the disease with him.

"Why didn't they just shoot 'em?" I asked. When you are twelve years old, the world is still simple, and most problems are easily solved.

"Well, Harley, the people along that river was a superstitious lot. Buzzards are sorta scary. Black, gloomy varmints setting like undertakers in the treetops waiting for things to die. I'm told that they smell bad, but I couldn't say, having only seen one up close. I've heard folks say that they didn't believe in killing them because they did a valuable service, sorta like garbage collectors in town. That ain't the real reason, though. Sometimes, people make up sensible reasons when they are ashamed to tell you the real reason. Most folks won't admit it, but they think something bad will happen to them if they kill a buzzard.

133

"Rush and me went to the meeting at Grizzard's. There was a big crowd there, and to tell you the truth, I enjoyed myself. The other women went out of their way to be kind to me, and we ended up talking gardens, canning and quilting. Then, Mr. Grizzard got up and started talking. He introduced some man who had come all the way from Little Rock to talk about cholera and how it had spread. Like you, he wanted to kill the buzzards."

"You bet," I said.

"Well, people got real uncomfortable. Nobody said anything, and it was pretty obvious that nobody was going to volunteer to start shooting. I had noticed that Mr. Grizzard seemed to be in pretty good spirits about the whole thing. Unlike the man from Little Rock, he kept grinning and cracking jokes like there was nothing to worry about. Then, we found out why. "All of a sudden, he hollers, 'Bring him in, Wendell.' Then, I seen this grinning peckerwood go out the front door. Grizzard tells us that he thinks he has the problem solved, and as soon as Wendell Tilley gets back, we will see why. Wendell come back dragging a big chicken coop, big enough to hold about twenty white leghorns. There was just one bird in it, though, and it was a buzzard.

"Wendell and Grizzard hefted it up on a stack of feed and we crowded in to get a better look. It was one ugly critter. 'Found it trapped in a tree-stump,' said Wendell. Wendell figured it had gone in after a sick rabbit and then couldn't get back out. Wendell managed to get it into a tow sack. Some of the folks close to the coop started to back up and look disgusted. The buzzard had puked a green and yellow mess all over the coop.

"Wendell said that buzzards puked a lot but it didn't mean that they was sick. He said that it was just a buzzard's nature. Coulda fooled me! To tell you the truth, I never thought about a buzzard being healthy, being as how they eat dead things. While I was trying to sort this out, I heard it.

"*Ding, ding. Ding, ding.*"

"That buzzard was wearing a bell. 'Give me a fit,' said Wendell. 'Between it pecking my fingers and puking, it took all morning, but I finally got it on. It's a sheep bell.'

"Grizzard explained that they intended to turn the buzzard loose that night. He said they was hoping that when the buzzard showed up on the rock cliffs above the river, the ringing of the bell would frighten the other buzzards, or at least make them nervous enough to leave. That crowd seemed pleased. Grizzard lifted a keg of Arkansas moonshine onto his counter, and everybody, including the women, drank a toast to the belled buzzard. Wendell dragged the coop onto the porch and opened the coop door. It took a while. That buzzard set there like a black anvil 'til Wendell poked him in the ribs. Finally, he stepped out of that coop and glared at us." Granny stopped talking for a minute. "Now, ain't that quare! I called that buzzard 'he,' like I knew he was a gentleman and not a lady. Well, he was, I'm sure of that! Wasn't afraid, he just waited. I think we all moved back a little, and watched him - or it - waddle to the end of the porch. Then, that bugger lifted off, *flap, flap* into the night. For a while, we heard the bell, *ding, ding*, and then he was gone, black into black."

Granny got out her Bruton's Sweet snuff can and her birch snuff brush. She dumped a teaspoon of snuff into her lower lip and began to scrub it around with the brush.

"Filthy habit," she said. "Don't ever take it up."

"I don't aim to," I said. "What happened to the buzzard?"

"Well, as you can imagine, we was all out on the road at daybreak watching the buzzards. Oh, there was thousands of them black buggers on them cliffs. Sure enough, the belled buzzard was there. Grizzard was right. No sooner would that poor devil settle down in a flock, than every one but him would take off. He was being shunned by his friends, and he didn't like it. Kept follering them about. I guess buzzards is no different from people in that regard. They don't relish becoming outcasts.

"Looking down that river was a sobering sight, Harley. Maybe hell looks like that. A muddy river full of corpses rolling between rock cliffs and them buzzards setting up there as far as you can see, waiting. Anyway, that bell did the trick. In a couple of hours, the sky was full of buzzards trying to get away from that bell. At first, they just moved from one cliff to another, but nothing was working. The bell follered them. *Ding, ding*. Before the week was out, they was all gone. Nothing but the belled buzzard flying up and down the river, or setting miserable and alone on the rocks. A few days later, he was gone, too."

"Where did he go?"

"Well, Harley, I don't rightly know. Stories come back, of course. People in Little Rock reported a buzzard migration follered two days later by the one with the bell. Then, he started showing up by hisself. He was in north Georgia for a while, and then he showed up in the Smokies. Then, he sorta vanished." The buzzards across the road were lower now. Finally, they disappeared behind the jack-pine thicket.

"Is that the whole story?"

Granny put a pinch of snuff on her hand and sniffed it up her nose. She blinked her eyes and winked at me. "Pretty much."

I got up and stretched. Then, I started into the house.

"Except for the one time he come back."

That stopped me. I went back and set down by Granny.

"The buzzard come back?"

"Well, that's what I heard. Rush and me was gone from Arkansas by then, but we heard about it. Lots of folks said it wasn't the same bird."

"How come?"

"Well, it had been a couple of years. Then, too, some said he was different. Bigger. Some folks said that he had red eyes that glowed in the dark. But there was that bell going *ding, ding*. Also, he seemed to know things."

"Like what?"

"He showed up where bad things happened. Lots of times, he showed up *before* they happened."

"Like he knew the future?"

"It were more like he were a judgment. A man in Georgia killed his wife and children. The buzzard circled his house for days and when curious folks showed up because of the bell, the man confessed. I heard he roosted on the courthouse in Savannah during a murder trial. Then, he would be seen in two or three different places on the same day. He finally went home though."

"Arkansas?"

"Yep. Went back to that rock cliff above the river. When Rush and me went back to visit years later, old man Grizzard told us about it. Said he set above the river for years, the only buzzard in the whole gorge. Sometimes, late at night, Grizzard heard the bell when the buzzard passed over on his way to a deathbed or a wake. That's what he done, you see. He circled houses where someone was going to die. Wendell Tilley said he wished that he had never put that bell on him. He kept saying he had 'set something in motion' when he did that. He thought he had made that buzzard into some kind of force."

"What happened to him?"

"Well, Harley, somebody finally took your advice and shot him. The man's name was Jonah Trull, and he lived on the Arkansas River. He killed his wife, tied her to a iron tractor wheel and sunk her in the river. Told his friends that she had run away with a drummer. He even got a lot of sympathy from his neighbors until the belled buzzard showed up. There he was each day, mournfully circling the same place, the bell ringing *ding, ding.* People noticed, of course, but they didn't connect anything to Jonah.

"But that bell was driving Jonah crazy. He started pretending he was hunting and took his dogs down to the river. The next time the buzzard showed up, Jonah blasted him out of the sky. Saw him fall. Then, he went home thinking all of his troubles was over. As luck would have it, the local preacher and his wife come by and Jonah tried to play the role of host, serving tea and cookies and the like. Then, setting there in the parlor with a tea-cup 'n saucer in his lap, he heard it." Granny stopped talking and winked at me.

"Heard what?"

"Why, the bell, Harley! Setting with the preacher and his wife, Jonah heard the bell. *Ding, ding.* Coming closer, *ding, ding.*

In the yard, on the porch and down the hall. *Ding, ding.*

Poor Jonah thought the buzzard had followed him home. When the bell reached the parlor, Jonah fell apart. Confessed the whole thing to the preacher. Old man Grizzard saw them lift the tractor wheel from the river with what was left of Jonah's wife lashed to the rim. There was a quick trial and Jonah was hanged." Granny hummed and tapped with her foot.

"When your granddaddy played "The Belled Buzzard," he used to pluck the fiddle string with his finger like this." Granny acted like she was holding a fiddle and plucking a string with her finger. "*Ding, ding,* to make the sound of the bell, you see."

"But what did Jonah hear?" I said.

"Oh, it was the bell! See, one of his dogs swum out into the Arkansas River after the buzzard fell and he retrieved the little collar with the bell. Brought it home in his mouth, and as he trotted, the bell rang. Across the field, into the house and down the hall *ding, ding* all the way. Dropped that bell at his master's feet."

"Ah, shoot! I don't believe it," I said.

Granny winked and raised her fiddle while her foot tapped the floor. Her little finger curled, hooking an imagined string. "*Ding, ding,*" she said. "*Ding, ding.*"

137

GRANNY STRETCHES THE BLANKET

Granny leaned so far over the coffin, her nose almost touched old man Dockery's.

"Don't look like hisself," she said. "Color's not right. Look at his face, all flattened out like somebody had let the air out of him." She was looking at the dead man with her eyes almost shut, the same way I had seen her look at her needle when she was threading it.

I could see one of the old man's hands laying across his heart, heavy as a hammer. His fingers looked like they had been shaped by a mud-dobber.

"Please, Mother Teester," whispered Momma, her face all flushed, "Don't make a spectacle of yourself."

Granny turned around. The room was so quiet, I could hear Momma's watch tick. I could smell fried chicken, too. Bertha Dockery sat at the foot of the coffin surrounded by flowers and grandchildren. Nobody seemed to have heard what Granny said, but if they didn't, it was because they weren't listening very hard. We were at the head of the line of mourners that made its way past Bertha to the coffin. Just as we turned to take our place among the silent folk, Tina Lou Dockery suddenly rose among the flowers with her Kodak aimed at her daddy. After the flash, we stood, helpless and blinded by the light. The room swarmed with blue hornets.

"It's for the family album," said Tina Lou.

With Momma acting as guide, we slowly made our way out of the room. Off to the left, the kitchen table was loaded down with covered dishes. Chicken, potato salad and banana pudding. Momma stopped outside the door, waiting for her vision to clear. The porch was covered with Dockerys, and bunches of men stood about in the dark yard, smoking and talking softly. Daddy broke away from one of the groups and came forward, taking Momma's arm.

"Ready to go, are ye?" he said.

"I certainly am," she said, giving Granny one of her killer stares. "Your mother managed to behave like a fool again." Daddy gave a weary sigh, and led us to the car. He had been listening to Momma and Granny argue for years. People nodded at us as we passed, and I heard pieces of talk about hog feed, pastures and white leghorns.

Granny and me got in the back of Daddy's car and waited while Daddy got Momma settled and got in hisself.

"I don't see what the big to-do is about," said Granny. "I don't think I showed any disrespect by commenting on the fact that the undertaker done a sorry job."

"It is hardly the thing to discuss at a funeral! I'll never be able to look Bertha Dockery in the face again!" Momma snapped open her pocket book and began to stir the contents. "Honest to God, Lyndon, she actually said that Ethan looked like somebody had let the air out of him! Everybody heard her!" She found a powder-puff and gave her nose a couple of pats. "I'm glad we left Frankie Jean at the Passmores." My little sister had been disappointed because she wasn't allowed to come.

"Well, he did," said Granny. "And I didn't announce it. I just said that he didn't look like hisself. Nobody heard me but you and Harley." Granny looked at me and winked. "At least, they had the funeral at home. I don't care for this new-fangled way of holding services at the undertakers. Them little rooms called 'parlors' with all them little metal chairs and that organ music. Too impersonal." She patted my knee. "Your Uncle Hoyt went to a funeral at the undertakers a while back, and didn't discover that he was at the wrong one 'til it was over. He said they had four funerals going at the same time in different rooms. 'Course, he said now that he knew about it, he was going back and just drift in and out of all of them. He said it was like getting more than one channel on the tv." Granny laughed.

"That's what I mean," said Momma. "Listen at her!"

"Times are shore changing," said Granny. She turned to me, smiling. "When I was a girl, folks with goiters used to show up at funerals and ask permission to let the corpse heal them."

"How could they do that?" I asked.

"Well, see, there was an old belief that a dead man's hand could cure a goiter. They would take hold of that cold, dead hand

and press it against the goiter." Granny took my hand and demonstrated. When I jerked my hand away, she poked me in the ribs and grinned.

"Ignorance and superstition," said Momma. "If that is what you mean by the old ways passing, then I say, good riddance."

"And that coffin," said Granny, attempting to change the subject, "that coffin was *cherry*. Probably cost as much as a Buick. Bertha will have to sell the bottom pasture to pay for that thing, and Ethan will just get to ride in it once."

"You can't fault the Dockerys for showing respect for their father," said Momma, but she sounded a little uncertain.

"Ethan was the color of a Christmas orange," said Granny. "It must be the embalming fluid." Granny stared out the window and shook her head. "Undertakers!" she said. "Lots of them prey on the weak. I'd hate to think that your daddy would do something like that when I die."

"You can stop worrying about that, Mother Teester."

Granny pretended not to hear that one.

"Hand-polished cherry, and after the funeral tomorrow, we will never see it again." Granny thought about that for a moment, and I saw her eyes twinkle. "I heard that Ethan wanted a telephone and a night-light in that coffin...just in case he wasn't really dead." She poked me again. "Can you imagine that, Harley? The phone ringing and when you answer it, you hear, 'This is Ethan. What's for supper?'" Granny chuckled. Momma give her a mean look and stared at my daddy like she was saying 'see what I mean!'

Granny patted my knee. "But Ethan won't be going anywhere. Well, not unless we have another one of them flash floods like the one in '31. Washed thirty coffins out of the Balm of Gilead churchyard above Glenville." She looked at me and waited.

"Coffins float?" I asked.

"Some do," said Granny. She had me.

"Where did they go?"

"Well, they got in the Tuckaseigee River and went merrily on their way. Just bobbed along like little boxcars right on through Jackson and Swain County. People gathered on the bridge in Bryson City to watch them pass. They eventually caught most of them. Some people started a rescue project and stretched nets across the river. Caught them like minnows in a seine. Took a dozen coffins back to East La

Porte and stored them in a church basement, so people could come and claim the runaway dead." Granny chuckled.

"I heard that two of them was never picked up. They just set there like them unclaimed packages at the post office." She give me a nudge with her elbow. "Wonder what happened to them?"
Granny got a peppermint out of her pocket, unwrapped it and popped it in her mouth.

"I heard that they never found a couple of 'em. Wouldn't surprise me if they made it to the Gulf of Mexico since they started their trip when that flood was at its peak. We all knew who was in them coffins, too. They washed out of a part of the graveyard with markers and numbers. The church had a record book. One of them was a man that courted me a bit before he was killed up at Cloudburst lumber-camp. A tree fell on him. His name was Troy Simmons. He used to tell me how much he wanted to see the world."

"I had just as soon you didn't fill the child's head with that kind of foolishness, Mother Teester," said Momma. Granny cackled and began humming "Did You Ever Go Sailing?" Momma adjusted the rearview mirror and stared at her own face. She didn't seem too happy with what she saw.

Daddy turned the radio on and we listened to a Holiness preacher talk about brimstone and eternal suffering. He said that the devil would bake the damned like cornbread and flip their smoking carcasses like flapjacks. After a while, Daddy turned the dial to WWNC and we listened to the Skyline Quartet sing "Listen to the Mockingbird." Finally, I prodded Granny's shoulder and whispered.

"But when people die, they stay dead, don't they?"

"Usually," said Granny.

"What do you mean 'usually'?"

"Now and then, somebody comes back. Like Lucinda Stillwell." Granny leaned forward and prodded Daddy's shoulder. "Slow down, Lyndon. I want to see who is on the porch at the county home."

Daddy slowed and Granny cranked down the window while Momma complained.

"Who was Lucinda Stillwell?"

"I'll tell you in a minute, honey. Your Granny wants to see who is on the porch at the County Home."

The county home was a big brick building with a porch that went all the way around the house. A long line of rocking chairs faced the highway, and the old folks sat talking and rocking. The porch lights were on and them people smiled and waved at the passing cars.

"There is Bertie Arwood," said Granny. "Third one from the end. That worthless boy of hers, Willard, he could have kept her at home." We were past the porch now, with nothing but pasture and trees.

"Guess Willard didn't want to be bothered," said Granny.

"We got the message," said Momma. "You don't have to beat it to death." I knew what that meant. Granny was afraid that she was going to end up in the county home.

"Who was Lucinda Stillwell?" I asked again.

"Well, she was Colonel Stillwell's daughter."

"The one who is in the library with the sword?" I was talking about a big picture of a fierce looking man on a horse that hung in the public library.

"That's him, Harley. Owned two thousand acres of timber and built a fine house up in the Balsams after the war. Just had one child, Lucinda, and he spoiled her rotten. Sent her to foreign countries and a fancy school up in New England."

"She died and come back from the dead?"

"Not so fast, honey. Let poor old Granny tell the story." She pinched me under my armpit.

"Ouch!"

"That'll be blue tomorrow." She smiled sweetly and got a peppermint out of her pocketbook.

"Lucinda was a puny thing as a child. Spent most of her time in her bedroom looking out the window. She rallied a bit in her teens, and finally got a bit of color in her face. Then, we seen her sporting that fellow around, a city-bred teacher named Roger Manley, who wore tweed coats and smoked a pipe. When her marriage was announced, nobody was surprised. 'Course, we weren't invited. Lots of folks from other places came, and the Stillwell clan descended in force. More folks than what showed up for the college dedication, I heard. The church was packed to the rafters with a goodly number out in the yard. Then, just as she started down the aisle with her daddy in this dress with a train that stretched clean outside, she keeled over. Just fell on her face. Dead as four o'clock, at least it looked that way. By dark, she was in her coffin and that mob of people was rushing around changing clothes. From white to black, and from carnations to lilies. She was buried the next day. Seems the Stillwells didn't put no truck in mortuaries, so the usual three days of mourning became one day. I'm going by hearsay now, since I wasn't at the funeral either, but the minister let it out that Lucinda was buried in enough jewelry to shame the queen of England! He said the wedding ring alone was worth enough to build a ten-room house with indoor plumbing."

"But, she came back from the dead?"

"Yes, Harley, with a little help, she did. The night after the funeral, that poor one-day widower heard something on the porch. Musta been around three o'clock in the morning, when there is thick fog in the Balsams and somebody was scratching on the door."

Granny made a claw and scratched my back, laughing when the gooseflesh spread down my arm. "Scritch, scritch," she said.

"When he opened the door, there stood Lucinda, blood streaming down that wedding dress and looking like she had seen something that would make her wake up struggling for breath for years to come." Granny stopped talking and began to hum again. Made me mad, the way she teased me, making me ask:

"Okay, what happened?"

"Why don't you tell me," she said. "Maybe you got it figured out."

"Well, there is no way she could have got out there! Not if she was in a nailed-shut coffin under a ton of grave dirt."

"You are right, Harley. No way she could have got out." Then, she whispered, "But what if somebody got in?"

"Somebody dug her up?"

"That's right! Remember all that jewelry? When they caught the two guys in Knoxville two days later, they were still a little pale around the gills. They wanted the ring, Harley. One of them cut her finger off with a pair of pinking shears. Work hands from Tennessee that had been doing chores for the Stillwells that summer. Lucinda sat up in that coffin screaming like a banshee....You know about banshees, Harley? Remind me to tell you some time. The two grave robbers had already collected the other stuff - watches, a necklace, one of them diamond tiaras. That is what they were trying to sell in Knoxville when they got caught."

"What happened to the finger?"

"Got lost for a while, but it was found the next day. Lucinda kept it on the mantle for years in a little cut-glass jar. Imagine it for a minute, Harley. What would it be like to wake up in that opened coffin and see some beady-eyed wretch with pinking shears and a lantern....to sorta take stock and realize that you were in a coffin...and your finger was gone." Granny shook her head. "Wonder who was more frightened - Lucinda or them grave-robbers?"

"So she wasn't dead."

"The doctor said that it was some kind of sleeping sickness that was called 'the little death,' and that it was possible that some folks got buried alive, and didn't have the good fortune to be dug up."

"So, that's it?"

"Pretty much." I rolled the window down, and watched the night sky where a half-moon floated in a cloudy sea. "Until Lucinda disappeared." There it was again. Granny's baited hook.

"Disappeared?"

"Vanished, Harley. About ten years after she came back, she *vanished*. It was during a party, one of those Stillwell affairs with catered food, a host of relatives and expensive presents; they really put on the dog. It was the kind of thing you usually only read about in the big city papers. It was a birthday party."

"Lucinda's?" Granny shook her head.

"Her daughter's. They had been playing 'Hide and Seek,' and in the middle of all the fun, Lucinda hid so well, no one could find her. Didn't find her for fifty years."

"Did she run away?"

"No, Harley, she was there all the time - up in the attic in an old trunk...a fancy one like people have who travel to foreign countries. Big as a coffin. The lid locked, you see. There she was back in the airless dark. I guess she thought nobody would ever think to look there, and she was right. They looked for her for days. Long after the party was over, Roger wandered about the house calling her. Then, he got the idea that she was alive somewhere and would write him. Waited each day for the letter until he died on the front porch of Stillwell Manor.

"Now, some folks thought that Lucinda was meant to die the first time and that is why she ended up in the trunk, like it was Fate, you know?"

My mouth was open, and Granny reached out, cupped my chin and gently closed it. Then, she laughed and turned to the window, watching the dark world flow by.

"You made that up!" I said. I prodded my daddy's shoulder. "Didn't she, Daddy? She made that up!" My daddy laughed. "That is the way she told it to me, too!" he said, "except, I don't remember the part about Roger waiting for the letter."

"Foolishness," said Momma. "Old lies to give you bad dreams. Telephones in coffins, runaway coffins, graverobbers! I never heard the beat."

Momma sounded like she was about to lose her temper. Daddy sighed and rolled his window down, watching the dark woods flow by. The cool night air flooded the car and I stared at the distant lights of farmhouses. Granny's old hand dropped on my head and pressed it against her cheek. Like always, she smelled of camphor, snuff and peppermint.

That was the last time we took a trip together, the four of us. In a few months, Daddy was dead, and then Granny had a stroke. Sometimes, in dreams, I'm back riding with Granny. Daddy rolls down the window and I can smell honeysuckle. When he flicks the lights on bright, the beams jump up the distant hillsides where startled eyes turn toward us. Momma adjusts the mirror so she can see Granny and me in the back seat, and we smile back at her.

BLIND HODUR

An Appalachian folktale

The idea for this story came from an old Japanese folktale, "The Story of Mimi-Nashi-Hoichi" that I heard over forty years ago. It also exists as a part of the Japanese film, "Kwaidan," which is based on a collection of traditional stories, collected (and rewritten) by Lafcadio Hearn.

In this story, I attempted to write without using quotation marks. The idea is certainly not original with me since Faulkner, Cormac McCarthy and Charles Frazier frequently omit them. Like Frazier, I simply use a dash (-) to indicate speech. I hope it doesn't confuse any readers, especially since the purpose of the simplification is to make the story more "readable."

G.C.

His earliest memories were of his mother's voice. In that still, dark world where he would always live, he lifted his child's fingers to her face and lightly traced the shape of her moving mouth. She said, -Listen, child, and I'll tell you a story. She told him of murdered children who became birds and sang; of imprisoned women, and a boy who did not know how to shiver. When he was old enough, he asked questions.

-Why does the little dead boy's sister fill her plate with tears?

-Because she thinks she killed her brother, said his mother.

-But, it was the mother, wasn't it?

-Yes, and the father ate the little boy in a stew, but he didn't know he ate his son.

-He didn't know what he was doing?

-Yes, people can do terrible things and not know it.

-And the little boy became a bird?

-A beautiful bird with bright red and gold feathers.

Then, she sang a little song.

Kywitt, kywitt, kywitt, I cry,
Oh, what a beautiful bird am I!

-Why did the fairy not want Rapunzel to see a man?

His mother laughed. -She thought they were evil, she said. -My mother felt the same way.

-The little boy who could not shiver, he wasn't afraid of anything?

-That's right. My goodness, you are filled with questions tonight!

-But that would be a good thing, wouldn't it, to never be afraid?

-Not always. There are times when your life may depend on being afraid rather than being brave.

-Tell me again how I got my name.

-You were named for a blind god, she said. He was called Blind Hodur and his brother was Balder, the Good. She told the story patiently although she had told it many times.

-And Hodur killed his brother?

-Yes, but he didn't know what he did.

-Because he couldn't see.

-That is right, child. A long time ago in another world.

He knew that his father rode away each morning to teach in a one-room school and that he returned in the evenings, angry and sullen. At night, he drank, lurching about the room, weeping and cursing in turn. Sometimes there were terrible fights and his mother ran into the woods with Hodur in her arms, and they listened to his father rage in the twice-dark woods. Perhaps they huddled together in a nest of roots at the base of a great water oak, and his mother said -Listen now, and I will tell you a story. She talked of white bears and a girl who carried her severed hands slung over her shoulders. There were witches who lived in gingerbread houses and clever Jack, who knew how to survive.

The soldiers came when he was seven. The night rang with the sound of horses and wagons, shouts and curses. The noise passed like a thunderstorm, and he heard it receding down the mountain until it became a part of the wind and rain.

147

-Where are they going?

-To some battle or other, his mother said. -Your father heard that they were on their way to Chattanooga. He whispered the name of the place for days. *Chattanooga*, like something a wild bird would say deep in the woods. *Chatta-noogaaaa.*

No one else came until that winter when the man named Dexter arrived one morning. He had six men with him and Hodur listened as their horses stamped in the yard. Amid the angry shouts, Hodur heard the sound of gunfire. Then, the men rode away.

-What happened? said Hodur, clutching his mother's legs. - Who did they shoot?

-The pig, said his mother. -The pig and the little calf.

-Why?

-To feed the soldiers. He said they were foragers for the Union, which means they can steal and kill our animals. After a moment, she added that they were lucky. Over the mountain, they killed people and burned houses. They called old farmers and young boys spies and shot them.

Hodur thought of the sounds the pig had made when it ate, and the bleat of the calf. His world was diminished without them. One cold evening several weeks later, his father came home with a tale about Dexter's Raiders. Angry farmers had driven them into a dead-end cove, and there amid a freezing rain and an ice storm, the foragers had perished.

-Froze to death, said his father with relish. -Had to pry them up with hayforks and shovels and stacked them up like fence posts. Dropped their bodies in Kitner's Cave, that bottomless pit on the backside of Windy Hill. They are all in hell now, where they should be. His father laughed and quoted Dante. That night, he played a new song on his fiddle.

-Listen, he said. This is "Kitner's Cave." The melody was wild and frenzied, and as he played, he shouted Dexter's story.

> *Down through the chilling mist they fell*
> *To lie forever in a frozen hell.*

One morning, his mother was no longer there. He had heard shouting in the night and his father's curses, but that was hardly unusual. Hodur searched the house, his fingers sliding along the walls, prodding the bedclothes. He called her from the porch.

-Hush, now, said his father. -Your mother can't hear you.

-Where is she? said Hodur.

-She is where the woodbine twines, my boy, said his father. Then, he whispered in his blind son's ear. -Beware the helping hand, Hodur. Learn to walk alone! Ye'll get no help from me. Then, he seized his battered fiddle and played the wild dissonant melody and sang the keening song about Dexter that sounded like a blend of madness, laughter and tears. In the following weeks, he raved about missed opportunities and the curse of lust. Hodur learned to sleep at odd hours, feed himself and avoid his father's presence.

One morning, the boy woke to silence and his questing fingers found the cold flesh of his father's face, his gaping mouth and eyes as sightless as his own. Finding his way to a neighbor's farm, he stood in the winter field until he was seen and brought to warmth and food where he told his story. A preacher was summoned and a rude coffin built. Hodur, wrapped in a homemade quilt, ate bleached apples and biscuits and listened to talk of cooling boards and jaw strings.

-We wouldn't want your dear father to rise on judgment day with his mouth a-gape, now would we! said the old woman who presided at the last rites. -Come, say goodbye to your daddy, lad. Hodur stood by the trestled box smelling pine shavings and cheap whiskey. His fingers traced the contours of the defeated face. -Bye, Papa, he said. When all was done, they brought him his father's fiddle.

-Can you play it, lad? said Giles, the farmer.

-No, but I'll learn. He was eight years old.

-So what will ye do now? the farmer asked. -Where will ye go? How will ye live?

Hodur didn't answer.

-Have ye no family? asked Jandie, the farmer's wife. -Where is your mother? Hodur turned away, his hands covered his sightless eyes. The farmer and his wife whispered together. Finally the old man came and spoke with mock gruffness. -Ye'll stay here with us for the time being, he said, - but ye'll have to make yourself useful.

It wasn't a bad life. Despite his blindness, Hodur was a clever boy. He learned to sweep, mend, milk cows and shell corn. He could weave, make brooms and repair broken tools. And he learned to play the fiddle, finding that he could even recreate his father's wild music.

-Pray tell, what was that? said farmer Giles.

-I don't know its name, said Hodur. -My father used to play it.

-Never heard such unhappy music, said Giles. - Don't ye know something a bit more uplifting? Hodur would play *Flow Gently, Sweet Afton* and *Abide With Me.*

-Ah, boy, I'm glad ye found your way to my cornfield. Here me and Jandie, we were facing a bleak prospect, no children and all that, but then, ye came. Giles's hand touched Hodur's head, and the old man said, -We're glad ye are here.

When he was ten, Giles told him about his mother.

-I wanted to wait till you were older, the old man said. -Me and the Tallent boys found her about a year after your daddy died. Nothing left but bones, son, said Giles. -She was buried in a sack at the foot of a big water oak. Her skull was crushed.

Hodur wondered if there was a brightly colored bird in the tree above her grave.

When he was twelve, Hodur began to tell stories - the ones that his mother had told him. Gradually, the stories began to change, the way clothing will alter to fit the form of a new owner. Evenings, he sat on the porch with Giles and Jandie, the three united by the darkness, and Hodur talked.

Once there was a man who had three sons. The older sons grew to manhood, asked for their father's blessings and their rightful share of inheritance, and vanished into the great world. But, the youngest son remained with his father. When the old man became blind and feeble, the youngest son said, - Father, it grieves me to see you grow old. Is there nothing I can do to bring you comfort? For a long time, the old man said nothing.

Then, he said, -A traveler who passed the night in this house once told me of a stream called the Elixir of Life. He said that one draught from the stream would make an old man young again. In an instant, his limbs would be renewed and his failing sight restored. Alas, I was young when he told me about the stream, and I had no need of it. Now, that I am old, I don't have the strength to make the journey.

-Where is the stream? said the son.

-Beyond the Blue Mountains, across the White Desert to an island in the Green Sea, said the old man. -There, in a deep cove guarded by two serpent angels, you will find it. The water

can only be caught in a silver flask that lies in the crook of an
apple tree that grows on the banks of the stream, and only those
deemed worthy by the angels can have the flask.

-*Father, I will go, said the son.*

When Hodur told the stories, he played his father's fiddle, and the music clothed his words, causing his audience to listen with rapt attention, to respond with laughter and tears. At first, it was only Giles and Jandie who sat in the dark shelter of their porch like prisoners of an enchantment; but word spread. People came to "borrow" Hodur.

Children came to lead him to other farms, other porches.

-Please, sir, the children said, can Hodur come to our house tonight? Giles enjoyed his new role as Hodur's protector.

-Now, who would you be? he would say sternly. -We can't have Hodur leaving with any stranger that chances by.

-Oh, sir, we ain't strangers! My father's Nick Kirby who owns the sawmill at Dark Corners, and he knows you. We'll bring Hodur home afterwards.

-Well, now, it's up to Hodur. Let's ask him if he wants to go traipsing off in the middle of the night with a passel of children.

Hodur always wanted to go.

And so it was. Hodur would depart, towed by a bevy of children and friendly dogs. Giles and Jandie sat in the dark, waiting for the gleam of an approaching lantern that signaled Hodur's return. Sometimes, on warm summer nights people came to the gate. -Could we hear the boy talk? They would say. Giles and Jandie bustled about finding chairs and offering refreshments. They sat in the darkness while Hodur talked, drinking his words like the cider that Giles gave them. Hours later, when they rose to leave, they spoke to the boy.

-Thank ye, Hodur, they said, their hands touching the boy's face or resting briefly on his head. The men left small objects: pocket knives, garnets and madstones. The women left jars of jelly, handkerchiefs and once an old man gave him a carved walkingstick with a serpent's head.

-Why, it's like an offering, said Giles. I'm not sure it's right.

-Hush, Giles, said Jandie, -It can do no harm.

When Hodur was fifteen, he made a strange request.

-Live by yourself! said Giles, his voice failing to hide the hurt, -What for?

-I can't explain it, said Hodur. -I just need some time alone.

151

-Don't you love us, Hodur? said Jandie. -Is it hard to live with two old dottering fools?

-You're my family, said Hodur. -Of course I love you. And I'll come home every day. I need a place, maybe up on the ridge with the wind and the rain crows. He could hear the old woman weeping. - I'll come down for breakfast every morning, he offered.

Giles helped him build a shelter on a windy ledge above the farm. There was barely room for Hodur, a chair and a cot.

-It seems so small, said Giles. -We could build a proper house.

-No, this is enough. Tell Jandie I'll be down for breakfast.

-I can come for ye, said Giles.

-No, I can manage. I've already walked it three times. He tapped the serpent stick on the porch. -It's easy.

They could hear the fiddle in the evening, the music plaintive and sweet.

In time, the evening visitors learned of Hodur's new home. and they merely called a greeting to Giles and Jandie as they trudged up the steep slope to the wind-blown shack on the ledge. On the return trip, Hodur called to them as he was led to hearths and front porches where children and patriarchs waited. Giles missed the visitors and sat late on the porch to witness Hodur's return. The lanterns ascended and descended the path like great fireflies.

-Our Hodur is famous, it seems, he said to Jandie.

-I'm afraid he isn't ours anymore.

-Why did he want to live up there, do you think?

-He said once he was called.

The old woman snapped beans in the dark and listened to the night-sounds. A lone owl questioned the darkness; a rain-crow mourned. She said that winter was coming.

Sitting in his aerie, Hodur waited. It was winter now, and wind raked the mountain precipice, carrying away root and limb, scouring away all but abiding rock, the bones of trees and Hodur. Sitting by his tiny fire, the blind boy listened to his chimney flute keen like an Aeolian harp. He had been playing a counter-point melody much like his father's sad, mad songs, but now he sat listening to the night. Beneath the wind, he felt, rather than heard, a knock.

-Come in.

He did not hear the door open, and he waited for the grate of the hinge. It did not come. He felt the floor thrum beneath him and sensed a presence.

-You must come. A harsh whisper close to his ear.

-You must come now. We are waiting.

-A bad night, said Hodur.

-But a good night for stories!

Hodur rose, clutching his fiddle, his hand groping for the serpent stick.

-You won't need that. Hodur heard the stick clatter against the chimney and fall to the floor.

- I will lead you.

Hodur found himself outside in the keening night. Accustomed to being led, Hodur gave himself over to his new guardian. Yet, as they began the descent, they suddenly veered from the trail and the blind boy felt himself to be surrounded by a quaking wilderness.

-Is this the way?

-A shorter one.

And on they went through laurel hells and hemlock coves. His guide moved effortlessly down familiar paths. Hodur had lost track of time when they stopped. The sound of the wind had diminished, suggesting that they had entered....what? A large building perhaps? Voices and laughter that quaked and echoed.

-Here. You must sit here.

He heard the pebbles rattling, falling, striking distant stones. And then, it came like the breath of a great animal, a cold exhalation, damp and fetid. His fingers grew numb and he drew them into his armpits.

-Play for us.

-But, you said, stories....

-Another night. Tonight, play your father's songs.

-How did you know....

-Play.

And he did, all the wild, wailing melodies that resembled sobs and mad laughter. Crazed and discordant, the sounds fled on the chill wind....

- - - - -

153

-Giles? Giles? Giles snapped from his reverie to find a man with a lantern on his porch.

-Yes, James, what is it?

-Where has Hodur gone?

-He isn't there?

-No, and he left his door open. Did you not see him pass? Giles shook his head, perplexed. He always saw the boy with his escorts; he always called a greeting.....

-The children will be disappointed.

Giles watched the farmer's lantern move down the path until it winked out. Then, he rose and ascended the hill. He found the open door and peered in to see the serpent stick on the floor.

Something is wrong.

Yet, Hodur was back the next morning. He came to sit at the trestle table in the kitchen, but he seemed distracted. When Giles asked where he had gone the night before, the boy did not answer.

That night Giles climbed to a spot below Hodur's windy rock and waited.

- - - - -

The next morning, the familiar tap of Hodur's serpent stick paused at the doorway to the kitchen.

-Someone else is here.

-Yes, Hodur. This is Nestor Flint. He is a preacher, said Giles. Hodur laid his stick across the table and sat in his accustomed place. His hands found unfamiliar shapes on the scoured oak planking before him. Books?

-Those are Rev. Flint's books, said Jandie, as she placed a steaming plate before the boy. Hodur's finger touched broken boards and dog-eared pages.

-They are very old, he said.

-And very powerful, said Flint softly.

-I smell new sausage and grape jelly. Hodur smiled and began to eat.

Finally, Giles broke the silence.

-I followed you last night, Hodur.

Immediately, the boy was alarmed.

-You shouldn't have. I was warned not to tell.....

-Who warned you? interrupted the preacher.

-The guide. The one who came to get me. He told me I must never tell anyone where we went.

-Do you know where you went? demanded Flint.

-Not exactly. It was a meeting of some sort and a large crowd.

-Giles, tell him where he went.

-Kitner's Cave, said Giles. -I followed you to Kitner's Cave.

For a moment, Hodur was perplexed. Then, he brightened.

-Then, you can tell me something. I am curious as to who the people are, and when I asked questions, they only said they would eventually explain everything.

-Listen, Hodur. I followed you down the mountain and through a wilderness of laurel and hemlock, and I followed you back home. Hodur, you were alone.

-But the guide....

-Alone, my boy, at least to these old eyes. I must admit that it did seem you had a guide, an invisible one. When I told Jandie, she said I should get Flint. That's why I walked to Big Bend last night in the dark.

-Your church is in Big Bend? said Hodur.

-I have no church.

Flint's voice grew louder. -It was burned years ago. Now I administer to the damned and lost who seek me out. Although you don't know it, you are in need of my services.

Hodur laughed. -Which am I, damned or lost?

-You consort with demons.

Giles' hand touched Hodur's head. -My boy, the thing that led you to Kitner's Cave....

-A demon. Flint spoke with total conviction. -I'm afraid I have seen this before. Tell me now, how did he come to you?

-I don't understand. You saw me go to Kitner's Cave alone?

-Yes, said Giles. -Whatever led you was not of human kin.

-Did you invite him? When he came, did you welcome him?

-He knocked at the door and I asked him to come in.

-That is all that is needed. How many times has he come for you?

-Twice. He said tonight would be the last time and then all my questions would be answered.

-What story did he ask you to tell?

155

- The old song my father sang and the story about the death of Dexter's Raiders.

There was silence then, and gradually, Hodur began to realize that, indeed, he had trafficked with something ...evil.

-Is my life in danger?

-Much more than that, said Flint.

-What if I simply refuse to return?

- You will be literally torn to bits. At least, that is what happened to the farmer in Dark Corners who played his fiddle for something that came to his home in the dark of the moon and asked him to play. Each visit increases the demon's power.

-And death comes with the third visit? Is there no defense at all?

-Perhaps there is one, and that is why I am here, said Flint. I will need goose quills and ink.

Twelve hours later, Giles, Jandie and Flint sat regarding their work.

-What makes you think this will succeed?

-I don't know that it will.

-Do you know of a case like this?

-Not exactly. There is an ancient story about a Buddhist monk that was saved by covering his body with religious verses. When the demons came to tear him to pieces, he was protected...clothed, as it were.

And so it was that naked Hodur sat, his arms twined about his knees, in the middle of the table. His skin had become a living parchment of holy writ. His thighs proclaimed Genesis and the soles of his feet recorded First and Second Kings while the palms of his hands proclaimed Psalms. The Song of Solomon encircled his genitals and Revelations and Exodus wrapped about his loins. His face and chest were darkened by Lamentations and the Book of Job covered his heart; Matthew, Mark, Luke and John wound like a tapestry around his back and shoulders. Flint's minute calligraphy had erased every vestige of flesh, even to the thin folds of Hodur's eyelids as Corinthians overlapped Judges and Acts emerged from Hodur's armpits to weave through tangled skeins of Numbers and Deuteronomy.

-Is this the whole Bible? said Giles.

-It is enough, said the preacher.

-Well, it is time, said Flint. Then, as an afterthought, he tore a page from one of the books, folded it into a tiny square and gave it to the blind boy.

-What is this?

-Put it under your tongue. Hodur did as he was told.

-Rev. Flint, do you know what you are doing?

-No, Giles. I can only hope.

-Then, what.....

-It is a little late for second thoughts. Why did you come to me?

-People have always said that you.....knew things.

-Tarback, the Baptist preacher was closer. Why not him?

-I felt I needed something special....an uncommon man.

-With an uncommon knowledge? Flint laughed.

-I heard you have driven demons from people. I heard about Johnson Lindsay, the poor boy that came home from Chattanooga laughing...

-Oh, yes. Poor Lindsay. I helped him, but he died.

-These books you have...they are not all Christian.

-No, this one is Egyptian, this, Greek and the one from which I tore the page, it is called The Kaballah.

-Some say that you are as bad as the things you destroy.

-Perhaps. Sometimes, it is too late, and the people die. Sometimes, I save their souls, but lose their flesh.

-Giles, said Jandie, -ask Hodur. Ask him if he wants to do this.

The boy sat, still as a stone, clutching his snake-stick in one hand and his fiddle in the other. As the sunlight faded and shadows spread across the kitchen, his inscripted flesh seemed to fade, absorbed by the coming night. He raised his stippled face and spoke with effort.

-What do you look like? The boy's questing fingers touched Flint's ravaged face.

Jandie answered. -The preacher's face is scarred, Hodur. Terrible things have happened to him, perhaps in the recent war.....

-There are all kinds of wars, said Flint ambiguously.

-His eyes are the worst, though, continued Jandie. -He has seen things, maybe done things that I'd rather not know about.

-Right enough, said Flint.

157

-But he came when Giles asked, and there are people in these mountains that consider him God's warrior.

-I guess I'm ready, said Hodur.

The four figures climbed the hill to where the last of the sunlight clung to Hodur's rock.

-Leave me outside. They placed him on the windy ledge and waited.

-Go away now.

-I want to speak to them when they come, said Flint.

The blind boy shook his head. -Go back, now.

Hodur listened to the retreating footsteps and waited, feeling the warmth of the sun withdraw as well. The wind faltered and stopped, suspended, expectant.

Like a cold tongue in his ear, the liquid whisper came.

-Time to go.

-I know who you are.

Laughter like stones dropped in a deep well followed by the shift and slide of something ponderous that came to rest by his side and breathed on his cheek. Then, anger bloomed; anger as palpable as fire in the night.

-What is this? What have you done?

-You can't harm me now. You're Dexter, aren't you?

In the ensuing silence, Hodur waited. Was it over so quickly? Was the voice gone? Then, the whisper came again, mocking.

-Dexter? Oh, yes, Dexter is here. Would you like to hear him speak?

An anguished scream.

-And all of his miserable band.....

A chorus then, a keening chant that mingled loss and despair and swelled to an explosion of fragmented cries.

-It is not so simple, you see. I am Dexter and his wretched men, but like your deity, I am much more. Listen........

Hodur heard his father's crazed laughter reverberating from some great depth accompanied by a trill of music.

-Poor blind Hodur! To think I am such a simple thing. No, storyteller, I was here before all things, asleep in the dark caves of these mountains. Your war awakened me, you see - that, and the mounting cruelty of your daily lives. I have grown strong, battened by a tide of pain and murder. Kennesaw, Stone Creek, Chattanooga! I am thousands of shackled souls.

-Why did you come to me?

-We need you, Hodur. We need a singer, a storyteller, a court jester. It is quite an honor, really.

-No.

A weary sigh and a mockish chuckling. Hodur placed his serpent stick across his lap and picked up his fiddle.

-It would have been better to have gone willingly, blind boy. Well, so be it.

Hodur began to play.

- - - - -

From the dark porch, Giles, Jandie and the preacher heard the music. It fell through the night air like snowflakes, covering the fields, the house, the porch with a palpable music.

-What is he playing? said Flint.

-Music that he alone can hear, said Jandie. -He used to worry about it. Wondered where it came from.

-It may be that all of my efforts were pointless.

-You think he is lost then?

-Oh, no. I meant that the music may have more power than all of those inscriptions.

-Perhaps, the two together, the written and the spoken, said Giles.

-Yes, said Flint, -Let us hope.

Eventually, the fiddle faltered and then grew silent. The wind revived and the night-birds returned.

They climbed through the dim woods to the moon-washed rock, hearing a faint muttering. It was Hodur's voice.

> *And the boy said, I will go for you, Father.*
> *I will journey beyond the Blue Mountains*
> *to the Blue Lake, and I will bring back the*
> *Elixir of Life.......*

Jandie placed her hand over Hodur's mouth. His eyes were closed and as her fingers covered his lips, she saw the blood. Jandie drew his head to her bosom. She began to cry.

-So, Hodur, we won, huh? Flint's voice was hopeful.

-He can't hear you, said Jandie. The old woman raised the boy's head in her hands. -His ears are gone.

Flint stared at the bleeding orifices and then, struck himself full in the face. Blood dripped from his nose.

-I forgot to write in his ears.

-It would seem so.

-They took the only part of him that was unprotected.

-But he is alive, said Jandie.

- - - - -

They wrapped the blind boy in their arms, and sat long in the dark. Flint removed the small, folded page from beneath the boy's tongue.

-What the hell was that, anyway? said Giles.

-The secret name of God.

-Did it help?

Flint shrugged. -I don't know.

-It helped. Everything helped, said Hodur.

-You can hear?

-Things are a bit faint, but yes I can hear.

-The pain must be awful, said Jandie. She tore the hem from her dress and bound his head with it.

-Not as bad as it was.

-I'm sorry about the ears, son, said Flint.

The boy smiled. -Didn't plan to wear glasses anyway.

-You need to be tended to, said Jandie. They rose as one and began the descent. Within a short distance, Giles fell.

-Can't see a damned thing.

-Take my arm, said Hodur. They began again, the preacher, Giles and Jandie, walking slowly at first, but Hodur walked quickly and they had to walk faster to keep up with him. So they went, the blind boy leading the way.

There are sections of Big Bend near the Tennessee/North Carolina line where there are stories about Blind Hodur. Some say he had "second sight" and was sought out for advice during drought or sickness. Even the love-lorn came to Hodur's Rock.

But most came to listen to the music and the stories. Here, an old grandmother talks:

-I seen him once, this old, white-headed man with a fiddle and no ears. Not a thing I'm likely to forget. When he talked the birds hushed and the wind grew still.

-When you heard him talk, do you remember the story?

-Oh, yes. It was the one about the youngest son, the one that went to get the Elixir of Youth for his dying father. And he played as he talked about the Blue Mountains, the White Desert, the Green Sea, and the angels and the silver flask.

-As I remember the story, he brought the elixir back and restored his father's youth. Is that correct?

-Well, yes, but he changed it somehow. It didn't end there.

-What do you mean?

-As the old man felt youth flood his body and as his once failing sight cleared, he leaped from his bed and turned to embrace his son. That is when he saw the change.

-Change?

-The youngest son had become old. The journey for the elixir had aged him. The son told his father that it was an exchange and that he had learned that things always balanced in the end.

-Ah, how sad!

-Not the way he told it. The son rejoiced in his father's youth, you see. He said it was a fair bargain.

-And that is how it ended?

-Yes, the young father and the old son sat on the porch in the evenings and talked. The son recounted the story of his journey again and again. When the son's health failed, the father tended him and they talked late into the night. When the son died, the father became a wanderer who traveled from town to town telling his story.

-What does it mean?

-Ah, how would I know that? I'm an old woman and sometimes foolish, but I do think about the balance of things now and again. If we harm each other, even the ones we love, we also help them, and that may be unwitting, too. At least, that is what Hodur said, the blind storyteller sitting on his rock with his white hair streaming. I remember it well, you see.

CHRISTMAS ON GUINEA TROT RIDGE

Some forty years ago, I read a wonderful little play by the North Carolina playwright, Bernice Kelly Harris. The play was called **Open House: The Story of An Evicted Family**. *By modern standards, the play is a "black comedy" with a liberal dose of the gothic. In addition to feeling that Mrs. Harris is one of the most neglected North Carolina writers, I have never forgotten the plot: a poor, rural family evicted on Christmas Eve! Throw in a dying baby, a bleak future and some corrupt rich folks, and you have a play that, to modern audiences, borders on bathos.*

I decided to take Harris' basic plot and do an Appalachian version with what I hope is a healthy dose of humor and courage. I have tried to reproduce the language of this region (western North Carolina), so bear with the dialect, misspellings, incorrect verb tense and the standard misuse of "sit" and "set." "Christmas on Guinea Trot Ridge" doesn't bear much resemblance to **Open House**, *but generates the kind of hope and good spirit that we associate with an Appalachian Christmas. Enjoy!*

Gary Carden, 1999

When the sheriff and his deputy carried the big red chair out of the house, Momma was still in it. The yard was already covered with stuff and it was beginning to snow. In no time at all, there was little snow doilies on everything, including Rydell's guitar case and the little battery-operated Philco radio that was setting on the Studebaker's fender. Our clothes was everywhere! Hanging on tree limbs and the car door handles. My sister Bug was setting in the back seat opening and closing her purse.

Our Christmas tree was in the middle of the yard. It was the saddest tree ever. It was a loblolly pine that Rydell had cut in the woods and it wouldn't stand up straight. It was in a bucket full of rocks, and it didn't have much stuff on it except some cotton balls. We cut pictures out of the Sears catalogue and hung them on the branches. The pictures was stuff we wanted for Christmas, but all of us knowed that the picture was as close as we would get. I think it ended up making us all sad. Momma kept saying, "We have each other - that is a great blessing."

That means "no presents".

We had quit talking about Christmas two days ago and everybody had tried to not look at that pitiful little tree. I noticed that snow was beginning to settle in the branches and it was looking better.

"I hope you can sleep tonight, Blighton Wooster," Momma yelled at the sheriff. "Putting poor folks out in the snow on the coldest night of the year." She laid a look on them two men that shoulda curled their toe nails. "And you, Horton Tolley! We went to school together," she said to the deputy, "Are you proud of yourself?" Horton blinked, shook his head and turned away. I felt kinda sorry for him.

Granny Wikle come out next in her big hickory rocker. They had to carry her, too. "My curse on you, Sheriff Wooster! You too, Horton! May your tongues shrivel and your teeth rot. Cruel and black-hearted Republican devils that you are!" They set her down by the car, and Blighton went back in the house and got her black walnut walking stick. When he give it to her, she took a swing at him with it, but he sidestepped it, and went back to padlock the door. He could move pretty good for a fat man.

Then, Daddy come 'round the side of the house with a piece of lead pipe, but Horton took it away from him and throwed in up in the woods. It didn't look like Daddy was trying real hard, but that it was kinda expected of him to do something. Wooster already took daddy's shotgun, and since there weren't no shells for it anyway, he put it in the car. Daddy started coughing and set down on the running board with his head in his hands.

"Is that everything?" Horton nodded.

"There weren't much anyway. The bedsteads, the stove and most of the furniture go with the house."

"Fine Christians you are," said Momma. "Putting a pregnant woman and three innocent chillern out in a snow storm."

163

I reckon that meant Bug, Rydell and me are the innocent children. Bug is six, I'm nine 'n Rydell is fourteen. Since Rydell had been in reform school, he might not be real innocent.

"Give it a rest, Ruth Ann." The sheriff pulled up his sagging pants and tucked in his shirttail and began shinning his boots on the back of his pants legs. "I'm doing what I have to do. Anyway, we mailed you the eviction notice a month ago. You and Westley chose to ignore it. I know for a fact that you ain't paid your rent in over a year. Further, the social service department has offered to move you into temporary housing til you got on your feet agin, and you ignored them, too."

Momma laughed. "One of them three-room fire-traps out on Garnet Hill. No, thank you."

"Better than setting out here in the snow."

Rydell got his guitar, leaned against the car, and started playing "Goin' Down That Road Feeling Bad." He did some fancy finger picking and sung that he wasn't goin' to be treated this a-way.

Horton said "Hey, that is pretty good, Rydell. Can you play 'Saint James Infirmary'?" I could tell that Horton felt bad about his part in putting us out, and he was trying to be friendly. Without even stopping, Rydell went into that song, and sung about his baby stretched out on a long, white table. Horton clapped and nodded. Rydell combed his hair and looked at Wooster. "Why don't you put us in jail? At least, we'd be fed and have a roof." The Sheriff shook his head. "You ain't broke any laws."

"Not yet, anyway." Rydell struck a match on the sole of one of his cowboy boots and lit a cigarette.

"Now, what does that mean?"

"If I knocked the winder-lights outta that house, would you arrest me?" Rydell looked for a rock.

"Hush, Rydell," said Daddy. "They'd just take you down to the jail and call that juvenile officer. We'd be left setting here in the snow. We need to stay together." Daddy walked over to where Momma was still arguing with Horton. "You hush, too, Ruth Ann. Let it be." He set down by her and looked at Horton, who ducked his head and got red in the face. Then, I decided to say something.

"As soon as you are out of sight, what's to keep me from knocking a window out, and crawling back in that house?" Everybody looked at me, and Rydell grinned. "Why, J. D., you so quiet, I'd forgot that you was here."

"We're going to drive by ever couple of hours just to see if you are still here," said the sheriff. I didn't know if that was because the sheriff was worried about us, or he was checking to see if we was back in the house.

Rydell started playing "Birmingham Jail." Lots of times, Rydell plays a song instead of talking. He says he gets in less trouble that way. His song is usually what he would have said though, only he's singing or playing 'stead of talking. Wooster come over and grinned at Rydell.

"You staying out of trouble?" Rydell nodded. Then he played and sung a little bit of "I Walk the Line." Wooster slapped Rydell on the back and said, "You a good boy." Then the sheriff pulled up his pants legs and said, "Rydell, I know you like fancy boots. How 'bout these?" Rydell was impressed. I was, too. The sheriff's boots was black and white and had what looked like little green eyes all over 'em. Rydell looked at his own scuffed boots.

"What kind of leather is that?" said Rydell.

"That's lizard skin."

"Musta took a lot of lizards," I said.

The sheriff laughed, and then I guess he remembered this was serious business. He and Horton got in the police car, and rolled down the windows and Wooster stared at Daddy. "That social service woman will be here any minute now. She'll find you a place to stay." He started the car. Then he said, "Hell, Westley, Wendell Turpin ain't a bad man. He even offered to let you move in that house he owns over on Norton Road. Pretty generous considering the fact that you don't pay rent. But he wants you out of this one." The car moved off. We watched it go slow and easy over the hill. Rydell played "Jingle Bells' and we watched it snow. Big old flakes that floated down like feathers.

"What you want for Christmas?" I asked Rydell.

"Them lizard boots," he said and laughed.

I got the feeling that maybe we'd just set there 'til we disappeared. The snow would keep falling, Momma, Granny and the Studebaker would be covered up. Maybe we'd all go to sleep to the tune of "Jingle Bells."

Then, Daddy said, "All right, let's get the hell out of here."

"Ain't we gonna wait for the social service lady?"

"Is that what you want?" Momma shook her head.

"Then we better go now."

165

"Where we going?" I said.

"I'm thinking."

"What about your brother, Truman?" said Momma.

"I dunno. Maybe."

The door of the Studebaker cracked open and Bug got out. She was wearing her Dale Evans hat and Daddy's big wool jacket, her head just barely showing above the collar. She had been setting in the back seat watching. She had her coin purse and I figured she'd been playing her favorite game. She closes her eyes, grits her teeth and says "Please!" Next, she opens the purse and looks in it. Then, she shakes her head and says "Nope."

Well, she come over to me and asked what was going on.

"We're trying to decide where to go, Bug."

"Why don't we go to Miami, maybe sleep on the beach?" Bug talked a lot about Floridy.

"The Studebaker would never make it."

"I think Truman's our only hope," said Momma. "If we don't get loaded and get out of here pretty quick, we won't be going nowhere."

Daddy sorta took control then, and we started loading stuff in the Studebaker. I guess we was in trouble, but it was nice to see Daddy up and about. Mostly, we just packed clothes in the car. Daddy said if it "wasn't important, it stayed behind." I got my little Philco radio and put it inside the bib on my overalls.

"All right, Rydell, put that guitar in the case and put it in the trunk. .J.D., you and Rydell put Granny in the back seat. We'll tie her rocker on the roof, I guess. Pack them clothes in the floorboard." He looked at me and said, "Put J. D.'s radio back there, too."

"I'll take care of the radio," I said.

"Ruth Ann and J. D. will be up front with me. The rest of you are in the back with Granny." I guess this is the way he used to talk when he was a foreman at the Red Fox textile mill in Bumkin.

" Ruth Ann, we'll have to leave the red chair."

Momma started crying and Daddy said maybe we could come back for it later. She got up real slow and stood for a while by the chair. She brushed the snow off and stroked it like it was a cat.

Granny had snow on her head when me and Rydell walked her to the car, and got her in the back seat. I brushed the snow off and put Momma's "Golden Rings" quilt around her. "Damned Republicans," she said.

Daddy and Rydell tied Granny's chair down with some twine.

Momma looked at the car. "Is this what we've come to, Westley? What we can cram into that car and it with a cracked block?"

Daddy put his arm around her and said, "We do seem to be down on our luck." Momma looked at him and then they both laughed. Sometimes I don't understand grownups.

Daddy told her again that we would come back for her chair. We stood for a minute looking at the car with stuff hanging out the windows and Granny's rocker on the roof. Daddy said, "I ain't sure we can all get in there." But we did. I set between Momma and Daddy with the Philco in my lap. "You and that radio!" said Daddy and grinned at me. I do like my radio.

We set for a minute, watching the snow cover Momma's red chair. Then Daddy said, "Let's go see Truman."

The motor went *wump, wump wump* and quit. Daddy said, "Everybody pray." In the back seat Bug said "Please," and on the next try, the engine caught. A big cloud of smoke come out from under the car, and the new snow turned black around us. Then, we crawled down the road in fits and starts, leaving a trail of black snow. When I looked through the back window, I couldn't see the chair or the Christmas tree, but I knowed that they was there with the other stuff we left. The rake, the old axe and the Sears catalogue.

"Westley, I don't think Truman will be glad to see us," said Momma.

"Oh, I dunno, he might. It's Tressie I'm worried about."

Tressie was Uncle Truman's wife. I'd only met her once but I could still see her face. Daddy took us to the Wikle reunion last summer, and we met some of Daddy's relatives. Truman has big buckteeth and white hair.

He was chubby and when he laughed, which he did a lot, his belly wobbled up and down. Tressie was just the opposite. Tall, skinny and looked like she'd been sucking a lemon all day. Never seen her smile.

On the way home from the reunion, Momma had been in a snit. That's what Daddy called it. Said Tressie had insulted her half a dozen times by talking about how hard she had tried to lift Truman above "his background," so he could amount to something. She didn't invite us to visit, and she didn't even ask us what our names was. So, I could see that us standing on Uncle Truman's doorstep might not be a welcome sight for Aunt Tressie.

"Well, it's Christmas Eve," said Daddy. "Some folks act different on Christmas. Brings out the best in them." Momma didn't look like she believed that.

So, on we went through the snow. I loved it. All the muddy red clay, tree stumps and lonesome fields was gone, buried under them big flakes that just kept falling. Rydell, since he didn't have his guitar, was humming "White Christmas," and Bug had given Granny her purse.

"Now, don't open it 'til I say," said Bug. She closed her eyes, gritted her teeth and whispered "Please." Then, she said "Now, Granny." Granny opened the little snap, turned it upside down, and shook it.

"Damned Republicans!"

"Maybe next time," said Bug.

"J. D., why are you so quiet?" Momma mussed my hair. I didn't say nothing, so she poked me with her finger. "What're you thinking about?"

"I'm always quiet."

"You got that dreamy look on your face again."

"I was just thinking how nice this is."

"Nice!" Daddy give me a sideways look, and Momma laughed. "Here we are in a snowstorm, no place to sleep, no money, no food, and you think it's nice!"

"But we're together in this old car. Granny, Bug, Rydell, Daddy, you and me. And it's snowing. Let's just keep driving."

Daddy put his hand on top of my head like it was a cap with the fingers holdin' tight. "I agree with you, son. That would be wonderful. But sooner or later, we'd run out of gas, or Bug would want to go to the bathroom, or we'd all get hungry. But, right now, for a little while, it is wonderful. It'll probably last as long as it takes to get to Truman's." Daddy looked at Momma. "Let's enjoy it while it lasts."

So, on we went, the moon peeping through the clouds and snow falling. Rydell hummed and sung "Silent Night," "Frosty, the Snowman," and "Silver Bells." Me and Momma hummed and sung along, too. Bug and Granny went to sleep. Once, Momma looked at Daddy and said, "Westley, are you scared?" He said, "Sure am!" and Momma said "Me, too."

Momma rode with her arm around me and watched the snowfall. It was deep now. Daddy said it might be two feet. Momma's other arm was around her stomach, and now and then, she'd say, "There!" Then, she'd put my hand and Daddy's hand on her stomach. Sure enough, I could feel the baby move. Daddy said, "If that baby knowed what was going on out here, I don't think he would come out." Momma laughed.

The little red light come on when we started up Guinea Trot Ridge. "What does that mean, Daddy?" I pointed at the dash.

"Means the poor ole car is feeling the strain," he said. "It ain't in the best of health, and it is hauling a pretty heavy load." Daddy slowed down a little. "If I give it a little extry attention, it'll be all right."

"Like me," I said.

Daddy looked at Momma and then at me. "Yeah, like you, J.D." He shifted to low gear and we creeped up Guinea Trot.

I've been sick a lot the last two years. The doctor at school said I had had rheumatic fever sometime or other. There was no telling when it happened since I'd never seen a doctor or a nurse 'except for the one that come to the school this year. I was real sick when I was six, but then I got well. I got sick again last summer, and stayed in the bed for five weeks. The school doctor said that I probably had "a touch of polio." That's what he said, like instead of jumping on me and making my legs shrivel up like Jody Smiley who is on crutches now, old polio just sorta tapped me like when the kids play tag at school. He said that I was lucky. He was right about that, I guess. I'm a little undersized though. What Granny calls "puny."

"Why do they call this ridge Guinea Trot?" I said.

"Well, J. D., that is a good story." He grinned at me, and Rydell and Bug leaned forward with their heads stuck over Momma and Daddy's shoulders. We all liked to hear Daddy tell stories.

"Well, about fifty years ago, your Granddaddy Wikle lived on this ridge. He tried farming but nothing worked. Hogs, cattle, chickens, nothing thrived on this ridge - but corn."

"So he raised corn?"

"Yep. Acres and acres of yeller corn. Your granddaddy took a lot of it to a mill where it become cornmeal. He traded some of it with his neighbors for stuff like firewood and chickens. The rest, he tried to sell."

"Who bought it?"

"Not much of anybody, if the truth be known. But, then your granddaddy made a discovery." Daddy paused and winked at Momma.

"What, Daddy, what?" said Bug.

"If he changed that corn to moonshine, it was easy to sell. It was also easier to haul, too."

"How come?" said Bug.

"Well, that corn, shucked and shelled, was worth about fifty cents a bushel, but the same corn in gallon jars was worth two dollars. A few gallons of corn ain't hard to haul at all, and it's worth a whole lot more. There was just one thing wrong."

"It was against the law," said Rydell.

"That's right. Now, that is one of the strangest laws in this country! Why, the damned government....."

"You are getting off the subject," said Momma, patting Daddy on the back of his head.

"Yes, well. Your granddaddy did real well for a while until the government revenuers started showing up. At first, they just broke all the gallon jugs and tore up your granddaddy's still, but later, they sent him to prison for six months."

"Papaw was in prison for six months?" said Rydell.

"Yes, he was."

"Damned Republicans!" said Granny. We didn't even know that she was awake.

"That's when your granddaddy decided he needed something to stand watch. Something to warn him if them revenuers come sneaking up the ridge. Something that would always be watching night and day." Rydell laughed.

"You mean guineas?"

"That's right! Of all of the critters on this earth, there ain't nothing like a guinea for warning you that somebody's coming. Nervous is the word. Them guineas are nervous. If they hear something, even if it's a walnut falling or a squirrel jumping, they holler. One hollers and then they all holler."

"When he heard the guineas cut loose, he would hide everything?"

"That's right. The gallon jars would be hid in the woods in nothing flat and the still would be took apart and hid, too. When the revenuers got to your granddaddy's house, he would be settin' on the porch reading the Bible. Course, them revenuers knowed the guineas had warned your granddaddy that they was coming, but there was nothing they could do. Couldn't get around them guineas. Over a hundred of them living out in the woods."

"Do guineas trot?" said Bug.

"No, honey. They run just like a chicken. But, like hogs, cows and chickens, they made a little trail across the ridge, and a trail is called a 'trot.'"

"Papaw was sorta famous then, if he is the reason that this hill is called " 'Guinea Trot'," I said.

"Well, I'm proud of him," said Daddy.

The Studebaker was hacking and coughing, like Daddy when he has a bad night. Momma breathed a sigh of relief when we topped the ridge.

"Not a minute too soon." Then, we saw the sign. "Thunderation!" said Daddy. "Look at that!" It hung over the road and there was lights shining on it. The letters was all loops and curls that said, "*Windsong Acres*," and under that, "*The Truman Tolleys.*"

"She's gone and changed the name of the place!" said Momma. "I guess Guinea Trot Ridge was too common for her."

We chugged under the sign, up a long drive with trees and a white fence. The trees was all decorated with colored lights that blinked on and off. There was a manger scene in front of the house with a crowd of cardboard people and all kinds of cute cows and horses. A dozen angels hung in the air above the manger blowing gold trumpets. "Never knowed the Baby Jesus had so much company," said Daddy. Truman's house was brick with big round posts like the courthouse in Bumkin, only Truman's house was bigger than the courthouse.

"Looks like Tara," said Momma. "The house in *Gone With the Wind*." Daddy coasted up to the steps. "Let's see if Scarlett and Rhett are home," he said. Daddy cut off the engine, and we sat and listened to the motor tick.

"I don't think we should all go in there," said Momma. "Westley, why don't you go and test the waters."

When Daddy knocked, nobody answered. He finally trudged off around the house, and we set looking at the blinking lights and the manger scene. We could hear music and people laughing, so there was a party in there somewhere. After a while, Rydell got bored. Him and Bug got out and went down to look at the angels and Baby Jesus. Then, Rydell got his guitar out of the back of the car and played "Oh Come All Ye Faithful" for the crowd at the manger. He sung like Perry Como and even sung in that foreign language, "Avast day Fe Da Lay." He looked good standing with the Three Wise Men in his fringed shirt and cowboy boots.

Then, Daddy come back with Truman and I could tell from the way Daddy held his head that things had not gone well. Truman was carrying a big basket full of oranges and tangerines. Rydell put up the guitar and crawled in the back seat. Him and Bug held the basket on their knees. Uncle Truman was real friendly and shook everybody's hand except Granny's. She stuck her walkingstick out the window and punched Truman in the belly. "Back off, Buster," she said.

Uncle Truman hugged Daddy. Then, he tried to put some money in his shirt pocket.

"I'm sorry, Westley. I guess I'm hen-pecked." He laughed like it was a joke. Daddy turned away from him. "Now, don't let pride hurt your family. You go on down to the Bumkin Motel in Bumkin. Tressie tried to get you folks room at the Holiday Inn but it was full-up. She called and made the reservations at the Bumkin Motel and everything is paid for, so all you gotta do is move in. Hell, stay 'til New Years if you want."

Daddy got in the car. The engine went *wump, wump, wump* and caught, all of a sudden. There was a backfire, and we was going back down Guinea Trot Ridge. I watched Uncle Truman wave goodbye, and then the blinking lights was gone as we chugged downhill through the snow.

"So, what happened?" said Momma. Daddy drove for a while, and then he told her.

"At first, it was fine. Truman didn't blink a eye when I told him what had happened. He said we could stay as long as we needed to, and he was getting ready to come back to the car with me when Tressie showed up. When she opened the door, I could see a crowd of people standing around with paper plates and cups. Tressie closed the door real quick.

'Well, Truman, I see we have an unannounced guest,' she said. Didn't even look at me. Truman told her about the eviction and then she said, 'Truman, we need to talk in private.' They went in the kitchen but Daddy said he heard most of it, anyway.

"It come down to the fact that she said that Truman's trashy relatives would never 'darken her doorway.' She would gladly pay the bill to put the whole crew up at the Holiday Inn, but they were not 'passing the portals of Wind Song.' I gathered that the house is in her name. She said something about 'one phone call to daddy' would make Truman more agreeable. He sassed her a little, but not much."

"Are we going to the Holiday Inn?" said Bug. Daddy didn't say anything. After a while, Bug said, "I guess not."

"They're full," said Daddy,

"No room at the Inn," said Rydell and laughed.

"Guess we'll have to go to Miami," said Bug.

"We can go to the motel in Bumkin."

"Maybe we should," said Momma. "You heard what Truman said about pride and hurting your family." Daddy stared at Momma and said, "We coulda waited for that social worker, too." Momma nodded.

"All right then, where are we going?" That's when the car quit. It shook, coughed, and died right there on a dark road somewhere between Guinea Trot Ridge and Bumkin. Wasn't any friendly lights in the distance, no porch lights or kerosene lamps saying "Welcome." Just cold, empty darkness. Momma cried a little and then she said, "All right, Westley, what are we going to do now?"

Bug said, "We shoulda gone to Miami."

Daddy set for a minute. Then he said, "Rydell, you get the guitar and move up here." Rydell did as he was told. Daddy said that we should keep on singing and talking 'til he got back. "Keep the door closed so the warmth will last," he said. "I'll find something, don't worry." He started walking down the dark road. I listened to the sound of his feet in the snow, then he was gone.

Rydell played "500 Miles Away From Home," and we sung along. Made me feel better, in a way. The guy in the song didn't have a shirt or a penny, and as bad as things was, we had more than that. I had three shirts and forty-seven cents. Momma looked so worried, I thought I'd try to talk to her and take her mind off what was going on. Then, too, I'd been thinking about all the questions I wanted to ask, but was afraid to.

"Momma, can I ask you something?"

The wind was blowing now, and she watched the snow whirl on the Studebaker's hood. There was some ice mixed with it, too, because it made little ticking sounds on the glass. "What do you want to know?"

"Lots of things we never talk about. Things that happen to us."

"Like what?"

"Daddy and Red Fox," I could tell Momma didn't want to talk about that. She set there with her eyes closed. Then she opened them and said, "All right, J. D. Rydell, you and Bug listen to this, too." Then she started talking.

"Three years ago, your Daddy had a good job at the Red Fox textile plant. We had a five-room house, a washing machine, indoor plumbing, and a telephone. Food was on the table and life was pretty good. All of you remember that. Then, your daddy started coughing. It was a soft little cough, but it would leave him pale and shaky. You all know your Daddy is sick, but we never put a name to it. The doctors call it 'brown lung,' a disease people get in textile mills where them fine little cotton fibers get in their lungs and their lungs turn brown. It can kill you. Westley quit his job, and for a while, it looked like he would get well. He got a little monthly check from Red Fox, and he was told that when he got better, the mill would give him a job in the office away from them cotton fibers.

"It didn't happen. Red Fox closed down and the checks stopped coming. Life went on, but it got worse a little at a time. We just sorta slid down inch by inch. Less money, more debts. J. D. here, he got sick. Rydell back there got in trouble with the law, and we went on food stamps. We moved a lot, and sometimes, we moved at night."

"I remember that," said Bug. "That was fun! Loaded the car and drove with the lights off." Rydell started playing "Folsom Prison."

"That's right, honey," said Momma. "That was the night we met the cow in the dark."

"Yeah! She was standing in the road and we bumped her!"

"That's right. Your Daddy turned on the headlights to see what it was and there was the cow. Didn't hurt her. Scared her though."

"She mooed," said Rydell. "Then, she come back and stuck her nose in Daddy's face." We all laughed. "Give him a big cow lick," said Bug.

I remembered the cow, too. She had a calf, and she had got out of somebody's pasture. She was lost out there in the dark, waiting for some-body to find her and take her to the barn. I don't think she was worried. It was a warm night, and she was grazing along the roadside. But, she was lost, sorta like we are now. Ain't no warm summer night now like there was for that cow, though.

We listened to Momma tell how Daddy found the pasture and put her and the calf back where they belonged.

Then, Rydell started playing "Can I Sleep in Your Barn Tonight, Mister?" and we all sung about the cold north wind blowing and we had no place to lay down. "Maybe there is a barn out there somewhere, a place for us," said Momma and then, Daddy was back.

He tapped on the window, and Rydell rolled it down.

"I found a place," he said. "Let's go."

We all got out of the car except Granny. Then, Daddy took control again.

"I'll go first," he said. "Ruth Ann, give me your hand. Now, Bug, you take Momma's hand. J.D., you hold onto Bug, and put Granny between you and Rydell. Hold on tight. It ain't far."

When we got Granny out of the car, she said, "Things has been bad and they're gonna get worse." That was one of her favorite sayings. She had been right, so far.

We did like Daddy said, and he started walking back down the road, tugging us along through the dark like kids playing "Crack the Whip," or "Pretty Girl Station." The snow had stopped and we could see stars. It was still dark, because the clouds was covering the moon. We run into laurel bushes along the road. Then, Daddy stopped and we sorta stacked up, knocking our heads together.

"We are going to turn here," he said. Then, we was walking down a little path that wound through the laurels. "Everybody hold on tight." We walked a good while it seemed. I got to thinking about how this morning, we had a house, and then we was in the Studebaker and now we was out in the dark walking through the snow. What next? Granny fell once, cussed the Republicans, and then we went on under the stars and falling snow until I seen it. Some kind of building, but it wasn't a house. It didn't have a porch, and there was no lights on inside. Then, the moon peeped out for a minute, and I seen the words on the big sign by the door.

GUINEA TROT CHURCH OF CHRIST

"A church!" said Momma.

"What kind is it?" said Granny. Daddy read the sign to her.

"Long as it ain't Baptists," said Granny. She had been mad at the Baptists ever since Papaw Wikle died, and the Baptist preacher refused to do the funeral 'cause Papaw cussed so much.

"Ain't it locked?" said Rydell. Daddy shook his head. "I tried the door and walked right in."

So, we all walked in. Daddy found a light switch, and there we was, standing in a big room full of pews. A big wood stove set in the middle of the floor, and there was even a Christmas tree and a piano over in one corner.

"You shore that this ain't Baptist?" said Granny. We all just stood there for a minute, a little uneasy, I reckon. We wasn't used to being in a church. Then Rydell went straight to the piano, like a bird dog to a quail's nest. He set down and started playing. The music didn't sound like anything I'd ever heard. It was something that sounded like snow falling and nighttime, and stars shining. It shore wasn't country and western! We all stood there in little puddles of melting snow and listened.

"What was that?" said Daddy, leading Momma to a pew and looking at Rydell like he'd never seen him before.

"Some fancy music I learned at reform school," said Rydell. "There was a piano there, and a teacher showed me how to read music. She taught me to play that."

"Well, it sure ain't Hank Williams," whispered Daddy.

"Some famous musician wrote it for a woman named Elise."

"Can you play it on your guitar?"

"I guess so. I just never did."

"Why are we all whispering?" said Bug.

It was true! We was all talking like we was afraid we'd wake somebody up. "Because we are in church," said Daddy. We laughed, but then Momma said, "Maybe we shouldn't be here. Ain't this like breaking and entering?"

"I don't think so," said Rydell. "The door was unlocked. We entered, but we didn't break nothing."

"The car broke down, and we ain't got no place to go," said Daddy. "We're just trying to get out of the weather, and we don't intend to steal anything." He looked around at us, and said, "I'm going to start a fire." That's what he done. There was still some coals in the stove, and in no time at all, the fire was roaring.

"I think I'll cut out the overhead lights," said Daddy. "No need to call attention to the fact that we're in here."

With the lights out, there was just the Christmas tree and the glow from the stove for light, but it was enough.

Daddy went back to the car and brought Uncle Truman's basket, and my radio. I turned it on and got Bing Crosby singing "I'll Be Home for Christmas."

"You're gonna run the battery down," said Momma.

"Let him play it," said Daddy. That is how I felt, too. If I had been saving the battery for something special, this must be it.

We all set close to the stove and eat oranges and tangerines. We set there and listened to the radio play Christmas music, and it was as nice as riding through the snow between Momma and Daddy in the Studebaker. Maybe nicer. But, like Daddy said, the real good times can't last. Granny dozed off. Momma and Daddy started talking about what was going to happen tomorrow. Bug went over and set under the Christmas tree. She peeked in her purse. "Nope," she said.

The next thing I knew, Rydell had disappeared. I went looking for him. In the front of the church there was the bell rope that went up through a hole in the loft and in one corner was a big ladder. I heard Rydell's guitar. Shore enough, he was up there. When I climbed up, there he was, setting next to the church bell, playing that Elise song.

"Hey, J.D., come on up."

The loft was cold and drafty, but Rydell didn't seem to mind. He just kept playing. Through the chinks in the wall, I could see moonlit snow that the wind blew up into the air and then it fell again.

"What you doing up here by yourself?"

"Sometimes, I need to be by myself."

"You want me to go?"

"No, you can stay."

"Can I ask you something?

"Let me guess. You want to know why I got sent to reform school."

"I guess. Nobody ever told me."

"Well, I got sent there because I broke into and robbed the Wacky Pool Hall."

"Gollee!" I said. "Did you have a gun?"

"Nope."

"Tell me about it."

177

"All right. When Daddy lost his job and things got bad around the house, I started hanging out in the pool hall. Like, I'm too young to work, but, if I made myself useful, like racking the balls, chalking the cues, and getting drinks out of the machine for the guys that was playing pool, why, they'd give me change. Quarters and dimes mostly, but it added up. I give most of it to Momma. She wasn't sure where I got it, but she left me alone about it.

" I just stayed out of everybody's way, and most of them liked me. Got to where they'd say, 'Rack 'em, Rydell!' like I worked there. There was just one problem, and that was old man Wacky."

Rydell stopped talking for a while. He tuned the guitar and peeped through the cracks at the snow. Just when I thought he wasn't going to say anything else, he went on.

"Since I was doing things that he was supposed to do, and he didn't even have to pay me, why, it seems like he would be pleased. For some reason, he wasn't. When I'd rack the balls and one of them sharks would flip a quarter in the air for me to catch, Wacky would give me a sour look. Started accusing me of stealing. Wouldn't come right out and say that I had took something. But, it was obvious what he meant. 'Rydell, I can't find my Philip's head screwdriver. Would you know anything about that?' Or he would announce to the whole room, 'My Ronson lighter seemed to have vanished!' Then, he would stare at me."

"Did you tell him you didn't take nothing?" Rydell shook his head.

"I guess I thought if I said anything, then he'd answer. Then, I'd say something else, and I'd be in trouble." Some of the regulars understood what he was suggesting and they told him, 'Elmo, that boy don't steal, or I'm a mighty poor judge of character.'"

"Well, good!"

"Didn't make any difference. I thought about staying out of the pool hall, especially since I knowed that Daddy would be mighty upset if he knowed I was hanging out there. But, we needed the money. Lots of times, the money I give Momma brought the groceries. So, I stuck it out.

"Then, one night, Elmo delivered his 'Nobody-steals-from-me" speech. He had a few too many, and got to bragging. At first, it was just big fish and bear stories, but finally, he got around to the pool room.

'I don't miss a trick,' he said. 'I sleep right up there,' he pointed at the roof, "If a mouse crosses the floor, or a drunk tries the door, I know it.'

"He told a couple of windies about catching 'young hoods' who had jimmied a window and came in. Said he nabbed them before they even had a chance to crack the moneybox on the candy machine. He kept looking at me as though all of this was a warning.

"That's when I decided to do it. That night, I left the window raised in the toilet and about two hours after the pool hall closed, I just dropped through that window. I didn't break into anything since I knowed where the keys for everything was. Took all of the money in the drink machine and the candy machine. Took the cash box from behind the cue rack. Took a burlap sack and filled it with pool balls. Carried everything out back and put it in the big garbage can. Covered it up with cans and bottles. Then I went home."

"Why didn't you take the stuff with you?"

Rydell laughed. "That would be stealing," he said.

That confused me right much.

"I didn't go near the pool hall until around seven, the next night when all the regulars would be there. When I went in, Sheriff Wooster and Horton Tolley was there. All the regulars was setting around watching and listening since they couldn't play pool. Wacky was holding forth about hearing footsteps and seeing three armed men disappearing into the night when he looked out the window. Then, he acted out the crime. He said that this was the work of professional criminals, and he talked about magnet keys and piano wires and stuff. I waited until Wooster and Horton left, and then I asked Johnny Revis to come out back with me.

"Johnny helped me carry it in. We dumped it all on a pool table, and I asked Johnny to tell Wacky where the sack had been. Well, you could have heard a pin drop for a minute. Then, one of them laughed. Then, they all laughed. The only one that didn't laugh was Wacky." Rydell smiled at me. "He called Wooster and charged me with breaking and entering."

"But why did you do that?" I said.

"I guess getting back at Wacky was part of it. All that bragging got to me. Said he could hear the little motor in the drink machine turn on and off, but he didn't hear me pour them balls into that sack! But the real reason was to prove that I wasn't a thief."

179

"You proved you wasn't a thief by stealing and then taking it back?"

"Something like that. When Wacky said that he was calling the law, the guys in the poolroom spoke up. Johnny said, 'Rydell might be guilty of bein' a smart-ass, but he ain't a thief.'"

"Let me think about that," I said. "It might even make sense."

"Wacky called Wooster anyway. He come over and listened to the whole story. He laughed, too."

"Brought it all back?" said the sheriff. Then, he laughed some more. Wacky was red as a beet.

"Anything missing?" said Wooster.

"I'm not sure yet. I haven't done a inventory."

"He brought it all back," said Johnny. "Hell, it didn't leave. Been out there in the trash can all the time."

"I don't care. Stealing is stealing."

Rydell played a little of "Birmingham Jail " and then said "Turned out the judge agreed with him."

That's when I seen the headlights through a chink in the wall. It was some kind of bus, and it was coming to the church. When it pulled up in front, I could read the letters on the side of the bus. GUINEA TROT RIDGE CHURCH OF CHRIST.

Me and Rydell watched as a big shepherd and three wise men got off the bus. Next come Mary, Joseph and the Baby Jesus who was a Raggedy Andy with a diaper on. I could see some angels still on the bus.

"Go tell the others," said Rydell. "Tell them we can hide up here."

I was down that ladder in nothing flat. Momma and Daddy was still whispering together in one of the pews when I told them.

"Quick, we have to hide in the bell loft. The members of this church just pulled up in a bus." So, here we went! Momma grabbed Bug, and we run to the ladder. Bug went up first with Momma, Daddy and me close behind. When Rydell pulled Bug into the loft, he said, "Where's Granny?"

We forgot her. She was asleep in one of the pews.

"Too late now," said Daddy. We all scrunched up round the bell just as the door opened.

"Hey, it's warm in here," said the big shepherd. I laid on the floor and peeped through the bell rope hole. In come the three wise men in bathrobes with towels on their heads. Then come Mary,

Joseph and the Baby Jesus. Everybody had fake beards except Mary and Jesus. I recognized Mary as the checkout lady at the Piggly-Wiggly. Then, the angels and shepherds trooped in followed by a little kid dressed in white. He had big red dots on his cheeks and he had long fake icicles for fingers. Everybody was laughing and cutting up, and the angels was pretending to fly, flapping their cardboard wings. Finally, a whole mob of people, little kids and grown-ups come in. Their faces was all red from the cold, and they was all smiling.

Then this man dressed like a Grand Ole Opry star come in. He had on a outfit that looked like it used to belong the Hank Williams, with musical notes all over it. "Look at that!" said Rydell, "It's the Reverend Jerry Bledsoe."

"Who is he?"

"He is about the best banjo picker in the world."

Turned out he was the preacher at this church, and he started in trying to get everybody settled. That is when one of the wise men spoke up.

"Hey, Preacher Bledsoe! There's a fire in the stove!"

It got real quiet. Then, it was like that story about Goldylocks and the three Bears with people hollering things.

"Somebody's been in here eating oranges and here are the peels!" said one of the angels.

"Somebody's been in here playing this radio," said the little kid with the icicles and then we could hear Gene Autry singing *Frosty, the Snowman.*

"Somebody is sitting back here asleep," said one of the shepherds. I guess Granny wasn't really asleep, 'cause she whacked him with her walking stick. We waited, but she didn't say anything about Republicans.

She just said, "Back off, Buster."

"Maybe whoever has been here is still here," said one of the three wise men. Next thing we knowed, one of them was standing at the foot of the ladder looking up at us. I guess he was Frankincense or Myrrh because he had a little glass bottle of perfume in his hand.

"Don't shoot!" said Rydell. "We're coming down."

Daddy went down first and then he helped Momma, who had some trouble. When we was all standing at the foot of the ladder, Daddy introduced us just like we was visiting.

"This here is my wife, Ruth Ann," he said. "My name is Westley."

"How do?" said the Preacher. Then Daddy introduced Rydell, Bug and me. Then, everything got real quiet again.

"What you all doing in here?" said the Preacher Bledsoe.

"Could we move inside by the stove?" said Daddy. "This is gonna take a while."

So he told it. It was kinda funny, in a way. Here these folks had come up to the church to see one kind of play, and we had give them another. When Daddy got through, the shepherd and the wise men looked at each other. Everybody had their mouth open.

"You ought not to come in here," said one of the shepherds. "You're trespassing!"

"I didn't know you could trespass in a church," said Momma. "If a-body is in trouble and looking for a place out of the cold, seems like a church is a place that would take you in." Then, she said, "Of course, I don't know much about churches."

I believe Momma saved the day. All of them shepherds and angels got embarrassed and uncomfortable. Some of them went off in a corner with Preacher Bledsoe and whispered. When the preacher come back, he said, "What you said is dead right, lady. Sometimes we forget who we are and what we believe." He laughed 'n shook his head. "We come here tonight to celebrate *another* night when a family had no place to go, and we found you folks."

"There wasn't no room for us at the inn, either," said Rydell. "The Holiday Inn, that is."

Then, all of a sudden, everybody was milling around, talking. The little kid with icicles for fingers told me he was Jack Frost and that he was in a play. "I get to freeze the girls just before Santa comes," he said.

"So, that is your car on the side of the road out there with the rocking chair on top," said a wise man.

"I'm afraid so," said Daddy. Then, he whispered to Rev. Bledsoe, "Ruth Ann is due."

"Well, I'll be dogged," said Rev. Bledsoe. Everybody looked at Momma and she blushed.

"You say Wendell Jenkins put you out?" said Rev. Bledsoe. "That troubles me the most, because Wendell is a member of this church. As a matter of fact, he is one of the shepherds." He turned around and said "Wendell!" Then, this man stepped forward from the back of the crowd. He had a real nice bathrobe, all red, blue and orange striped with a great big blue towel wrapped around his head and tied back with string. He had a big staff that looked a lot like Granny's walking stick.

"You put these folks out in the cold?" said the Preacher.

"This is embarrassing," said Wendell, the shepherd.

"Why did you do it?" said the Preacher.

"If memory serves, they hadn't paid rent in a year."

"He's right about that," said Daddy.

"How come?" said one of the wise men.

"I've had a lot of problems," said Daddy.

"Howdy do," said Wendell, "Pleased to meet you." He shook Daddy's hand.

"I don't know 'bout that," said Daddy.

"You never met this man?" said the Preacher.

"I have a lot of tenants," said Wendell. "Are you the guy with Brown Lung?"

"That's me," said Daddy.

"You put a sick man with...." the Preacher started counting us. "Five dependents out in the cold on Christmas Eve? An unemployed man with a pregnant wife?"

"I gotta admit the timing was bad," said Wendell.

"Well, far be it from me to tell you your business Wendell, but..."

"It's my brother-in-law. He showed up on my doorstep with his family. I decided that I would move him into one of my houses, 'cause him and his kids was driving me crazy. Told my wife that they couldn't live with us."

"Sounds familiar," said Daddy.

"Listen, I'm sorry about what's happened."

"Not your fault," said Daddy. "Besides, I didn't pay you any rent."

The angels had gathered around Rydell and he struck up *We Wish You a Merry Christmas*. The angels sung along and clapped. It turned out that two of them was in a little string band, and they went back to the bus to get their instruments. When they got back, one had a fiddle and the other one had a mandolin. They had intended to play *Santa Claus is Coming to Town* just before Santa came in with the presents for the little kids.

"Maybe you can help us," said the angel with the mandolin. They huddled up around the piano and whispered to each other. Then, they all went over and whispered to Rev. Bledsoe, and he come over and said, "You folks socialize for a little while. We're planning a play party over here." Off he went.

Well, the next thing I knowed, all of these people was talking to Bug and me. Some of the older folks went back and talked to Granny. When they told her they wasn't Baptists, she brightened up and said to one of them, "Are you a Clawson? You look like one." Turned out she was. The ladies fussed over Momma. Then, Daddy and Wendell went outside and talked. When they come back, Daddy was smiling.

I don't know when I've had such a good time. Some ladies went back to the bus and started carrying in food. Leather britches and canned corn, stack cake, cornbread, potato salad, and banana pudding. When Rydell, Bug and me just set there, one of the ladies brought us plates and pointed at the food on a big table in the corner. "Don't be bashful," she said. Well, we wasn't.

Then, they did the play. Rev. Bledsoe read about the shepherds watching their flocks, and we watched the shepherds as they listened to the angels, and then he walked over to the manger scene. Then, the wise men come down the aisle and sung about the "star of wonder." Rydell, he played along with them. He showed out a little bit. He was good, and they stopped the play and clapped for him. Everybody gathered around the manger, and Rev. Bledsoe played "Away in the Manger." Rydell started playing, too, and I could tell that Rev. Bledsoe liked what he heard.

Then we all set down and Jack Frost run up and down the aisle freezing people. He would poke little kids with that icicle finger, and they would squeal and giggle. All of a sudden, the door opened and we heard "Ho, Ho, Ho!" There was Santa with sacks of stuff. He even had a elf helping him! Where did he come from?

I went over and looked out the window. Maybe I thought I was gonna see Santa's reindeer. What I saw was Sheriff Wooster's police car. It took me a minute to put it together.

"Ho, Ho, Ho," said Santa as he came down the aisle. He was calling all the little kids by name, and then he saw Daddy, and he stopped dead in his tracks. He sorta looked around, and I guess he saw all of us. "Merry Christmas!" he said. He started passing out presents. He even had presents for us. He stopped and act like he was reading a name on a list and that it was hard to make out. Then, he said, "J.D. Tolley," and give me a present. Then, he goes over to Rydell and said "Have you been a good boy, Rydell?" Rydell said that he had. Santa slapped him on the back and said, "I know you are a good boy." Then, he saw Bug setting by the Christmas tree. Her little purse is under the tree, and Santa just picked it up and said, "Little girl, is this your purse?" She nodded, and he handed her the purse.

She opened it and it was full of quarters! Old Santa is slick. I never saw him put them quarters in there.

"Golleeee!" said Bug.

Then Rev. Bledsoe got up, rubbed his hands together and said, "Now, let's make some music." Then, he cut loose on "Jingle Bells." They played them all. Everybody sung, clapped and patted their feet. I set between Momma and Daddy and it was better than riding in the snow or setting in the dark with Momma and Daddy by the church stove. All of that was wonderful, but this was the best. Us and music and other people.

Santa and his helper disappeared for a while, but then they come back. Santa went over to Rydell and said, "I hear you like cowboy boots." Then, he handed Rydell this pair of boots that looked just like the ones that the Sheriff had on today.

"Genuine lizard skin," he said.

"Looks a lot like Sheriff Wooster's boots," I said.

"Oh, no," said Santa, "These used to be mine, but my helper here, he gave me a new pair." Santa pulled up his red pants. 'Rattlesnake skin," he said. Then, he was gone.

Rydell put his boots on right away.

Lots of nice things happened that night. Daddy said that Mr. Jenkins said for us to move back in the house, and then he give Daddy a job "overseeing" his rental property. Rev. Bledsoe asked Rydell if he wanted to play back-up guitar in his band. Santa's helper brought me new batteries for my radio. Daddy winked at me and said, "Didn't I tell you! People are at their best at Christmas!" I didn't want that night ever to end. But it did.

In the middle of everything, Mamma said, "Westley! It's time." Ever thing stopped while we stared at her.

I guess you know what she meant.

IDAHO

When Granny used to drive me crazy, I'd sometimes sneak around the side of the house and crawl through the tomatoes until I get to the cornfield where I could vanish between the rows of sunflowers and cornstalks, beans and morning glories.... until I got to the barn where I could climb up the steps to the loft and read my new Captain Marvel. I guess Granny knew where I was, but she didn't say nothing about it. Just set there watching the mail-box.

That's the problem, you see, the damned mailbox. About once a week all this summer, I have had to go clip the boxwood while Granny hollers at me.

"More off the left side, Harley. That's right. Take a couple of inches off just to your left." There is this pile of little dead leaves on the ground where I have been clipping every week.

"Granny, this box-wood ain't shaped right, and the more I cuts the worse it looks."

"I don't care how it looks, Harley. I need to see the mail-box."

"Sure is gonna be one ugly bush if I keeps clipping the left side."

"That's alright."

"All si-goggled 'n crooked."

"Just cut the bush, Harley."

So, I cuts. Sometimes, I would go and set on the porch with Granny, and we would talk about the mailbox.

"I can see it pretty good, Granny."

"From the left side of the porch, yes. But, if you move to my little blue rocker down there by my Wandering Jew, you can't see it a-tall."

"Why don't we just cut it down?" I have asked this before, but I keep hoping Granny will change her mind.

"Harley, I raised that box-wood from just a sprig. It is eighteen years old come this fall."

"Maybe it would rather be dead than ugly."

"That is a bush, Harley. It wouldn't rather "be" anything. What a quare thing to say! Reading them funny books is going to rot your brain. Besides, I sometimes sell clippings to Balzora Melton down at the flower shop."

"Why don't we get her to come get some clippings?"

"She don't need them, "cepting around Easter and Christmas."

"You must have a hundred box-woods."

"That ain't no reason to go killing one."

This all started when Granny put this ad in the *Farmers' Friend*, this little magazine that prints recipes, letters about seeds and poems. The poems are mostly about sunsets, birds' nests and snow falling. Granny always reads the "Swap Shop" where people trade seeds and stuff. She sent in this recipe for "leather-britches" beans, and offered to swap her Mountain Joy daylilies for other kinds of flowers. The mail started coming the next week.

"Well, I swan. I want you to listen! This woman lives in Sego, Nebraska, and she has sent me twelve Love Lies Bleeding seeds. Now, ain't that something. She is a widow lady like me with two grown daughters."

Granny not only sent the seeds, she wrote her a letter about her own children. Next thing, they are swapping pictures. Sometimes, when we are setting on the porch at night, Granny says, "Tell me again where Nebraska is," and I show her the map in my fifth-grade geography book. Other people wrote, too, and Granny wrote all of them 'cept for this "lonely farmer" in Georgia. "I know what he is up to," said Granny, throwing his picture into the fireplace. "Don't need no seeds from him."

I guess I have to accept credit for what happened next. I mean, Granny kept asking me questions about where all of these people lived.

"This one is from California. Cambria. Well, who would have thought it! She has Jacob's Cattle beans. A retired school teacher and she is deaf."

The letter writing was turning into a nightlong chore, but Granny was writing all of them people. That is when I got the idea. I asked

187

Miss Katie Mae Coggins, my fifth-grade teacher, about the map and she gave me one. It was a big thing that used to roll up, but the roller quit. She just tore it off that wooden rod and give it to me. Well, Granny had a fit. She put it up on her bedroom wall and she started putting these colored thumbtacks in the places where people lived.

"Help me find Medford, Kansas, Harley. That is where this blind woman lives that has Stump of the World apples." I put the thumbtack in Medford.

"Way over there? Well, who would have thought it."

I guess you see where this is going. Granny's whole life seemed to be them letters and the people she wrote. What she called her "little stroke" three years ago had stopped her gardening. She could still get around though, cook and clean house. And write letters. She would set on the porch and read them to me. Sometimes, at night, she would set in her bedroom and look at that map. She had put white thread around them thumbtacks and run the line to Sylva, North Carolina. It looked like a web built by a drunk spider.

"Now, where did you say Sandia Peak was?" I showed her the tack in New Mexico. "Raises Hollyhocks. Lost both of her legs." Sometimes, she would just shake her head at the wonder of it all. "Never been out of Jackson County. I was twelve years old before my daddy brought me to Sylva from Big Ridge. Now, look at all of these people that know me and I know them." After a minute, she would say, "I always wanted to travel."

That damned boxwood is beginning to look like a backward "C." Otis Frady, the mailman knows all about it. He toots the horn when he leaves the mail and raises the little red peg on the top, and Granny starts hollering before he is out of sight.

"Harley! Mail time!" I haul them letters in. First off, Granny reads the postmarks. "Eugene, Oregon; Livingston, Texas; Bradenton, Florida." She polishes her glasses with the hem of her dress. "Here, honey," she says, "The sun is in my eyes. Read them postmarks to me." And I do. Then, she says the same thing she has been saying for months now.

"No Idaho?"

"No, Granny, no Idaho." That is the one state she lacks. On her map, she has clusters of tacks in Tennessee, Virginia and Kentucky. In fact, she has a tack in every state...except Idaho. In the middle of all that white thread and brass tacks, Idaho was bare. "Maybe no one lives there," said Granny.

She reads all afternoon, chuckling and nodding, sometimes dabbing her eyes when the news is bad. "Tilda Hicks in Arizona? Dead grandbaby. Not six months old. I'll send her some Balm of Gilead." Granny wrote replies with a pencil on a Blue Horse tablet and a couple of nights each week, we would address the envelopes and I would lick the stamps. Of course, she was back on the porch the every day, staring at her little wooden mailbox and she rocked and read *The Farmers' Friend* and *The Grit*.

Granny had another stroke a week ago. I had been told what to do if that happened, so I called Uncle Asbury. Within minutes the ambulance came. That night, I listened to the doctor as he told Asbury about Granny. He kept saying words like "critical" and "serious." When we went down to her room in the hospital, she was curled up on her side and she looked smaller than usual. She knowed us though, and brightened up when she saw the mail that I had brought.

"Idaho?"

"Yep, Idaho." She give me a hard look.

"Did you write this letter, Harley?"

"No, Granny. It come in the mail." It did, too. I got Miss Katie May Coggins to write that letter. I ain't a dummy. She sent it to her sister in Idaho who mailed it back to Granny. I got the idea a couple of weeks ago, and asked Miss Katie if she would help. The letter asked for some Eden's Joy daylilies.

"Well, I swan." She held the envelope like it was one of her old teacups. "I ain't got my glasses."

"That's all right, Granny. I'll read it to you."

Granny died last night. The nurse said her last words were "wondrous strange." We have already been down to the Abiding Arms funeral home to see Granny. I was glad to see that she had on her glasses.

"That's the way everybody remembers her," said Asbury. "With them little specs half-way down her nose."

That's when I knew what I wanted to do. I needed to steal something from Uncle Asbury's service station. If I asked him, he would give me what I wanted, I guess. I would have to explain why I wanted it, though, and it ain't worth it. It is easier to steal it. It is the Esso Travelers' Atlas, and it has maps of every state in the U.S. with all of the roads and towns and cities. It even has Idaho. I figure I can sneak it into Granny's coffin. She used to say that she always wanted to travel if she got the chance.

A THING WITH FEATHERS

I have a character named Haskett that will probably end up with his own collection of short stories someday. This one owes a significant debt to Gabriel Garcia Marquez.

I was in the Green Lizard with six empty long-necks on the counter and the beginning of a bad mood when Hicky Dobbs sidled over and said, "Professor, I got something I want to show you." Hicky always has some-thing to sell.

"Don't call me 'professor,' Hicky."

Hicky grinned. "Okay, Haskett." He leaned closer. "I got something that you need."

"Don't need anything, Hicky."

"Haskett, you might not need it, but you'll want it."

"What is it?"

"Can't tell you. Have to show you."

"You got somebody's lost coon dog out in the truck?"

"No and No. It's at home."

"How come?"

"Can't bring something like this out in public."

Well, I was curious, so I rode home with Hicky clear to the top of Windy Gap. His old rusty trailer was canted up on one side where it had fell off the cinder blocks, and Hicky said that anything he dropped in the living room found its way to the back bedroom. "Knee-deep in base-balls, basket balls, and bowling balls," he said.

"You got another albino coon?" Hicky grinned and shook his head. Then, he pointed at this rickety old chicken-house.

"If you brought me all the way out here to look at some game chickens, I will definitely be upset." Hicky pulled one of them four-celled flashlights from under his truck seat and we trudged through briars to the chicken-house.

It was sitting on the roost with a dozen game-chickens. At first, I thought it was a swan. The big wings trembled and then it looked at me. It had a human face. Well, sort of. Pale, blue eyes. Whimpered like a beaten dog, a sort of mewling whine. The big wings closed down over its face.

"What is it?"

"Damned if I know." Moving to the back wall, Hicky unhooked a chain and pulled. He had a dog collar on it, so it fell, crashing to the floor and then stood in a half-crouch, the wings held like a shield before its face.

I'll have to go on calling it, "it," since it wasn't either he or she. The place where it should have had some kind of sex was as bare and bald as a Barbie doll. It was sort of a hybrid, I guess. Breastless, but with a sort of soft, vulnerable flesh on the chest - and them wings that sprouted where the arms should have been. Strong legs, but blood flowed from a dozen wounds on the thighs. The toenails looked dangerous - like yellowed horns that curved under and made standing upright near impossible. And on top of it all, that cringing face that shied from the light like an owl in the sunshine.

Before I could ask, Hinky said, "Dogs caught it." He told me about waking in the night to the baying of his hounds. The racket made sleep impossible, so he got his twelve-gauge and his flashlight and climbed the ridge. It was in a locust tree, and the dogs had backed off a bit. The old blue-tick, Uncle Dave, had a few rips in his sides where that thing spurred him like a fighting cock.

"When I shined the light on it, it give that pitiful cry. I had a time getting it out of the tree, but I got the collar on it and mostly dragged it down the hill since it can't walk worth a damn." I touched the wings and several feathers fell away. "It's losing them feathers. I think it is sick, and I can't get it to eat. Tried cracked corn, oats and dog food."

Well, finally, I just went ahead and said it. "Hicky, maybe this is an angel." Hicky said he had thought that himself, but he had changed his mind.

"I'd expect more of an angel," he said. "Something bigger, stronger than this. Something that don't whimper."

"Maybe it is a *fallen angel*."

191

"Well, it sure ain't used to walking. Wouldn't be worth much as a field hand. Can't fetch and carry. Can't milk cows. As near as I can tell, it don't talk." We watched it for a while, as it beat its head and body with those bedraggled wings. "Mites," said Hicky. "Chicken mites. Covered with them." After a while, Hicky said, "So, what would you give me for it?"

"Why do you want to sell it?"

"Well, I can't talk to it or sleep with it, don't think I want to eat it."

"What makes you think I want it?"

"Haskett, as long as I have knowed you, you was always reading, or listening to that high-tone music or quoting poetry. You don't keep dogs, but, hell, everybody needs a pet, or something for company -even ex-English teachers."

"A muse?"

"A what?"

"Never mind. No, Hicky, I don't want it."

We started back to the truck and I asked Hicky what he was going to do with it. He gave a reluctant sigh.

"I could clean it up, delouse it and charge people to look at it."

"You mean like a side-show?"

"Yeah. The old Cherokee Fair used to have stuff like that. Two-headed babies, geeks, bearded women. I might could sell it to a carnival."

"But, it ain't a freak."

"Looks like one to me."

On the way back to the Green Lizard, I thought about what Hicky was going to do. I conjured up a picture of the cage, the crowd and the bright lights. The growing mound of feathers beneath the perch. The gawking crowd.

"It'll die."

"Well, of course, it will. It was dying when I found it."

"But you might make a buck before it croaks."

Hicky nodded. "I just might."

"Turn around."

I traded Hicky my outboard motor and two weed-eaters for Gabriel. That is what I decided to name him until I could think of something better. Besides, if I called it Gabriel, I could also call it "he." I swore Hicky to secrecy. "If you start talking about it, one of them organizations that is against cruelty to animals will be up here."

"The ASPCA?"

"Then, the ministers and the civil liberties people."

Hicky sighed. "You are probably right."

"The media, newspapers, tv. Don't say another damned word."

He didn't. I cleaned Gabriel up with a garden hose, deloused him and brought him in the house. I discovered that he did have hands of a sort; cunning little claws on the underside of the wings, wonderfully adapted to either ripping flesh or holding a fork. He has benefited much from a good pedicure and a macrobiotic diet. I play music for him and he seems to have a preference for Beethoven and Wagner. He is putting on a little flesh, too, and the feathers have a nice, glossy sheen. He sits erect now, his eyes a-glitter with intelligence. No trouble at all. He doesn't seem to have bodily functions. A little flatulence that smells like lavender and occasional small droppings that do wonders for my tomatoes. And he hums. Wonderful little melodies that seem to fill my head with ideas, metaphors and sonnets. I haven't been in the Green Lizard in months.

I've taken the collar off. Gabriel sits in a little swing close to the ceiling and wafts back and forth. Doesn't sleep as near as I can tell. Ever vigilant. Last night, he spoke for the first time. A single word. I had just said, "Well, Gabriel! I'm thinking about doing a poem about you. Maybe even an epic."

"*Azazel*," he whispered, in a beautiful, liquid dialect. At least, I think that is what he said. It was late and we had both been into the brandy.

THE SWINETT

The Sylva Barbershop, circa 1945

    Since we don't have indoor plumbing in Rhodes Cove, Uncle Albert sometimes goes to Wimpy's Barbershop for "the Saturday Special." It is a terrifying thing. First he goes in this back room where there are bathtubs, huge sinks and boiling water. When anybody opens the door, steam boils out and I see men walking around with nothing on but big white towels wrapped around their waists. When Albert comes out, he gets in Wimpy's chair and gets a shave. Wimpy puts hot towels on his face, shaves him with a straight razor and sprinkles this bottle of green gunk on his head. All of this is because Albert has a "hot date," and he is awful pleased about it. Between towel-wrappings, he keeps singing and grinning and winking at himself in the mirror.

    I went with Albert to Wimpy's last Saturday, and you will never guess who was sitting in there! Willard, Ardell and Boogie, these three old guys that are sorta famous in Sylva for telling lies. Usually, they set on the bench in front of the post office and tell lies to people from Florida. They was setting in the barbershop big as day! Willard had his spit can and Ardell's hearing aids was whistling and twittering like two birds. Boogie was making faces at the mirror. Three guys, one huge, one deaf and one a little crazy. I think the only reason they were in there was because it was raining. They sure didn't get a "Saturday Special." They talked to everybody that got a shave or a haircut, mostly kidded them and asked them questions. Albert vanished into the back room and left me with three Captain Marvels and a Smiling Jack. I lost interest in my funny books though. There was this big stack of "Front-page Detectives" on the bench full of pictures of dead people and bloody knives! Wow! Granny would take a fit if she knew I was looking at them. That's when the college professor came in.

Right off, I could tell that Willard didn't like him. The guy had on a sports coat and a tie, and he kept asking Wimpy questions about Sylva. He said it was "quaint" and "picturesque." I'd never heard them words before, but he said them so many times, I remembered them when I got home and looked them up. Sounded like he was bragging on us, as near as I could tell. He said his name was Stanley, and he told Wimpy that he was collecting things like old fiddles and dulcimers and if anyone in the barbershop knew where he could buy some "rustic instruments," he would be obliged. Well, the Liars' Bench guys sure got quiet when this guy was talking. Then all of a sudden, Willard spoke to him.

"In your collection of rustic instruments, do you have a swinett?" It got real quiet then. I could hear the razor scraping on somebody's jaw. Then, Stanley said, "I beg your pardon?"

"A swinett," said Willard. Then he spelled it.

"I'm afraid I've never heard of a ...swinett? Is it a wind or a percussion instrument?"

"If you mean, do you blow it or beat it, well, most swinett players squeeze 'em." He looked at Ardell. Don't they usually squeeze 'em, Ardell?"

"OH YES!" yelled Ardell. "SQUEEZE 'EM! YES!"

Stanley got out a little notebook and a pen and started making notes. "Like an accordion, then?"

"No," said Willard. "More like a pair of pliers. Professional swinett players use pliers." Boogie nodded wisely. "That they do."

Stanley looked confused. Could you give me some specific details? For example, is it shaped like a zither or a trumpet?"

"I've seen round 'ens," said Willard. "You ever seen a round swinett, Boogie?"

"I have. They brought one up to the Balm of Gilead Baptist church last year and played it at a revival. Never forget it."

"ME NEITHER," said Ardell. "MADE ME CRY."

"Played 'The Old Rugged Cross," said Boogie.

"But, most of 'em are square or rectangle. About 20 feet by 40 feet." Stanley stopped writing. "See, what you do is, you fill a swinett with pigs. Little pigs that go wee-wee, and big boars that go Oink, Oink. Forty pigs will give you a pretty good musical range. Then, you bore holes around the top of the box. Pull their tails through the holes 'n anchor 'em down." Stanley stared at the Liars' Bench guys who all nodded solemn as owls.

"You try to arrange them pigs according to scale, like, do, ray, me fai, soo, you know."

"THE CHORDING IS THE HARD PART!" said Ardell. Boogie nodded. "Take about six men to play a swinett right, and they've got pliers in both hands."

"Hit is a wondrous thing when it is done right," said Willard.

Stanley put his pen up and closed his notebook. Then, he left. Nobody said anything for a while.

Then Ardell said, "SOME FOLKS CALL EM HOGOLAS!"

"He's gone, Ardell, " said Willard. Ardell was surprised. "MUST HAVE JUST REMEMBERED SOMETHING HE HAD TO DO!"

"You guys are something else," said Wimpy. "Maybe you ought to go on the road. See if you could get on the Opry."

"Is it true?" I said. "A hymn sung by squealing pigs?"

Everybody stared at me. "Well, Harley, hit's true if you believe it," said Willard.

"Don't tell him that!" said Albert. He was under a steaming towel and sounded all muffled. "He already probably believes in snipes. When did he come back? Must have been when I was looking at that bloody hatchet that was used to dismember the 'Tampa Temptress'."

"What's a snipe?"

Willard grinned. "Put down that gory magazine and I tell you."

Albert made little clucking noises under that towel. I think he was laughing.

MY GRANDFATHER'S BROTHER

(a poem)

They tell me he died in Morganton
Repeating the names of rivers and mountains.
"Never thought he was crazy," my grandfather said,
"But he had a certain.....quareness.
Just not quite right, you know?
Remember working by him in the field once.
I seen him bend to pull a morning glory from a corn stalk;
Then, all-of-a-sudden, he drops his hoe,
Cocks his head like a bird listening;
Then, he took off walking like he was going somewhere definite.
It would be days, sometimes weeks, before he would come back,
Acting like he had just left a few minutes ago.
He might work steady the next day, or maybe a whole week
Before his head would give that funny little tilt again, listening,
And his feet would already be moving toward the road."

In later years, he couldn't keep a job,
Always leaving his shovel in a ditch
Or his hammer on a plank,
Not even hearing the foreman's angry call behind him.
Neighbors told of seeing him on distant ridges,
Striding along logging roads,
Or fording mountain streams.
But then, when he didn't come home for a month,
Returning only when a kindly farmer from another county
Led him home, up through the cornfield, past the spring-house
To where great-grandmother sat waiting with tears in her eyes,
The family decided to do "something."
So, finally, he came to Morganton;
Came to a cell with barred windows and a locked door.
A nurse told my grandfather that his brother was "well-behaved;"
Except for those days when he moved
between his window and the door,
Muttering the names of mountain places.
Without the sun, he paled; wouldn't eat.
Visiting relatives found him sitting in a darkened room,

Whispering the names of places he'd been:
"Cowee...Leatherman's Gap...Blaze Creek and Goshen,
Standing Indian, Nantahala and the Winding Stairs."
On and on, a litany of water, wooded hills and stone,
Until he died like a wing-cropped raven,
Peering through the bars.

When my grandfather talks of his dead brother,
He makes vague allusions to a "quareness in our blood."
Speaking of great-grandfather's "peculiar habits,"
And my own father's penchant for wandering.
Sometimes, when I raise my eyes from reading,
I find my grandfather staring at me -
As though waiting for my head to tilt, listening.

LEARNING TO SWIM

(a poem of sorts)

Austin never knew that he had been moved to the terminal ward.
It was quieter, so he slept most of the time.
A weak sunlight, strained through glass and plastic,
inched up the wall,
Momentarily touched his face, and then vanished through the roof.
He felt suspended, floating in a wavering subterranean light.
There was the smell of new-turned earth
and a sense of budding trees.
Despite the medication and the whirring pumps, he knew:
It was spring.

He remembered another spring and the all-night drive;
500 miles with Eustis Shepherd and Manard Potts
To see the ocean.
Such a foolish thing to do!
He smiled behind the plastic sheets.
Ten hours non-stop from Murphy to Nag's Head.
As they drove from the mountains to the piedmont,
And from the piedmont to the coast,
The rich manure and loam smell of spring gave way
To the sweet rot of ocean.
In the last light before sunrise,
They waded into the surf at Nags Head.
Eustice and Manard stopped, but Austin kept going.
Waded straight out until the water was at his armpits.
Then, the undertow dragged him under.
The world churned away.

Then, he was on the beach,
His eyes and throat racked with burning brine
As he coughed, gagged, struggled for breath.
Eustis was angry. "Goddam fool," he said.
"Do a thing like that and you can't even swim!
You are lucky that Manard can."
He never told them that he thought he could, too,
Even though he had never tried.

He had been filled with absolute certainty as he waded,
Toward the bruised sunrise, that he could swim.

All these years, he had remembered that feeling:
Knowing that when his feet no longer touched the bottom,
Some instinct would take over. He would simply..... swim.

Now, in the dimness of his room, he returned to Nag's Head;
Felt that green, heavy water move up his body;
Heard that great ebb and flow that sounded like distant shouting.
And once more, he felt his toes
lose their final purchase with this world.
The water closed over him,
.....And slowly, cautiously, he began to swim.

Uncle Reece Talks About His First Wife

This one is supposed to be a poem.
I could be wrong about that.

She meant to kill me, I reckon; Frankie, I mean.
Meant to kill us both.
Later, in the hospital, she denied it.
Said the sun was in her eyes, and the next thing she knew,
She had broadsided that concrete bridge.
Tell you what I remember: the little sign by the bridge.
Said, "Cuberson, Georgia," and it came through my windshield
Like one of those stealth missiles on TV.
Just before we hit, the car speeded up, and I looked at her.
She smiled. Goddamned if she didn't!
It was like she was saying, "Here we go Reece! Whoopeee!"
When I come to, it was dusky dark and I could hear cowbells.
I was in the floorboard, my head crammed up in the heater-vents
And my legs kinda jack-knifed under the seat.
Then, I seen two ugly faces sorta floating where the front window
On the driver's side ... where it used to be.
One said, "They dead, I reckon."
The other said, "No, the man, he just moved."
Somewhere, a long ways off, I heard people singing.
"Yes, We Shall Gather at the River."
Then, the first one said, "He won't move long," and they were gone.
Laid and listened to crickets and bullfrogs, and the ticking of the engine.
Finally, the hearse came. No ambulance, mind you, no sirens.
Found out later that those two fools that looked in the window,
They were on their way to a tent meeting on up the road.
They called the funeral home and reported two dead folks
Down at the Cuberson bridge.
So, the hearse came and these two guys with flashlights checked us out.
Frankie had a bad cut on her head, a ruptured artery in her leg.
I had a face full of glass and a door handle embedded in my butt.
The two guys didn't know what to do when we turned out to be alive.
They laid us out on in this pasture where some cows came to look at us.
They talked it over for a while.
Told me that they would take us to the hospital, but it would cost me.

I paid them in advance.
It was Thanksgiving Day, and we were on our way to Bryson City.
Neither of us had slept in two days,
Just stood in the kitchen, drank coffee and glared at each other.
I told her she ought to stay in Bryson City with her Momma;
Let me come on back and finish out the year at Toccoa High.
Said I thought this marriage thing wasn't working out.
That was a mistake.
"I know what you are doing, Reece," she said.
"With me in Bryson, you can screw all of them cheerleaders."
Yeah, she was convinced I was sleeping with half of my students.
That's when she decided to kill me.

Three days later, I told her daddy that Frankie had tried to kill me twice.
Told him I didn't aim to give her another chance.
Well, the old man takes me out behind the house.
Never forget what he said.
"The first little problem and you want to quit." Mad, he was.
"Life is not easy, Reece. But you stick with it. Now, you and Frankie,
You two go on back to Georgia, try to make a life together."
Decided then that I was talking to a crazy man.
Walked out to the street and put up my thumb. I was in Atlanta
        before dark.
Never went back. Quit teaching.
My second wife was crazy, too, but she wasn't dangerous.
Now, I feel like I have sorta "wifed out," you know.

THE TRUNK IN THE ATTIC

The attic in the house that my grandfather built was never finished. The windows were papered over with newsprint and most of the floor was exposed joists. In summer, the attic was filled with the drone of groggy wasps that flew through the dim light like lost pilots searching for a landing strip. In winter, wind-driven snow filtered through the eaves and settled in wavy strips across the rope bed, the stacks of *Farmers' Almanacs* and my grandmother's dried leather-britches. The old trunk, a strange white and yellow assemblage, was set against a brick chimney that rose through the roof like a red tree.

When I was a child, the attic had all the allure of an exotic land, and on rainy days I came here to explore Africa and Mars. Sometimes, I read. Often, I opened the trunk. The leather straps, brass hinges and formidable locks were purely decorative. I always raised the lid in slow inches so that my grandmother would not hear, although I think she usually did.

The trunk contained all that was left of my father. Here, cushioned in little padded compartments were his cuff-links, ornate belt-buckles and a collection of pork-pie hats. Dozens of picks made of amber, wood and ivory glittered in the dim light. A photograph album with hundreds of pictures; many of my father holding guitars, mandolins and banjos - always smiling. His nick-name was "Happy." The mandolin was in the bottom of the trunk. It smelled of rose oil and when I lifted it, it glowed, all buffed wood and polish.

Always, I would pluck a string, and a single note, bright as a firefly in the darkness, would hang in the air with the droning wasps. I came to feel that the wavering note was as close as I would ever come to hearing my father speak. Often, I would hear my grandmother below. "What are you doing?"

I would answer, "Nothing."

And she would say, "Not in that trunk, are you?"

I would assure her that I wasn't. I realize now that it was a game that we played. Certainly, she knew that the mandolin was in my lap.

"Come down now and do your homework."

I would bury the mandolin, close the lid and retrace my steps, emerging in the bright, sunlit kitchen where my grandmother stoked the fire in the old Home Comfort stove.

As the years went by, I began to put my own objects in the trunk, each with a story to tell. When Toby, my favorite dog, became rabid and had to be shot, I buried him in the cornfield. The following year, my grandfather's plow turned up Toby's skull, delicate as an eggshell. I wrapped it in an old shirt and put it in the trunk along with the hood ornament from a wrecked, '53 Chevrolet, a gaudy pin that I bought for a cheerleader and never had the nerve to give her, a bicuspid I lost in a fight and a tarnished Saint Christopher medal. Each had a story to tell. I could pick them up and hold them to the light and hear Toby's bark and see the little mole on the cheerleader's neck.

After my grandparents died and I moved away to teach, the old house sheltered a series of families. Other women cooked on the Warm Morning, and on rainy days, other children explored the attic. A few token items found their way to me: pictures of stern relatives and my smiling father.

The trunk and the mandolin vanished. However, one of my most pleasant dreams is of the trunk in the attic. Again, I can raise the lid, unwrap the mandolin and pluck the string that resonates in the darkness.

In a sense, I still have the trunk, and, figuratively I continue to place objects in it. I'm talking about memory, of course, a writer's most valuable tool. I continue to store faces, moments and emotions, which, like Wordsworth's injunction, can be "recollected in tranquillity." Lifting the lid, I reach down through layers of pain and joy, mandolins and memories.

We all have a trunk in the attic, I guess. Perhaps you have forgotten yours; however, like a faithful servant, it is there, waiting. All it takes is a moment of quiet introspection, and you are lifting the lid, sifting through layers and layers of memories; unlike my original trunk in the attic, this trunk is bottomless.

THE MAN WHO DIDN'T LISTEN

This one is ... personal, I guess

He was more than just "hard of hearing," no question about it. "You have 90% hearing loss," said the audiologist. "What?" said Roger.

"I'll write it down for you." The audiologist wrote, "You are now classified as 'profoundly deaf.' Roger smiled. "I like that. Sounds like something I worked long and hard for." The audiologist stared at him for a moment. "Perhaps a sense of humor will prove helpful," he said.

For the past decade, his hearing had grown steadily worse, and one by one the wonderful sounds went: wind, crickets and running water; the mourning doves on the ridge above his house. The turn signal in his car. Rain on the roof. He began to talk louder, perhaps in order to hear himself speak. In restaurants, his wife would nudge him beneath the table. "Roger, please!" she would whisper, and he would look up to see faces turned toward him, cups and forks frozen in mid-air. "Everybody can hear you!" He would grin and nod at his listeners. "Sorry," he would say. "Deaf, you know."

"Turn on your hearing aids, for God's sake," his wife whispered. And he would do so, and sit listening to an avalanche of discordant sounds. He was a trial to his wife. "What?" he said at the movie and at the Neil Simon play, "What did he say?" His wife began to complain of headaches, and she and the cats retreated to the garage when he played Wagner or watched "Wheel of Fortune." Finally, she packed the car and left. "I have an apartment, Roger," she wrote him, "and I can hear myself think. Goodbye."

He had always felt guilty about the problems he had caused her, but now, he went on an orgy of crescendos and thunder. "The Ride of the Valkyries" and "Siegfried's Rhine Journey." Boxcar Willie and Merle Haggard. But, eventually, he was sated. Yes, that is the word, "sated." He no longer went to visit friends, for he seemed to be forever straining, leaning forward to grasp some fragment of meaning. He turned his hearing aids up to maximum.

"Sir, you will have to leave. Either that or cut your hearing aids off. They are whistling."

"What?"

And he was led away to the lobby, embarrassed by the fact that he had added the high-decibel whine of his hearing aids to a Vivaldi concert, or the romantic music on the movie soundtrack. Better to stay home. His friends were relieved when he quit visiting, and little by little they stopped visiting him. "Nice, guy, that Roger," they would say, "but talking to him can be a real ordeal." He took up gardening, foreign films (the ones with the captions) and murder mysteries. But it wasn't enough.

Roger began to tell stories. First, at civic clubs and then to small gatherings, hospice groups, church retreats. He liked to hear his amplified voice boom and roll in auditoriums, and to his surprise, he discovered that he was good at it. He talked about his childhood, his deafness, and his favorite relatives. "You have a wonderful ear for dialect," listeners told him. "What?" he would say. "Your stories are a marvelous mix of sadness and joy." "Yes!" he would say, hoping his answer was appropriate. And so, for a time he was content.

But it was not enough. And little by little, a shadow came over him, and he felt alone, even in the midst of crowds. For although he could perform, he couldn't listen. He found himself yearning for a personal communication. "No one wants to talk to me," he lamented, "Not even God."

"That's not true," said God.

"What?"

"Never mind, I'll tell you in a dream." And God did.

"Roger, I have something to tell you."

"Well, it is about time," said Roger. "Kind of neglected me, haven't you?" Roger didn't mean to sound petty, but he said, "Where the hell have you been?"

"Roger, I've been talking to you. You just don't listen."

"Well, you should certainly know why!"

"No, Roger, it has nothing to do with that. In fact, it was necessary to make you deaf so you *would* listen."

"I hate that kind of talk," said Roger. "Next thing I know, you will be telling me that being deaf is a gift."

"It is."

"Hey, I don't want to offend you, but bullshit!"

"Could be."

"What do you mean? You are in charge aren't you."

"Not really. I'm just saying that you have an opportunity here."

"Sounds like one of those ads: 'Make thousands in your own home assembling our product.' It is a little late for that, don't you think?"

"Roger, I don't want to hurt your feelings, but you were never a 'quick study.' But, now after all this time, you just might be ready."

"Meaning?"

"Tell me about being deaf."

"Well it is lonely. I can't mix with crowds, talk, sing. I have audiences, but I don't have friends. And no...well, no special ladies, you know?"

"I can't help you with the ladies, Roger, but what happens to the sounds that you have lost, and the friendships that you once had?"

"I have memories. In my memories I can hear them, and yeah, I guess, in my dreams it all comes back. I sometimes write down things."

"So there you are!"

"Are you saying I'm supposed to write? After all of this time, I am supposed to write! Why didn't you tell me this thirty years ago?"

"You didn't have anything to say then. Now you do."

"Oh, I get it. 'Suffering enriches!'"

"Perhaps. If you work hard, learn a little discipline and revise, revise, revise. Gotta go Roger."

"Hey, if all of this was preparation, IT WASN'T WORTH IT!"

God mumbled something.

"What?" But he was gone.

So, Roger wrote, and as he wrote, he heard the rain crows again, heard wind in the poplars around the house, crickets in the night, the laughter of children. The music scores from a hundred movies returned and even the voice of the girl in the ninth grade who said, "I love you, Roger. I will always love you."

And it was true. She would always love him. Each time he remembered her, he heard her say it. "Roger, I love you."

He wrote it down. Then, he described the sounds of wind, rain, his grandfather's laughter and his grandmother's singing.

"You are doing it," said God.

"Yeah, well, I had still rather hear."

"But, all things considered, since you can't do that...,"

"Yeah, it is a pretty good deal."

And it was.

Some of the works in this collection have appeared in a variety of anthologies and magazines. In some instances, they have been modified or expanded from their first publication.

"My Grandfather's Brother" appeared in <u>Step Around the Mountain</u>, an anthology of Appalachian literature published by Seven Buffaloes Press, Big Timber, MT 59011. In the Fall issue, 1982, this poem also appeared in <u>The Chattahoochee Review</u>, DeKalb College, Dunwoody, Georgia 30338.

"Learning to Swim" appeared in <u>Grab a Nickel</u>, an Appalachian poetry anthology published by Alderson-Broaddus College, Philippi, West Virginia, 1998.

"Nick-names" was published in the literary magazine, <u>Lonzie's Fried Chicken</u>, published in Dunn, North Carolina, 1998.

"Mason Jars in the Flood" appeared in <u>The Lost State of Franklin</u>, a literary magazine devoted to regional writing and folklore, 1999.

"Babby" appeared in <u>Now and Then: The Appalachian Magazine</u> in the Summer issue, 1993 under the title, "Babby's Trunk."

"A Stone, A Leaf, A Door," published by <u>Ink Literary Review</u>, 11 Spring Hills Terrace, Somerville, Maine 02143, November, 1997.

"When the Music Stopped" appeared in a greatly modified form in <u>Southern Exposure</u> some ten years ago under the title of "The Raindrop Waltz."

"Shazam!" in a greatly modified format once won a literary contest sponsored by the North Carolina Writers' Network and was subsequently published in six North Carolina newspapers (circa 1990).

OTHER WORKS BY THE AUTHOR

Belled Buzzards, Hucksters, & Grieving Specters: Appalachian Tales Strange, True and Legendary by Gary Carden and Nina Anderson, Down Home Press, Asheboro, NC 27204. Published in 1994.

Papa's Angels: A Christmas Story by Gary Carden and Collin Wilcox Paxton. New World Library: Novato, California, 1996.

From the Brothers Grimm: A Contemporary Retelling of American Folktales and Classic Stories by Tom Davenport and Gary Carden. Highsmith Press: Fort Atkinson, Wisconsin, 1992.

Native American Myths and Legends, "The Southeast" by Gary Carden. Salamander Press: London, 1994

PLAYS

The Raindrop Waltz, Palmetto Play Service, P. O. Box 123, Pendleton, S.C. 29670-0123

Land's End, Palmetto Play Service, P. O. Box 123, Pendleton, S. C. 29670-0123

The Uktena and the Nunnihi: two Cherokee ritual dramas. (Available only in manuscript from the playwright.)

FILMS

Blow the Tannery Whistle, written and performed by Gary Carden. Davenport Film, Route 1, Box 527, Delaplane, VA 22025

Willa: An American Snow-White, scripted by Gary Carden, Devenport Film, Route 1, Box 527, Delaplane, VA 22025